U0084661

序 言

　　「ECL測驗」的文法題，大部份都很簡單，但也有幾條題目較難，如果你不徹底研究，總是會有幾條題目答錯。

　　「ECL文法題庫①」，目標就是讓你在ECL的文法題中得到滿分。建議讀者每一回先做一遍，把錯的部份加以研究，完全徹底了解出題的目的為止。學文法是學英文的捷徑，很難將一本文法書，從頭到尾看完，不斷地做文法題目，是一個學英文法的好方法。

　　本書共有60回，每一回有10題，版面經過特殊設計，讀者一看，就有要做題目的衝動。每一條題目都有詳細的解答，並附翻譯和註釋，節省您查字典的時間。每做一回，都是一項挑戰，剛開始也許困難，無法全部答對，整本書做了一半以後，就會愈做愈快，到最後，10題都可以全部答對。即使題目很簡單，也要重複檢查，要練習到每一回，在最短時間內，完全答對為止。

　　把不會的題目做一記號，考前只要複習答錯的題目即可。對於書中不懂的文法規則，可查閱劉毅老師主編的「**文法寶典**」，裡面都有詳細說明。

　　本書雖經審慎編校，疏漏之處，恐在所難免，尚祈各界先進不吝指正。

編者 謹識

All rights reserved. No part of this publication may
be reproduced without the prior permission of
Learning Publishing Company.

本書版權爲學習出版公司所有，翻印必究。

TEST 1

Directions: *Of the four choices given after each sentence, choose the one most suitable for filling in the blank.*

1. The woman was _____ her dessert.
   - (A) had
   - (B) have
   - (C) having
   - (D) had having ( )

2. Work hard, _____ you will achieve success.
   - (A) and
   - (B) whether
   - (C) or
   - (D) as if ( )

3. He made an interesting _____ about comic books.
   - (A) speaks
   - (B) spoken
   - (C) speech
   - (D) speaking ( )

4. You look uneasy. What _____?
   - (A) happened
   - (B) happening
   - (C) was happened
   - (D) did you happen ( )

5. The weather here is _____ all the time.
   - (A) the same
   - (B) the same as
   - (C) same
   - (D) as same as ( )

6. Tommy : I haven't bought the book we need in music class.
   Susan   : _____
   (A) Neither have I.
   (B) Neither do I.
   (C) So have I.
   (D) So do I.   (   )

7. When Henry _____ enough money, he's going to
   open a flower shop.
   (A) made
   (B) makes
   (C) is made
   (D) will make   (   )

8. They're going to get married, _____ is a surprise
   to all of us.
   (A) that
   (B) who
   (C) which
   (D) whom   (   )

9. We _____ there soon; otherwise, we will be late
   for the movie.
   (A) can get
   (B) have got
   (C) were getting
   (D) should get   (   )

10. Patricia works _____ that she is certain to get the
    promotion she wants.
    (A) hardly
    (B) so hard
    (C) hardly so
    (D) good enough   (   )

TEST 1 詳解

1. (**C**)　The woman was <u>having</u> her dessert.

那位女士正在吃她的甜點。

「was/were + 現在分詞」爲「過去進行式」，表「在過去某一時間正在進行的動作」，故選 (C) *having*。

have〔hæv〕*v.* 吃（have 的主要意思是「有」，在此作「吃」解。）　　dessert〔dɪ'zɜt〕*n.* 甜點

2. (**A**)　Work hard, <u>and</u> you will achieve success.

努力工作，你就會成功。

$\left\{\begin{array}{l}\text{祈使句, } \textit{and} + \text{S.} + \text{V.（and 表「就會」）}\\\text{祈使句, } \textit{or} + \text{S.} + \text{V.（or 表「否則」）}\end{array}\right.$

本句等於：*If* you work hard, you will achieve success.

achieve〔ə'tʃiv〕*v.* 達到；獲得
success〔sək'sɛs〕*n.* 成功

3. (**C**)　He made an interesting <u>speech</u> about comic books.

他發表了一篇很有趣的演講，關於漫畫。

make a speech 發表演說　　speech〔spitʃ〕*n.* 演講（可數名詞）而 (A) speak「說」爲動詞，(B) spoken「口語的」爲形容詞，(D) speaking〔'spikɪŋ〕*n.* 演講（不可數名詞）；*adj.* 演講的；說（某種語言）的，則句意與用法均不合。

interesting〔'ɪntrɪstɪŋ〕*adj.* 有趣的
comic book 漫畫書

4. (**A**) You look uneasy. What <u>happened</u>?

你看起來很不安的樣子。發生了什麼事？

happen〔'hæpən〕*v.* 發生 爲不及物動詞，限用主動。
若要選 (D)，須改爲 What happened to you? (你發生
了什麼事？)。不及物動詞沒有受詞，所以沒有被動。
uneasy〔ʌn'izɪ〕*adj.* 不安的；焦慮的

5. (**A**) The weather here is <u>the same</u> all the time.

這裡的天氣始終都一樣。

> *the same* 一樣的
> A *is the same as* B A 和 B 相同

weather〔'wɛðɚ〕*n.* 天氣   *all the time* 一直；始終

6. (**A**) Tommy : I haven't bought the book we need in
music class.
Susan   : <u>Neither have I.</u>

湯米：我還沒買我們上音樂課需要的書。
蘇珊：我也還沒。

依句意，選 (A) *Neither have I.* (我也還沒。) 這句話
是由 Neither have I *bought the book we need in
music class.* 省略而來。   neither〔'niðɚ〕*adv.* 也不

7. (**B**) When Henry <u>makes</u> enough money, he's going to
open a flower shop.

等亨利賺夠了錢，他將開一家花店。

表時間或條件的副詞子句，須用現在式表示未來，不可
用 will 表示未來，且依句意爲主動，故選 (B) *makes*。
make money 賺錢

8. (**C**) They're going to get married, <u>which</u> is a surprise
to all of us. 他們即將要結婚了，令我們大家很驚訝。

> 代替前面一整句話，關係代名詞 ***which***。凡是關代
> 前面有逗點，不可用 that，只能用 ***which***。
>
> （詳見「文法寶典」p.161）
>
> ***get married*** 結婚
>
> surprise〔sə'praɪz〕*n.* 令人驚訝的事

9. (**D**) We <u>should get</u> there soon; otherwise, we will be late
for the movie.
我們應該趕快到那裡；否則我們看電影就要遲到了。

> 依句意，選 (D) ***should get***「應該到達」。而 (A) can get
> 「能夠到達」，(B) have got「已經到達」和 (C) were
> getting「當時就要到達」，均不合句意。
>
> ***get there*** 到那裡   otherwise〔'ʌðə͏,waɪz〕*adv.* 否則
>
> late〔let〕*adj.* 遲到的

10. (**B**) Patricia works <u>so hard</u> that she is certain to get the
promotion she wants. 派翠西亞工作非常努力，她
一定可以獲得她想要的升遷。

> ***so…that~*** 如此…以致於~
>
> { hard〔hɑrd〕*adv.* 努力地
> { hardly〔'hɑrdlɪ〕*adv.* 幾乎不
>
> 依句意，選 (B) ***so hard***「如此努力」。
>
> certain〔'sɝtn̩〕*adj.* 一定的
>
> promotion〔prə'moʃən〕*n.* 升遷

TEST 2

Directions: *Of the four choices given after each sentence, choose the one most suitable for filling in the blank.*

1. Kent usually works on weekends. _____ Frank.
   - (A) So does
   - (B) Neither does
   - (C) Either does
   - (D) So too   (   )

2. _____ you meet us at the snack bar?
   - (A) Have
   - (B) Ought to
   - (C) Couldn't
   - (D) Maybe   (   )

3. Did you hear that Jennifer is _____ marry?
   - (A) about
   - (B) about for
   - (C) about to
   - (D) about for to   (   )

4. How _____ you like the weather in California?
   - (A) do
   - (B) are
   - (C) have
   - (D) must   (   )

5. The trail is so narrow that _____.
   - (A) I must walk behind you
   - (B) I walking behind you
   - (C) to walking behind you
   - (D) must walk behind you   (   )

6. Meat is usually cut and _____ one piece at a time.
   - (A) eat
   - (B) eaten
   - (C) ate
   - (D) eating   (   )

7. Making friends with Americans _____ you an opportunity to speak English.
   - (A) to give
   - (B) given .
   - (C) giving
   - (D) gives   (   )

8. The report was ready for _____.
   - (A) to print
   - (B) printing
   - (C) printed
   - (D) be printed   (   )

9. You can always count _____ Carrie to do the right thing.
   - (A) on
   - (B) by
   - (C) to
   - (D) for   (   )

10. In the future, _____ to improve your listening?
   - (A) will you trying
   - (B) have you try
   - (C) will you try
   - (D) are you tried   (   )

TEST 2　詳解

1. (A) Kent usually works on weekends. <u>So does</u> Frank.

肯特通常在週末工作。法蘭克也是。

> 這句話是由 So does Frank *usually work on weekends.*
> 的省略，so 在句意上等於 also。用這種方法，什麼附和
> 句都會做。
>
> weekend〔'wik'ɛnd〕*n.* 週末
> ***on weekends*** 在每個週末

2. (C) <u>Couldn't</u> you meet us at the snack bar?

你不能和我們在小吃店碰面嗎?

> (A) Have 後面須接過去分詞，故不合;又此題為問句，
> 故 (D) Maybe「或許」不合，(B) Ought to「應該」，若
> 用於問句，須改為 Ought you to meet us at the snack
> bar?(詳見「文法寶典」p.319)，故選 (C) ***Couldn't***。
>
> meet〔mit〕*v.* 和～見面
> snack〔snæk〕*n.* 小吃;點心
> ***snack bar*** 小吃店

3. (C) Did you hear that Jennifer *is **about to*** marry?

你有聽說珍妮佛就要結婚了嗎?

> ***be about to V.*** 即將～
>
> hear〔hɪr〕*v.* 聽說　　marry〔'mærɪ〕*v.* 結婚

4. (**A**) *How <u>do</u> you like* the weather in California?

你覺得加州的天氣如何？

How do you like～? 你覺得～如何？

（詢問對方的看法）

weather〔'wɛðɚ〕*n.* 天氣
California〔ˌkælə'fɔnjə〕*n.* 加州

5. (**A**) The trail is so narrow that <u>I must walk behind you</u>.

這條小道很窄，所以我必須走在你後面。

that 所引導的子句中，須有主詞與動詞，依句意，選
(A) *I must walk behind you*「我必須走在你後面」。

behind〔bɪ'haɪnd〕*prep.* 在～之後

trail〔trel〕*n.*（荒野中踏成的）小道
so…that～ 如此…以致於～
narrow〔'næro〕*adj.* 狹窄的

6. (**B**) Meat is usually *cut* and *<u>eaten</u>* one piece at a time.

肉通常要切過，再一次吃一片。

and 為對等連接詞，須連接文法地位相等的單字、片語，
或子句；前面是 be 動詞 is，接過去分詞 cut，為被動語態，
故空格應填過去分詞，又 eat 的三態變化為 eat-ate-eaten，
故選 (B)。

meat〔mit〕*n.* 肉
cut〔kʌt〕*v.* 切（三態變化為：cut-cut-cut）
piece〔pis〕*n.* 片   *at a time* 一次

7. (**D**) Making friends with Americans <u>gives</u> you an
opportunity to speak English.
和美國人交朋友，能讓你有機會說英文。

空格應填動詞，又動名詞片語 Making friends with
Americans 當主詞，視爲單數，故 (D) *gives*。凡是
不定詞、動名詞，或名詞子句當主詞，都用單數動詞。

make friends with 和～交朋友
American〔əˋmɛrɪkən〕*n.* 美國人
opportunity〔͵ɑpɚˋtjunətɪ〕*n.* 機會

8. (**B**) The report was ready for <u>printing</u>.
報告已經準備好，可以印了。

for 爲介系詞，其後須接動名詞，故選 (B) ***printing***。
print〔prɪnt〕*v.* 印刷
report〔rɪˋport〕*n.* 報告　　ready〔ˋrɛdɪ〕*adj.* 準備好的

9. (**A**) You can always ***count on*** Carrie to do the right thing.
你可以信賴凱莉，她一定不會做錯事。

count on 依賴；信賴（= *depend on* = *rely on*）
right〔raɪt〕*adj.* 正確的

10. (**C**) In the future, <u>will you try</u> to improve your listening?
未來你會想要改善你的聽力嗎？

依句意爲未來式，又助動詞之後，須接原形動詞，故選
(C) ***will you try***。　　***try to*** *V.* 試圖～；努力～
in the future 未來　　improve〔ɪmˋpruv〕*v.* 改善

TEST 3

Directions: Of the four choices given after each sentence, choose the one most suitable for filling in the blank.

1. I prefer to write a paper _____ an examination.
   - (A) than take
   - (B) than taking
   - (C) rather than take
   - (D) to taking   (   )

2. I'm so bored and feel like _____.
   - (A) left
   - (B) to leave
   - (C) leaving
   - (D) leave   (   )

3. I _____ my lunch when you phoned me.
   - (A) had been having
   - (B) had
   - (C) was having
   - (D) could have   (   )

4. The Chen family _____ watching TV now.
   - (A) may
   - (B) are
   - (C) has
   - (D) have   (   )

5. He is _____ that we all like him.
   - (A) such a good person
   - (B) so a good person
   - (C) a such good person
   - (D) such good a person   (   )

6. Nowadays travel _____ faster and safer than ever before.
   - (A) will become
   - (B) becomes
   - (C) is becoming
   - (D) can become   (　)

7. I dislike _____ when I am absorbed in my studies.
   - (A) disturbed
   - (B) being disturbed
   - (C) to disturb
   - (D) disturbing   (　)

8. By the end of last year, I _____ this book three times.
   - (A) should read
   - (B) read
   - (C) have read
   - (D) had read   (　)

9. _____ students are Americans.
   - (A) This both
   - (B) Both these
   - (C) These both
   - (D) Both this   (　)

10. Tom and John are brothers. They are _____ same.
   - (A) very the
   - (B) the much
   - (C) the quite
   - (D) much the   (　)

TEST 3 詳解

1. (**C**) I prefer to write a paper <u>rather than take</u> an examination.
   我寧願寫份報告,而不要參加考試。

   > prefer〔prɪˈfɜ〕*v.* 寧願(選擇);更喜歡
   >
   > $\begin{cases} \textit{\textbf{prefer}} + \textit{\textbf{to}}\ V_1 + \textit{\textbf{rather than}} + V_2 \ \text{寧願}\ V_1,\text{而不要}\ V_2 \\ = \textit{\textbf{prefer}} + V_1\textit{\textbf{-ing}} + \textit{\textbf{to}} + V_2\textit{\textbf{-ing}} \end{cases}$
   >
   > paper〔ˈpepɚ〕*n.* 報告
   > examination〔ɪgˌzæməˈneʃən〕*n.* 考試
   > ***take an examination*** 參加考試

2. (**C**) I'm so bored and feel like <u>leaving</u>.
   我覺得很無聊,想要走。

   > ***feel like*** + ***V-ing*** 想要~
   > bored〔bord〕*adj.* (人)感到無聊的
   > leave〔liv〕*v.* 離開

3. (**C**) I <u>was having</u> my lunch when you phoned me.
   你打電話給我的時候,我正在吃午餐。

   > 兩個發生在過去的動作,比較短的動作以過去簡單式表達,
   > 而比較長的動作以「過去進行式」表達,即「was/were
   > +現在分詞」的形式,表示「在過去某一時間正在進行的
   > 動作」,故選 (C) ***was having***。
   >
   > have〔hæv〕*v.* 吃　　phone〔fon〕*v.* 打電話給~

4. (**B**) The Chen family <u>are</u> watching TV now.

陳氏一家人現在正在看電視。

「am/is/are＋現在分詞」為「現在進行式」，表「現在
正在進行的動作」，故選 (B) *are*。而 (A) may 為助動詞，
後面須接原形動詞，(C) has 和 (D) have 後面接過去分詞，
形成「現在完成式」，用法皆不合。

the Chen family 陳氏一家人

5. (**A**) He is <u>such a good person</u> that we all like him.

他是一位非常好的人，所以我們全都喜歡他。

「so…that～」和「such…that～」均表示「如此…
以致於～」，但 so 為副詞，後面接形容詞或副詞，
such 為形容詞，後面須接名詞。

$$\begin{cases} \cdots\textit{such a good senior that}\sim \\ =\cdots\textit{so good a senior that}\sim \end{cases}$$

6. (**C**) Nowadays travel <u>is becoming</u> faster and safer than
ever before.

和以往相比，現在旅行變得愈來愈迅速、而且也更安全。

nowadays〔'nauə,dez〕*adv.* 現在；現今 與現在式動詞
連用，又 become 用於現在進行式，是表示「逐漸」、
「越來越」的意思，故選 (C) ***is becoming***。而 (B) becomes
為現在簡單式，表示不變的事實，與句意不合。

（詳見「文法寶典」p.343）

travel〔'trævl〕*n.* 旅行　　safe〔sef〕*adj.* 安全的
ever〔'ɛvə〕*adv.* 以往；從來（用於強調）

7. (**B**)　I dislike <u>being disturbed</u> when I am absorbed in my studies. 當我在專心唸書的時候，不喜歡被打擾。

　　　dislike + *V-ing*　不喜歡～
　　　disturb〔dɪsˈtɝb〕*v.* 打擾
　　　依句意爲被動，故選 (B) *being disturbed*。
　　　absorbed〔əbˈsɔrbd〕*adj.* 專心的；全神貫注的 < *in* >
　　　studies〔ˈstʌdɪz〕*n. pl.* 課業

8. (**D**)　By the end of last year, I <u>had read</u> this book three times. 在去年年底之前，我已經看了這本書三次。

　　　by the end of last year「去年年底之前」，爲表過去的時間，而發生在過去之前的動作，須用「過去完成式」，故選 (D) *had read*。
　　　end〔ɛnd〕*n.* 最後部分；末尾　　time〔taɪm〕*n.* 次數

9. (**B**)　<u>Both these</u> students are Americans. 這兩個學生都是美國人。

　　　both「兩者都」的位置：
　　　① both + the/these/those/所有格 + 名詞
　　　②人稱代名詞主格 (we, you, they) + both
　　　③ both + of + 人稱代名詞的受格 (us, you, them)

10. (**D**)　Tom and John are brothers.　They are <u>much the</u> same. 湯姆和約翰是兄弟。他們幾乎一樣。

　　　much (*about*) *the same*　幾乎一樣
　　　cf. the very same　完全相同

TEST 4

Directions: *Of the four choices given after each sentence, choose the one most suitable for filling in the blank.*

1. Martha prepares breakfast for _____ and her child.
   - (A) himself
   - (B) herself
   - (C) she
   - (D) hers   (   )

2. The dead police officer _____ in the chest three times.
   - (A) had been stabbed
   - (B) was stabbing
   - (C) had stabbed
   - (D) is stabbing   (   )

3. If you stop at the BX, _____ me a Coke.
   - (A) buy
   - (B) would buy
   - (C) will buy
   - (D) should have bought   (   )

4. Kelly would like _____ a new house.
   - (A) for get
   - (B) to get
   - (C) is getting
   - (D) of getting   (   )

5. My mother _____ to Texas.
   - (A) didn't not fly
   - (B) don't fly
   - (C) didn't fly
   - (D) didn't never fly   (   )

6. Laura was born early in the year 1966. She was born
   _____.

   (A) in February
   (B) at 1 o'clock
   (C) in New York
   (D) on Sunday   (   )

7. You should use a pen instead of a pencil _____ your
   checks.

   (A) to writing
   (B) of writing
   (C) for writing
   (D) for write   (   )

8. Have you met the _____ scholar who is visiting
   our department today?

   (A) has learned
   (B) had learned
   (C) learns
   (D) learned   (   )

9. It was winter _____ he moved to San Francisco.

   (A) where
   (B) what
   (C) when
   (D) why   (   )

10. "Was Jamie having dinner when the phone rang?"

    (A) "No, she is."
    (B) "No, she was."
    (C) "Yes, she was."
    (D) "Yes, she will."   (   )

TEST 4 詳解

1. (**B**) Martha prepares breakfast for <u>herself</u> and her child.
   馬莎爲她自己和小孩做早餐。

   > 依句意，爲「她自己」和小孩，應用反身代名詞，故選
   > (B) **herself**。而 (A) himself「他自己」，指男性，在此不
   > 合句意；(C) she 是主格，(D) hers 是所有代名詞，用法不合。
   > prepare〔prɪˈpɛr〕v. 準備；（用原料）做成

2. (**A**) The dead police officer <u>had been stabbed</u> in the chest
   three times.
   那名殉職的警官，死前胸部曾遭人用刀刺了三下。

   > 被刺的動作，發生在死亡之前，死亡是過去的事，
   > 比過去某時更早發生的動作，須用「過去完成式」，
   > 即「had + p.p.」，且依句意爲被動，故選 (A) **had**
   > **been stabbed**。　　stab〔stæb〕v.（用刀）刺
   > officer〔ˈɔfɪsɚ〕n. 警官（= *police officer*）
   > time〔taɪm〕n. 次數　　chest〔tʃɛst〕n. 胸部

3. (**A**) If you stop at the BX, <u>buy</u> me a Coke.
   如果你有停在福利社，那就幫我買罐可口可樂。

   > 依句意，幫我買罐可樂，是祈使句，故空格應填原形動詞，
   > 選 (A) **buy**。本句的 If 子句是表條件，是直說法，不是假設
   > 法。（詳見「文法寶典」p.356）　**buy** *sb. sth.* 買某物給某人
   > **BX** （空軍、海軍的）福利社（= *base exchange*）
   > Coke〔kok〕n. 可口可樂（= *Coca-Cola*）

4. (**B**) Kelly *would like **to** get* a new house.

　　　凱莉想要買一棟新房子。

　　　　　would like to + *V.* 想要 (= *want to* + *V.*)

　　　　　get〔gɛt〕*v.* 買

5. (**C**) My mother <u>didn't fly</u> to Texas.

　　　我媽媽沒有搭飛機去德州。

　　　　　My mother 是第三人稱單數，故助動詞須用現在式的
　　　　　does，或過去式的 did，否定則用 doesn't 或 didn't，
　　　　　故選 (C) *didn't fly*。　　fly〔flaɪ〕*v.* 搭飛機

　　　　　Texas〔'tɛksəs〕*n.* (美國) 德州

6. (**A**) Laura was born early in the year 1966. She was
　　　born <u>in February</u>.

　　　蘿拉在一九六六年初出生。她出生於二月。

　　　　　依句意，在年初出生，故選 (A) *in February*「在二月」。

　　　　　February〔'fɛbru͵ɛrɪ〕*n.* 二月

　　　　　be born 出生　　early〔'ɝlɪ〕*adv.* 在初期；在早期

7. (**C**) You should use a pen instead of a pencil <u>for writing</u>
　　　your checks. 你應該用原子筆寫支票，而不是用鉛筆。

　　　　　⎰ *use sth. **for*** + *N.* / *V-ing* 使用某物做～
　　　　　⎱ = *use sth. **to*** + *V.*

　　　　　pen〔pɛn〕*n.* 原子筆 (= *ballpoint pen*)

　　　　　instead of 而不是　　pencil〔'pɛnsḷ〕*n.* 鉛筆

　　　　　check〔tʃɛk〕*n.* 支票

8. (**D**) Have you met the <u>learned</u> scholar who is visiting our department today?

你認不認識，今天要來我們部門參觀的，那位很有學問的學者？

空格應填形容詞，修飾其後的名詞 scholar，故選 (D) ***learned*** 〔ˋlɜnɪd〕 *adj.* 博學的（注意發音）。

（如果是動詞 learn 的過去式 learned，就要唸成〔lɜnd〕。）

meet〔mit〕*v.* 認識 scholar〔ˋskɑlɚ〕*n.* 學者

visit〔ˋvɪzɪt〕*v.* 拜訪；參觀

department〔dɪˋpɑrtmənt〕*n.* 部門

9. (**C**) It was winter <u>when</u> he moved to San Francisco.

他在冬天時搬去舊金山。

表「時間」，關係副詞須用 ***when***，故選 (C)。

move〔muv〕*v.* 搬家

San Francisco〔͵sænfrənˋsɪsko〕*n.* 舊金山

10. (**C**) "Was Jamie having dinner when the phone rang?"
"<u>Yes, she was.</u>"

「當電話鈴響時，潔咪正在吃晚餐嗎？」

「是的，她正在吃晚餐。」

依句意為過去式，且在答句中，「Yes + 肯定內容」，「No + 否定內容」，故選 (C)。

have〔hæv〕*v.* 吃 phone〔fon〕*n.* 電話

ring〔rɪŋ〕*v.*（鈴）響（三態變化為：ring-rang-rung）

TEST 5

Directions: *Of the four choices given after each sentence, choose the one most suitable for filling in the blank.*

1. Tommy wanted his brother _____ his shoes for him.
   (A) ties
   (B) to tie
   (C) tie
   (D) tying   (   )

2. The movie star put on her fur coat.
   (A) She wore it.
   (B) She sent it to the cleaners.
   (C) She hung it on the rack.
   (D) She put it in the washing machine.   (   )

3. Tom is _____ to get a job.
   (A) enough old
   (B) old enough
   (C) age enough
   (D) enough age   (   )

4. How about _____ a muffin for dessert?
   (A) to having
   (B) to have
   (C) have
   (D) having   (   )

5. These young kids know how to _____ the time.
   (A) tell
   (B) say
   (C) speak
   (D) talk   (   )

6. We prefer to visit you tomorrow morning if _____ convenient for you.

   (A) you are
   (B) it's
   (C) it will be
   (D) I'm   (   )

7. Tony quit _____ because he was not interested in it anymore.

   (A) draw
   (B) to draw
   (C) drawing
   (D) drew   (   )

8. Stella needs a motorcycle, but she doesn't have enough money to buy _____.

   (A) it
   (B) this
   (C) one
   (D) motorcycle   (   )

9. In the contest, each boy must build a sand castle _____.

   (A) on himself
   (B) by his own
   (C) in oneself
   (D) on his own   (   )

10. The accumulation of mud on our tires was _____ than we thought.

   (A) as worse as
   (B) more worse
   (C) worst
   (D) worse   (   )

TEST 5 詳解

1. (**B**) Tommy wanted his brother <u>to tie</u> his shoes for him.

湯米要他大哥爲他綁鞋帶。

> ***want sb. + to V.*** 要某人做
>
> tie〔 taɪ 〕*v.* 打（結）；繫上

2. (**A**) The movie star put on her fur coat.

電影明星穿上他的毛皮大衣。

> 依句意，「穿上」毛皮大衣，故選 (A) ***She wore it.***
>
> （她穿著它。）
>
> ⎰ ***put on*** 穿上（強調動作）
>
> ⎱ wear〔 wɛr 〕*v.* 穿著（強調狀態）
>
> star〔 stɑr 〕*n.* 明星　　fur〔 fɝ 〕*adj.* 毛皮製的
>
> ***fur coat*** 毛皮大衣
>
> send〔 sɛnd 〕*v.* 寄；送（三態變化爲：send-sent-sent）
>
> cleaners〔'klinɚz 〕*n.* 乾洗店
>
> hang〔 hæŋ 〕*v.* 把…掛起（三態變化爲：hang-hung-hung）
>
> rack〔 ræk 〕*n.* 架子　　***washing machine*** 洗衣機

3. (**B**) Tom is <u>old enough</u> to get a job.

湯姆年紀夠大了，可以找一份工作。

> 副詞 enough 須置於所修飾的形容詞之後，用於
>
> 「*adj.* +enough + to V.」的句型，表「夠～，
>
> 足以…」，故選 (B) ***old enough***。
>
> job〔 dʒɑb 〕*n.* 工作　　age〔 edʒ 〕*n.* 年紀

4. (**D**) How about <u>having</u> a muffin for dessert?
要不要吃個瑪芬做甜點？

> ***How about + V-ing?*** ～如何？
> (=*What about + V-ing?* =*What do you say to* + *V-ing?*)

muffin〔'mʌfɪn〕*n.* 瑪芬鬆餅
dessert〔dɪ'zɝt〕*n.* 甜點

5. (**A**) These young kids know how to <u>tell</u> the time.
這些年紀幼小的孩童知道如何看時間。

> ***tell the time*** 看時間（=*tell time*）

young〔jʌŋ〕*adj.* 年幼的　　kid〔kɪd〕*n.* 小孩

6. (**B**) We prefer to visit you tomorrow morning if <u>it's</u>
convenient for you.
如果你方便的話，我們希望明天早上才去拜訪你。

> convenient 是非人稱形容詞，不可修飾人，故中文說
> 「如果某人方便的話」，英文要用 if *it's* convenient for
> *sb.* 不可說成 *if sb. is convenient*（誤）。又在表時間或
> 條件的副詞子句中，須用現在式表示未來，不可用 will
> 表示未來，故選 (B) *it's*。

prefer〔prɪ'fɝ〕*v.* 比較喜歡；寧願
convenient〔kən'vinjənt〕*adj.* 方便的

7. (**C**) Tony quit <u>drawing</u> because he was not interested in
it anymore. 湯尼放棄畫畫，因為他對畫畫不再有興趣了。

> ***quit + V-ing*** 放棄～；停止～
>
> draw〔drɔ〕*v.* 畫畫　　***not…anymore*** 不再…
> ***be interested in*** 對～有興趣

8. (**C**) Stella needs a motorcycle, but she doesn't have enough money to buy <u>one</u>.

史黛拉需要一輛摩托車，可是她沒有足夠的錢買摩托車。

代名詞 one 代替前面已提過的名詞，以避免重複，故選 (C) ***one*** (= *a motorcycle*)。而 (A) it「它」指「特定的那一個」，(B) this「這個」，用法均不合。

【比較】

Stella needs ***the motorcycle***, but she doesn't have enough money to buy ***it***. (史黛拉需要那輛摩托車，可是她沒有足夠的錢買那一輛摩托車。)

motorcycle〔ˈmotə‚saɪkl̩〕*n.* 摩托車

9. (**D**) In the contest, each boy must build a sand castle <u>on his own</u>. 在那場比賽中，每個男孩都必須自己蓋一座沙堡。

$\begin{cases} \textbf{\textit{on one's own}} \ \ 靠自己；獨力 \\ = \textbf{\textit{by oneself}} \end{cases}$

contest〔ˈkɑntɛst〕*n.* 比賽   build〔bɪld〕*v.* 建造
sand〔sænd〕*n.* 沙   castle〔ˈkæsl̩〕*n.* 城堡

10. (**D**) The accumulation of mud on our tires was <u>worse</u> than we thought.

我們輪胎上所堆積的泥巴，比我們想像中的還嚴重。

從 than 得知此為表「比較」的句型，bad 的比較級為 ***worse***，故選 (D)。而 (A) as…as～「像～一樣…」，為原級比較，中間須放原級形容詞，故用法不合。

accumulation〔ə‚kjumjəˈleʃən〕*n.* 堆積
mud〔mʌd〕*n.* 泥巴   tire〔tɪr〕*n.* 輪胎

TEST 6

Directions: *Of the four choices given after each sentence, choose the one most suitable for filling in the blank.*

1. Kevin went to France _____.
   - (A) on Saturday, 1995, May 2
   - (B) on May 2, on Saturday
   - (C) on May 2, Saturday, in 1995
   - (D) on Saturday, May 2, 1995   ( )

2. It's no use _____ about it. Go and ask the teacher.
   - (A) to argue with me
   - (B) arguing with me
   - (C) that you argue with me
   - (D) that you should argue with me   ( )

3. Never _____ a man more selfish and mean than Peter.
   - (A) have I seen
   - (B) do I see
   - (C) I have seen
   - (D) I do see   ( )

4. Give me _____ bread. I am very hungry.
   - (A) few
   - (B) a few
   - (C) little
   - (D) a little   ( )

5. How much _____ to buy that notebook?
   - (A) did it cost him
   - (B) did he cost
   - (C) he cost
   - (D) was he cost   ( )

6. He cannot be a successful businessman because he is
   devoid _____ foresight.
   (A) with
   (B) from
   (C) of
   (D) in ( )

7. I could see something _____ behind the bush, but
   I did not know what it was.
   (A) moving
   (B) has been moving
   (C) is moved
   (D) to move ( )

8. If we have too many things on the desk, we will feel
   _____ easily.
   (A) tiring
   (B) tire
   (C) tires
   (D) tired ( )

9. His lecture _____ students to a better understanding
   of political science.
   (A) leaded
   (B) leads
   (C) lead
   (D) leading ( )

10. The causes of World War II are _____: nationalism
    and imperialism.
    (A) followings
    (B) as follows
    (C) as following
    (D) as follow ( )

TEST 6 詳解

1. (**D**) Kevin went to France <u>on Saturday, May 2, 1995</u>.

凱文在一九九五年五月二日星期六那天，前往法國。

> 日期的排列順序，須從小到大，故選 (D)。
>
> France〔fræns〕n. 法國

2. (**B**) It's no use <u>arguing with me</u> about it. Go and ask the
teacher. 跟我爭論那件事沒有用。去問老師。

> *It's no use* + *V-ing* ～是沒有用的
> argue〔ˈɑrgjʊ〕v. 爭論

3. (**A**) Never <u>have I seen</u> a man more selfish and mean than
Peter. 我從來沒看過比彼得更自私、更卑鄙的人。

> 否定副詞 Never (從未) 置於句首時，主詞與動詞須倒裝，
> 依句意為現在完成式，表示「從過去持續到現在的動作或
> 狀態」，故選 (A) *have I seen*。
>
> selfish〔ˈsɛlfɪʃ〕adj. 自私的　　mean〔min〕adj. 卑鄙的

4. (**D**) Give me <u>a little</u> bread. I am very hungry.

給我一些麵包。我非常餓。

> few 和 a few 用於修飾可數名詞；little 和 a little 用於
> 修飾不可數名詞。few 和 little 均表「很少」，指少到幾
> 乎沒有，相當於否定字；a few 和 a little 則表「一些」，
> 沒有否定意味，等於 some。依句意為肯定，且 bread
> 〔brɛd〕n. 麵包 為不可數名詞，故選 (D) *a little*。

5. (**A**)　How much <u>did it cost him</u> to buy that notebook?

那本筆記本花了他多少錢？

cost「花費」須以物做主詞，接人做受詞，依句意爲疑問句，須倒裝，故選 (A) *did it cost him*，it 爲虛主詞，代替 to buy that notebook。

notebook〔'not,buk〕*n.* 筆記本

6. (**C**)　He cannot be a successful businessman because he is devoid <u>of</u> foresight.

他無法成爲一位成功的商人，因爲他缺乏遠見。

devoid〔dɪ'vɔɪd〕*adj.* 缺乏的；沒有的
be devoid of 缺乏；沒有

successful〔sək'sɛsfəl〕*adj.* 成功的
foresight〔'for,saɪt〕*n.* 遠見

7. (**A**)　I could see something <u>moving</u> behind the bush, but I did not know what it was.

我看見灌木叢後面有東西在動，但是我不知道那是什麼。

see「看見」爲感官動詞，其用法爲：

see＋受詞＋　　原形 V. (表主動)
　　　　　　　現在分詞 (表主動進行)
　　　　　　　p.p. (表被動)

依句意，某物「正在動」爲主動進行，故選 (A) *moving*。
move〔muv〕*v.* 移動

behind〔bɪ'haɪnd〕*prep.* 在…的後面
bush〔buʃ〕*n.* 灌木叢

8. (**D**) If we have too many things on the desk, we will feel
   <u>tired</u> easily.

   如果書桌上有太多東西，我們就會容易覺得疲倦。

   > feel「覺得」是連綴動詞，後面須接形容詞做補語，又
   > tire〔taɪr〕v. 使疲倦 是情感動詞，「人」做主詞，須
   > 用過去分詞 tired「疲倦的」修飾，「非人」做主詞，則
   > 用現在分詞 tiring「令人疲倦的」修飾，故選 (D) *tired*。

9. (**B**) His lecture <u>leads</u> students to a better understanding
   of political science. 他的演講引領學生更了解政治學。

   > lead〔lid〕v. 引領；導致（三態變化為：lead-led-led）
   > 主詞 His lecture「他的演講」為第三人稱單數，故選
   > (B) *leads*。
   >
   > lecture〔'lɛktʃɚ〕n. 演講；講課
   > understanding〔ˌʌndɚ'stændɪŋ〕n. 了解
   > political〔pə'lɪtɪk!〕adj. 政治的
   > science〔'saɪəns〕n. 科學　　*political science* 政治學

10. (**B**) The causes of World War Ⅱ are <u>as follows</u>: nationalism
    and imperialism.

    第二次世界大戰的起因如下：民族主義和帝國主義。

    > *as follows* 如下
    > 此片語的動詞 follow，為非人稱動詞，不論主詞為何，
    > 都用第三人稱現在式，故選 (B)。
    >
    > cause〔kɔz〕n. 起因
    > nationalism〔'næʃən!ˌɪzəm〕n. 民族主義；國家主義
    > imperialism〔ɪm'pɪrɪəlˌɪzəm〕n. 帝國主義

TEST 7

Directions: *Of the four choices given after each sentence, choose the one most suitable for filling in the blank.*

1. I'm not sure what John is _____.
   - (A) interesting
   - (B) interested
   - (C) interested in
   - (D) interesting in   (   )

2. A person is usually judged by _____ he does.
   - (A) what
   - (B) however
   - (C) that
   - (D) which   (   )

3. Keep an eye on the kids for me while I _____.
   - (A) go to shop
   - (B) go shopping
   - (C) go the shopping
   - (D) going shopping   (   )

4. What flowers are you _____ in your garden?
   - (A) fertilize
   - (B) fertilizes
   - (C) fertilized
   - (D) fertilizing   (   )

5. Tony said he was going to take a bath.
   - (A) He's going to walk.
   - (B) He's going to sleep.
   - (C) He's going to wash.
   - (D) He's going to eat.   (   )

6. Whatever Mr. Brown does, he does it with an eye to
_____ more money.
- (A) make
- (B) making
- (C) be making
- (D) have made   ( )

7. David often fails to do his homework, which
_____ his father angry.
- (A) makes
- (B) make
- (C) had made
- (D) have made   ( )

8. The number of animals in San Diego Zoo is larger than
_____ in Taipei Zoo.
- (A) this
- (B) that
- (C) those
- (D) ×   ( )

9. All the dinner _____ before they finished the
conversation.
- (A) are eaten
- (B) had been eaten
- (C) has eaten
- (D) been eaten   ( )

10. I can't find my umbrella, but I remember _____
it at the back door.
- (A) putting
- (B) to put
- (C) put
- (D) have put   ( )

TEST 7 詳解

1. (**C**) I'm not sure what John is <u>interested in</u>.
　　　我不確定約翰對什麼有興趣。

> $\begin{cases} \text{interested} \text{ ('ɪntrɪstɪd) } \textit{adj.} \text{ (人) 有興趣的} < in > \\ \text{interesting} \text{ ('ɪntrɪstɪŋ) } \textit{adj.} \text{ (人或物) 有趣的} \end{cases}$
>
> what 引導的名詞子句中，以 *interested* 修飾約翰，
> 介系詞 *in* 不可省略。
>
> sure〔ʃʊr〕*adj.* 確定的

2. (**A**) A person is usually judged by <u>what</u> he does.
　　　要評斷一個人，通常是看他的所作所為。

> 複合關係代名詞 *what* 是本身兼做先行詞的關係代名詞，
> 等於 the thing(s) which。而 (B) however〔haʊ'ɛvə〕
> 「無論如何」為連接詞，(C) that「那個」為代名詞，
> (D) which 為關係代名詞，用法均不合。
>
> judge〔dʒʌdʒ〕*v.* 判斷；評定

3. (**B**) Keep an eye on the kids for me while I <u>go shopping</u>.
　　　我去購物的時候，幫我看一下小孩。

> while 引導副詞子句，須有完整的主詞和動詞，故 (D)
> 不合，又「go + V-ing」表「從事~（活動）」，故選
> (B) *go shopping*（ = *do the shopping* = *do my*
> *shopping*）。
>
> *keep an eye on* 留心；注意

4. (**D**) What flowers are you <u>fertilizing</u> in your garden?

你在花園裡爲什麼花施肥？

fertilize〔ˈfɝtḷˌaɪz〕*v.* 施肥

依句意，爲現在進行式，即「be 動詞＋現在分詞」的
形式，故選 (D) *fertilizing*。

garden〔ˈgɑrdṇ〕*n.* 花園

5. (**C**) Tony said he was going to take a bath.

湯尼說他要去洗澡。

依句意，選 (C) He's going to wash.（他即將去洗澡。）

take a bath 洗澡　　wash〔wɑʃ〕*v.* 洗澡

6. (**B**) Whatever Mr. Brown does, he does it with an eye
to <u>making</u> more money.

布朗先生不論做什麼，都是爲了要賺更多的錢。

with an eye to + ***V-ing*** 目的是爲了（ = *with a view*
to + *V-ing* = *with the purpose of* + *V-ing*）

make money 賺錢

whatever〔hwɑtˈɛvɚ〕*pron.* 無論什麼事

7. (**A**) David often fails to do his homework, which
<u>makes</u> his father angry.

大衛經常沒寫作業，這一點讓他爸爸很生氣。

which 代替前面一整句話，引導形容詞子句，在子句中
做主詞，並視爲單數，故空格應填入單數動詞 *makes*，
選 (A)。

fail to V. 未能～　　angry〔ˈæŋgrɪ〕*adj.* 生氣的

8. (**B**) The number of animals in San Diego Zoo is larger than <u>that</u> in Taipei Zoo.

聖地牙哥動物園的動物數量，比台北動物園的動物數量多。

為了避免重複前面提過的名詞，單數名詞可用 ***that*** 代替，複數名詞可用 ***those*** 代替，依句意，選 (B) ***that***，在此代替 the number of animals。

number〔ˋnʌmbɚ〕*n.* 數量　　animal〔ˋænəm!〕*n.* 動物
San Diego〔͵sændiˋego〕*n.* 聖地牙哥（美國加州一城市）
zoo〔zu〕*n.* 動物園

9. (**B**) All the dinner <u>had been eaten</u> before they finished the conversation.

所有的晚餐在他們結束談話之前，就已經吃完了。

「吃完晚餐」的動作發生於 finished the conversation「結束談話」之前，比過去式更早的動作，以「過去完成式」表達，其形式為「had ＋ 過去分詞」，又依句意為被動，即「be 動詞＋過去分詞」的形式，eat 的過去分詞為 ***eaten***，be 動詞的過去分詞為 ***been***，故選 (B) ***had been eaten***。

finish〔ˋfɪnɪʃ〕*v.* 結束
conversation〔͵kɑnvɚˋseʃən〕*n.* 談話

10. (**A**) I can't find my umbrella, but I remember <u>putting</u> it at the back door.

我找不到我的雨傘，但我記得我把雨傘放在後門。

$\left\{\begin{array}{l}\textit{remember} + \textit{V-ing}\text{ 記得做過（動作已完成）}\\\textit{remember} + \textit{to V.}\text{ 記得要去做（動作未完成）}\end{array}\right.$

umbrella〔ʌmˋbrɛlə〕*n.* 雨傘　　***back door*** 後門

TEST 8

Directions: *Of the four choices given after each sentence, choose the one most suitable for filling in the blank.*

1. All the _____ ID cards are listed in the computer.
   - (A) issued
   - (B) issues
   - (C) to issue
   - (D) is issuing   (   )

2. The airplane was forced _____ an emergency landing.
   - (A) made
   - (B) to make
   - (C) make
   - (D) to making   (   )

3. The brave soldiers fought _____ sunrise.
   - (A) in
   - (B) until
   - (C) in spite of
   - (D) by means of   (   )

4. Kevin walked _____ the path.
   - (A) at
   - (B) with
   - (C) between
   - (D) along   (   )

5. Billy and David _____ their lessons.
   - (A) study
   - (B) are studied
   - (C) were studied
   - (D) studying   (   )

6. John would not go to school yesterday, but he
_____ go to school today.
- (A) will
- (B) won't
- (C) always
- (D) sometimes   (   )

7. In baseball, the first ball of the season _____
by the president.
- (A) throwing
- (B) have thrown
- (C) does throw
- (D) is often thrown   (   )

8. The candidate, _____ by many, decided to run.
- (A) to support
- (B) supports
- (C) supported
- (D) supporting   (   )

9. Do you _____ if I turn off the radio?
- (A) want
- (B) wish
- (C) like
- (D) mind   (   )

10. _____ is his estimated time of departure?
- (A) Why
- (B) Who
- (C) What
- (D) Whose   (   )

TEST 8 詳解

1. (**A**) All the <u>issued</u> ID cards are listed in the computer.
所有發出去的身分證，都被列在電腦中。

> 空格應填形容詞，修飾其後的名詞 ID cards，依句意，
> 選 (A) *issued*「發出去的」。 issue〔ˋɪʃju〕*v.* 發行
> ***ID card*** 身分證 (= *identification card*)
> list〔lɪst〕*v.* 列出　　computer〔kəmˋpjutə〕*n.* 電腦

2. (**B**) The airplane ***was forced to*** <u>make</u> an emergency
landing. 這架飛機被迫緊急降落。

> force〔fors〕*v.* 強迫
> ***be forced to V.*** 被迫～
> airplane〔ˋɛr͵plen〕*n.* 飛機
> emergency〔ɪˋmɛdʒənsɪ〕*adj.* 緊急的
> landing〔ˋlændɪŋ〕*n.* 降落
> ***make an emergency landing*** 緊急降落

3. (**B**) The brave soldiers fought <u>until</u> sunrise.
這些勇敢的士兵，一直奮戰到日出。

> 依句意，選 (B) *until*「直到」。而 (A) in 須改為 at，
> at sunrise 才是指「在日出時」，(C) in spite of「儘管」，
> (D) by means of「藉由」，則不合句意。
> brave〔brev〕*adj.* 勇敢的
> soldier〔ˋsoldʒə〕*n.* 士兵；軍人
> fight〔faɪt〕*v.* 戰鬥 (三態變化為：fight-fought-fought)
> sunrise〔ˋsʌn͵raɪz〕*n.* 日出

4. (**D**) Kevin walked <u>along</u> the path.

　　凱文走在小徑上。

　　依句意，選 (D) **along**「沿著」（ = *down* ）。

　　path〔pæθ〕*n.* 小徑

5. (**A**) Billy and David <u>study</u> their lessons.

　　比利和大衛研讀他們的功課。

　　空格應填複數動詞，且依句意為主動，故選 (A) **study**。

　　lessons〔'lɛsn̩z〕*n.pl.* 課業

6. (**A**) John would not go to school yesterday, but he <u>will</u>
　　go to school today.

　　約翰昨天不會去上學，但是他今天會去。

　　he 為第三人稱單數代名詞，但空格後為原形動詞 go，
　　所以空格應填助動詞，故 (C) always「總是」和 (D)
　　sometimes「有時候」，皆為副詞，在此用法不合。
　　且由連接詞 but 可知，前後語意有轉折，「昨天沒去
　　上學，但是今天會去」，所以 (B) won't 不合句意，
　　選 (A) **will**。

7. (**D**) In baseball, the first ball of the season <u>is often thrown</u>
　　by the president.

　　在棒球方面，通常球季一開始，都是由總統負責開球。

　　球是被投出去的，為被動語態，故選 (D) **is often thrown**。
　　throw〔θro〕*v.* 投擲（三態變化為：throw-threw-thrown）
　　baseball〔'bes,bɔl〕*n.* 棒球　season〔'sizn̩〕*n.*（球）季
　　president〔'prɛzədn̩t〕*n.* 總統

8. (**C**) The candidate, <u>supported</u> by many, decided to run.

那名候選人受到很多人的支持，所以決定要參選。

> 本句是由 The candidate, *who was* supported by many, decided to run. 省略關代 who 和 be 動詞 was，簡化而來。 support〔 sə'port〕*v.* 支持
>
> candidate〔'kændə,det〕*n.* 候選人
>
> many〔'mɛnɪ〕*pron.* 很多人（= *many people*）
>
> decide〔 dɪ'saɪd〕*v.* 決定
>
> run〔 rʌn〕*v.* 參選

9. (**D**) Do you <u>mind</u> if I turn off the radio?

你介意我關掉收音機嗎？

> mind〔 maɪnd〕*v.* 介意
>
> ***Do you mind if~?*** 如果~你介不介意？
>
> ***turn off*** 關掉（電器）【↔ *turn on* 打開（電器）】

10. (**C**) <u>What</u> is his estimated time of departure?

他預計要什麼時候離開？

> 空格應填疑問代名詞，依句意，「什麼」時候離開，選 (C) ***What***。
>
> estimated〔'ɛstə,metɪd〕*adj.* 估計的；推測的
>
> departure〔 dɪ'partʃɚ〕*n.* 離開

TEST 9

Directions: *Of the four choices given after each sentence, choose the one most suitable for filling in the blank.*

1. He listened to them _____ about their boss.
   - (A) talking
   - (B) talked
   - (C) to talk
   - (D) to talking   (   )

2. It is _____ that he should send his own son to prison.
   - (A) to surprise
   - (B) to be surprised
   - (C) surprised
   - (D) surprising   (   )

3. I really recommend that restaurant. You _____ try it.
   - (A) must not
   - (B) ought to
   - (C) would
   - (D) may   (   )

4. When you are tired, you'll feel _____.
   - (A) sleepy
   - (B) sleep
   - (C) slept
   - (D) sleeping   (   )

5. I wish it _____ yesterday.
   - (A) has not rained
   - (B) did not rain
   - (C) will not rain
   - (D) had not rained   (   )

6. Rick got married to Nancy _____ he left the university.

   (A) as soon as
   (B) as far as
   (C) as often as
   (D) as long as   ( )

7. "What _____?" "Nothing."
   (A) was happened
   (B) did he happen
   (C) happened
   (D) he happened   ( )

8. I need _____ my trousers.
   (A) to iron
   (B) ironing
   (C) iron
   (D) ironed   ( )

9. _____ are very warm-hearted people. They volunteer to help homeless people.

   (A) The Benson's family
   (B) The Benson
   (C) The Bensons
   (D) Benson family   ( )

10. Mary didn't bring enough money and didn't know _____ to do.

   (A) when
   (B) what
   (C) how
   (D) where   ( )

TEST 9　詳解

1. (**A**)　He listened to them <u>talking</u> about their boss.

他聽他們談論他們的老板。

listen to「聽」為感官動詞，其用法為：

listen to + 受詞 + $\begin{cases} 原形 V.（表主動）\\ 現在分詞（表主動進行）\\ p.p.（表被動）\end{cases}$

依句意，他們「正在談論」為主動進行，故選 (A) *talking*。

talk about 談論

boss〔bɔs〕*n.* 老板

2. (**D**)　It is <u>surprising</u> that he should send his own son to prison.　令人驚訝的是，他竟會讓自己的兒子去坐牢。

surprise〔sə'praɪz〕*v.* 使驚訝 是情感動詞，「非人」
做主詞，須用現在分詞 surprising 修飾，「人」做主詞，
則用過去分詞 surprised 修飾。It 為虛主詞，代替後面
的 that 子句，故為「非人」，空格須填 *surprising*
〔sə'praɪzɪŋ〕*adj.* 令人驚訝的，選 (D)。而 (C) surprised
「（人）感到驚訝的」，則不合句意。

should〔ʃud〕*aux.* 竟然
send〔sɛnd〕*v.* 使（某人）去…
own〔on〕*adj.* 自己的
prison〔'prɪzn̩〕*n.* 監獄

3. (**B**) I really recommend that restaurant.　You ought to
try it.　我真的推薦那家餐廳。你應該試一試。

> ***ought to V.*** 應該~
>
> 而 (A) must not「絕對不能」，(C) would「將」（will 的
> 過去式），(D) may「可以；可能」，用法均不合。
>
> recommend〔ˌrɛkəˈmɛnd〕v. 推薦

4. (**A**) When you are tired, you'll feel sleepy.
當你疲倦的時候，你會覺得想睡覺。

> feel「覺得」是連綴動詞，後面須接形容詞做補語，故選
> (A) ***sleepy***〔ˈslipɪ〕*adj.*　想睡的。而 (B) sleep〔slip〕*n. v.*
> 睡覺（三態變化為：sleep-slept-slept），則用法不合。

5. (**D**) I wish it had not rained yesterday.
但願昨天沒有下雨。

> I wish「我希望；但願」後面須接假設語氣，且依句意，
> 希望昨天「沒有下雨」，為與過去事實相反的假設語氣，
> 故 that 子句中的動詞時態須用「過去完成式」，即「had
> + 過去分詞」的形式，選 (D) ***had not rained***。

6. (**A**) Rick got married to Nancy as soon as he left the
university.　瑞克一從大學畢業後，就和南西結婚。

> 依句意，選 (A) ***as soon as***「一⋯就~」。而 (B) as far as
> 「遠至」，(C) as often as「多達⋯（次）」，(D) as long
> as「只要」，皆不合句意。
>
> ***get married to sb.***　和某人結婚
>
> university〔ˌjunəˈvɝsətɪ〕*n.*　大學

7. (**C**)　"What <u>happened</u>?" "Nothing."

　　「發生了什麼事？」「沒事。」

　　happen〔'hæpən〕*v.* 發生 為不及物動詞，限用主動。

　　又「*sth. **happen** to sb.*」表「某人發生某事」，故 (D)

　　須改為 What *happened to him*? 才能選。

8. (**A**)　I need <u>to iron</u> my trousers.　我需要燙褲子。

　　need（需要）的用法為：

　　$\begin{cases} 人 + \textbf{\textit{need}} + \textbf{\textit{to V.}} & 某人需要～ \\ 物 + \textbf{\textit{need}} + \textbf{\textit{V-ing}} & 某物需要被～ \end{cases}$

　　　（= 物 + *need to be* + *p.p.* ）

　　iron〔'aɪən〕*v.* 熨燙

　　trousers〔'traʊzɚz〕*n. pl.* 褲子

9. (**C**)　<u>The Bensons</u> are very warm-hearted people.　They

　　volunteer to help homeless people.

　　班森一家人非常熱心。他們自願幫助無家可歸的人。

　　表「姓～的一家人」，姓氏後要加 s，且前面要加定冠詞

　　the。***the Bensons*** 班森一家人（= *the Benson family*）

　　warm-hearted〔'wɔrm'hɑrtɪd〕*adj.* 熱心的

　　volunteer〔ˌvɑlən'tɪr〕*v.* 自願

　　homeless〔'homlɪs〕*adj.* 無家可歸的

10. (**B**)　Mary didn't bring enough money and didn't know

　　<u>what</u> to do.　瑪麗帶的錢不夠，所以不知該怎麼辦。

　　依句意，選 (B) ***what to do***「怎麼辦」，在此相等於 what

　　she should do。而 (C) how 為副詞，在此用法不合。

TEST 10

Directions: *Of the four choices given after each sentence, choose the one most suitable for filling in the blank.*

1. Tracy had the table _____ from the classroom.
   - (A) removes
   - (B) to remove
   - (C) removing
   - (D) removed ( )

2. We had better eat dinner.
   - (A) Dinner was good.
   - (B) We should eat dinner.
   - (C) Dinner isn't ready.
   - (D) We ate dinner. ( )

3. Was the pilot _____ by the bright lights?
   - (A) confusing
   - (B) to confusing
   - (C) to confuse
   - (D) confused ( )

4. Select the correct sentence.
   - (A) The car to me belongs.
   - (B) The car belongs to me.
   - (C) To me belongs the car.
   - (D) The car me belongs to. ( )

5. I _____ write a letter to her if I knew her address.
   - (A) like
   - (B) can
   - (C) would
   - (D) will ( )

6. If Robert hadn't known how to swim, he _____
have drowned when the ship sank.

   (A) did
   (B) should
   (C) must
   (D) might   (   )

7. Generally speaking, the weather is good. The weather is
_____.

   (A) sometimes clear
   (B) too good
   (C) usually good
   (D) seldom clear   (   )

8. The class is made up _____ students from many
different countries.

   (A) from
   (B) with
   (C) in
   (D) of   (   )

9. Isn't the exam _____ by the instructor?

   (A) gave
   (B) given
   (C) to give
   (D) be given   (   )

10. Mr. Clark _____ in that school for five years.

   (A) is studying
   (B) been studying
   (C) has been studying
   (D) is being studied   (   )

TEST 10 詳解

1. (**D**) Tracy had the table <u>removed</u> from the classroom.
   崔西叫人把那張桌子，從教室裡移出去。

   > have 為使役動詞，其用法為：
   >
   > have + 受詞 + $\begin{cases} 原形 V. （表主動） \\ p.p. （表被動） \end{cases}$
   >
   > 依句意，讓桌子「被移出去」，為被動，故選
   > (D) *removed*。　remove〔rɪ'muv〕*v.* 移除

2. (**B**) We had better eat dinner.
   我們最好吃晚餐。

   > We should eat dinner. （我們應該吃晚餐。）
   > *had better V.* 最好～
   >
   > ready〔'rɛdɪ〕*adj.* 準備好的

3. (**D**) Was the pilot <u>confused</u> by the bright lights?
   飛行員有因為明亮的燈光，而感到困惑嗎？

   > 依句意為被動語態，故空格應填過去分詞，選
   > (D) *confused*。　confuse〔kən'fjuz〕*v.* 使困惑
   >
   > pilot〔'paɪlət〕*n.* 飛行員　　bright〔braɪt〕*adj.* 明亮的
   > light〔laɪt〕*n.* 燈光

4. (**B**) Select the correct sentence. 選出正確的句子。

   > The car belongs to me. （那部車是屬於我的。）
   > *belong to* 屬於

5. (**C**) I <u>would</u> write a letter to her if I knew her address.

如果我知道她的住址，我就會寫信給她。

依句意為「與現在事實相反的假設」，if 子句用過去式
動詞或 be 動詞 were，而主要子句則用 should, would,
could, 或 might 加原形動詞，故選 (C) *would*。

address〔ə'drɛs,'ædrɛs〕*n.* 地址

6. (**D**) If Robert hadn't known how to swim, he <u>might</u> have
drowned when the ship sank.

如果羅伯特當時不會游泳，那當那艘船沉沒時，他可能
早就淹死了。

依句意為「與過去事實相反的假設」，其用法為：

$$\text{If + S. + had + p.p.}\cdots\text{, S. +} \begin{Bmatrix} \text{should} \\ \text{would} \\ \text{could} \\ \text{might} \end{Bmatrix} \text{+ have + p.p.}$$

依句意，「可能」早就淹死了，選 (D) *might*。
而 (B) should have + p.p.「早該～」，表過去該做而未做，
(C) must have + p.p.「當時一定～」，表對過去事實肯定
的推測，均不合句意。

drown〔draʊn〕*v.* 淹死   sink〔sɪŋk〕*v.* 下沉；沉沒

7. (**C**) Generally speaking, the weather is good. The weather
is <u>usually good</u>. 一般說來，天氣都很好。天氣通常都很好。

依句意，選 (C) *usually good*「通常都很好」。

generally speaking 一般說來

weather〔'wɛðɚ〕*n.* 天氣   clear〔klɪr〕*adj.* 晴朗的

8. (**D**) The class *is made up of* students from many different countries.

這個班級，是由許多來自不同國家的學生所組成的。

> ***be made up of*** 由～組成
> = *be composed of*
> = *consist of*
> country〔ˈkʌntrɪ〕*n.* 國家

9. (**B**) Isn't the exam <u>given</u> by the instructor?

這場考試不是那位老師舉行的嗎？

> 依句意，考試是被舉行的，故須用被動語態，選 (B) ***given***。
>
> 【比較】
> { ***give an exam*** （老師）舉行考試
> { ***take an exam*** （學生）參加考試
>
> exam〔ɪgˈzæm〕*n.* 考試（= *examination*）
> instructor〔ɪnˈstrʌktɚ〕*n.* 教師；教官；講師

10. (**C**) Mr. Clark <u>has been studying</u> in that school for five years.

克拉克先生在那所學校唸書，已經唸了五年了。

> 由表時間的副詞片語 for five years（持續五年）可知，
> 動作從過去一直持續到現在，須用「現在完成式」，如
> 強調該動作仍在持續進行中，則用「現在完成進行式」，
> 選 (C) ***has been studying***。

TEST 11

Directions: *Of the four choices given after each sentence, choose the one most suitable for filling in the blank.*

1. My mother is _____ that I am in college.
   - (A) pleasing
   - (B) pleased
   - (C) to please
   - (D) pleasant   (   )

2. I haven't heard from him _____ last year.
   - (A) between
   - (B) for
   - (C) as
   - (D) since   (   )

3. I appreciate _____ able to study in peace and quiet.
   - (A) being
   - (B) to be
   - (C) can
   - (D) be   (   )

4. Did you finish _____ your report last night?
   - (A) writing
   - (B) to write
   - (C) written
   - (D) wrote   (   )

5. We would like to go to Canada for a vacation.
   - (A) We don't enjoy vacations in Canada.
   - (B) We are allowed to go to Canada.
   - (C) We must go to Canada.
   - (D) We want to go to Canada.   (   )

6. The wind _____ his hat down the street a while ago.
   - (A) was blown
   - (B) has blown
   - (C) has been blown
   - (D) blew   ( )

7. He _____ by us not to come here again last night.
   - (A) has been told
   - (B) had told
   - (C) is told
   - (D) was told   ( )

8. The trouble _____ by that mechanic pretty soon.
   - (A) was located
   - (B) was locating
   - (C) was to locate
   - (D) located   ( )

9. It was cloudy this afternoon, but _____.
   - (A) it doesn't rain
   - (B) didn't it rain
   - (C) it didn't rain
   - (D) it rains   ( )

10. We avoided _____ wet.
    - (A) get
    - (B) to get
    - (C) getting
    - (D) be getting   ( )

TEST 11 詳解

1. (**B**) My mother is <u>pleased</u> that I am in college.

   我媽媽很高興我在大學唸書。

   > 依句意，選 (B) *pleased*〔 plizd 〕*adj.* (人) 高興的。
   > 而 (A) pleasing〔'plizɪŋ〕*adj.* 令人愉快的，(C) please
   > 〔 pliz 〕*v.* 取悅；使高興，(D) pleasant〔'plɛznt〕*adj.*
   > 令人愉快的，均用法不合。
   >
   > college〔'kɑlɪdʒ〕*n.* 大學

2. (**D**) I haven't heard from him <u>since</u> last year.

   我從去年以來，就沒有收到他的消息。

   > 介系詞 *since* 表「自從」。而 (A) between「在 (兩者)
   > 之間」，(B) for「持續 (多久)」，(C) as「當作」，則
   > 不合句意。
   >
   > *hear from sb.* 收到某人的信；得知某人的消息

3. (**A**) I appreciate <u>being</u> able to study in peace and quiet.

   我感激能夠在安靜的環境中唸書。

   > appreciate〔 ə'priʃɪˌet 〕*v.* 感激
   > *appreciate* + *V-ing* 感激～
   > *be able to V.* 能夠 (= *can* + *V.*)
   >
   > peace〔 pis 〕*n.* 安靜   quiet〔'kwaɪət〕*n.* 安靜
   > *peace and quiet* 安靜

4. (**A**) Did you finish <u>writing</u> your report last night?

你昨晚有寫完報告嗎？

> ***finish + V-ing*** 完成～
>
> report〔rɪˈport〕*n.* 報告

5. (**D**) We would like to go to Canada for a vacation.

我們想去加拿大渡假。

> 依句意，選 (D) We want to go to Canada.
>
> （我們想去加拿大。）
>
> ***would like to V.*** 想要～（= *want to V.*）
>
> Canada〔ˈkænədə〕*n.* 加拿大
>
> vacation〔veˈkeʃən〕*n.* 假期
>
> allow〔əˈlaʊ〕*v.* 允許

6. (**D**) The wind <u>blew</u> his hat down the street a while ago.

不久之前，風把他的帽子吹到街上。

> 從 a while ago「一會兒之前」可知，空格須填過去式
> 動詞，又 blow〔blo〕*v.* 吹動；吹走 的三態變化為：
> blow-blew-blown，故選 (D) ***blew***。
>
> wind〔wɪnd〕*n.* 風　　hat〔hæt〕*n.* 帽子
>
> down〔daʊn〕*prep.* 沿著

7. (**D**) He <u>was told</u> by us not to come here again last night.

他昨天晚上被我們告知，不要再來這裡。

> 從時間副詞 last night 判斷，動作發生在過去，須用
> 過去式動詞，且依句意為被動，故選 (D) ***was told***。

8. (**A**) The trouble <u>was located</u> by that mechanic pretty soon.
故障處很快就被那名技工找到。

依句意，「故障被找到」，為被動語態，即「be 動詞
＋過去分詞」的形式，故選 (A) *was located*。

locate〔loˊket〕*v.* 找出；確定…的地點
trouble〔ˊtrʌbl〕*n.* 故障
mechanic〔məˊkænɪk〕*n.* 技工
pretty〔ˊprɪtɪ〕*adv.* 非常地

9. (**C**) It was cloudy this afternoon, but <u>it didn't rain</u>.
今天下午多雲，但是並沒有下雨。

依句意，天氣多雲，應該會下雨，但是沒有，且為
過去式，故 (A) 不合，選 (C) *it didn't rain*。

cloudy〔ˊklaʊdɪ〕*adj.* 多雲的

10. (**C**) We avoided <u>getting</u> wet.
我們避免弄濕。

avoid + V-ing 避免～

avoid〔əˊvɔɪd〕*v.* 避免　　wet〔wɛt〕*adj.* 濕的

TEST 12

Directions: *Of the four choices given after each sentence, choose the one most suitable for filling in the blank.*

1. I wish I _____ my time when I was young.
   - (A) have not wasted
   - (B) had not wasted
   - (C) did not waste
   - (D) were not wasting ( )

2. It _____ him $5,000 to fix the house.
   - (A) took
   - (B) spent
   - (C) cost
   - (D) paid ( )

3. It's time for lunch; let's _____.
   - (A) stop to work
   - (B) to stop working
   - (C) to stop to work
   - (D) stop working ( )

4. At first sight I mistook him _____ a teacher.
   - (A) to be
   - (B) for
   - (C) as
   - (D) as being ( )

5. He charged me the same price _____ he charged you.
   - (A) like
   - (B) as
   - (C) such as
   - (D) just like ( )

6. If his plane is arriving at noon, he _____ home
   by five o'clock.
   - (A) would have been
   - (B) will be
   - (C) would be
   - (D) could have been   (   )

7. When he _____ May next Friday, he will tell her
   all about it.
   - (A) saw
   - (B) to see
   - (C) sees
   - (D) will see   (   )

8. It's high time that the government _____ the law
   strictly.
   - (A) should enforce
   - (B) for enforcing
   - (C) will enforce
   - (D) enforces   (   )

9. Carrie is considering _____ to Vancouver this
   coming spring.
   - (A) to go
   - (B) goes
   - (C) going
   - (D) of going   (   )

10. We went to inspect the house _____ buying it.
    - (A) in order to
    - (B) so as to
    - (C) with a view to
    - (D) for to   (   )

TEST 12 詳解

1. (**B**) I wish I <u>had not wasted</u> my time when I was young.
　　　但願我在年輕的時候，沒有浪費時間。

> I wish「我希望；但願」後面須接假設語氣，依照句意，
> 希望在年輕的時候「沒有浪費」時間，爲與過去事實相反
> 的假設語氣，故 that 子句中的動詞時態須用「過去完成式」，
> 即「had + 過去分詞」的形式，故選 (B) *had not wasted*。
> waste〔west〕*v.* 浪費（詳見「文法寶典」p.368）

2. (**C**) It <u>cost</u> him $5,000 to fix the house.
　　　修理房子花了他五千元。

> 「花費金錢」的表達方式有：
>
> $$\begin{cases} 事或 It + cost + (人) + 金錢 + to\ V. \\ 人 + spend + 金錢 + \begin{cases} (in) + V\text{-}ing \\ on + N. \end{cases} \end{cases}$$
>
> 而 (A) take「需要（時間）」，(D) pay「付費」，主詞
> 須爲人，故句意與用法皆不合。
> fix〔fɪks〕*v.* 修理

3. (**D**) It's time for lunch; let's <u>stop working</u>.
　　　該吃午餐了；咱們停止工作吧。

> *Let's* + 原形動詞　咱們～
>
> $$\begin{cases} stop + V\text{-}ing\ 停止做～ \\ stop + to\ V.\ 停下來，去做～ \end{cases}$$
>
> 依句意，是「停下手邊的工作」，去吃午餐，故選 (D)
> *stop working*。

4. (**B**) At first sight I mistook him <u>for</u> a teacher.

第一眼見到他的時候，我把他誤認為是老師。

    mistake A ***for*** B　將 A 誤認為 B

    sight〔saɪt〕*n.* 看見　　***at first sight*** 初見；乍看之下

5. (**B**) He charged me the same price <u>as</u> he charged you.

他跟我收和你同樣的價錢。

    the same…as ~　和～同樣的…

    charge〔tʃɑrdʒ〕*v.* 收費　　price〔praɪs〕*n.* 價錢

6. (**B**) If his plane is arriving at noon, he <u>will be</u> home by five o'clock.

如果他的飛機是在中午的時候抵達，他將在五點以前到家。

    從 If 子句中的 is arriving 可知，If 所引導的是直說法的
條件句，並非假設語氣，故主要子句的動詞用未來式，故
選 (B) ***will be***。而 (A) would have been 和 (D) could have
been 用於「與過去事實相反的假設語氣」，(C) would be
則用於「與現在或未來事實相反的假設語氣」，均用法不合。

    plane〔plen〕*n.* 飛機　　arrive〔ə'raɪv〕*v.* 抵達
noon〔nun〕*n.* 正午　　by 表「在～之前」。

7. (**C**) When he <u>sees</u> May next Friday, he will tell her all about it.

他下星期五看到梅的時候，將會告訴她全部的事情。

    next Friday「下星期五」為表未來的時間片語，但在
表時間或條件的副詞子句中，不能用 will 表未來，須用
現在式表示未來，故選 (C) ***sees***。

8. (**A**) It's high time that the government <u>should enforce</u> the law strictly. 是政府應嚴格執行法律的時候。

$$It's\ (high)\ time + (that) + S. + \begin{cases} 過去式動詞或\ were \\ (should) + 原形\ V. \\ to\ V. \end{cases}$$

該是～的時候了（詳見「文法寶典」p.374）

enforce〔ɪn'fɔrs〕*v.* 執行

government〔'gʌnvənmənt〕*n.* 政府

law〔lɔ〕*n.* 法律　　strictly〔'strɪktlɪ〕*adv.* 嚴格地

9. (**C**) Carrie is considering <u>going</u> to Vancouver this coming spring. 凱莉考慮在即將到來的春天去溫哥華。

consider〔kən'sɪdɚ〕*v.* 考慮

consider + V-ing 考慮～

Vancouver〔væn'kuvɚ〕*n.* 溫哥華（加拿大一城市）

coming〔'kʌmɪŋ〕*adj.* 即將到來的；下一個的

10. (**C**) We went to inspect the house <u>with a view to</u> buying it. 我們為了買房子，所以才去查看那間房子。

$$\begin{cases} \textbf{\textit{with a view to}} + \textbf{\textit{V-ing}}\ \ 目的是為了～ \\ = with\ an\ eye\ to + V\text{-}ing \\ = with\ the\ purpose\ of + V\text{-}ing \end{cases}$$

$$\begin{cases} = in\ order + to\ V. \\ = so\ as + to\ V. \end{cases}$$

$$\begin{cases} = in\ order\ that\ 子句 \\ = so\ that\ 子句 \end{cases}$$

inspect〔ɪn'spɛkt〕*v.* 檢查

TEST 13

Directions: *Of the four choices given after each sentence, choose the one most suitable for filling in the blank.*

1. He spent thirty minutes _____ for his girlfriend.
   - (A) to wait
   - (B) waiting
   - (C) waited
   - (D) wait   (   )

2. Please _____ the form immediately.
   - (A) have filled out
   - (B) filling out
   - (C) fill out
   - (D) to fill out   (   )

3. When I was young, I _____ play tennis quite well.
   - (A) was used to
   - (B) used to
   - (C) get used to
   - (D) use to   (   )

4. I have to mail the letter.
   - (A) I needn't mail the letter.
   - (B) I won't mail the letter.
   - (C) I have mailed the letter.
   - (D) I must mail the letter.   (   )

5. The man _____ at the corner is my grandfather.
   - (A) whom is seated
   - (B) that is seat
   - (C) whose sits
   - (D) who sits   (   )

6. Michelle _____ a course in News English this
semester.

(A) is taken
(B) is taking
(C) taking
(D) may be taken ( )

7. If you ask politely, Mother will probably _____
a piece of cake.

(A) let you to have
(B) let you have
(C) allow that you have
(D) allow you have ( )

8. Shakespeare arrived in London about 1586, _____
he became a player.

(A) how
(B) which
(C) where
(D) why ( )

9. This book had better _____ to the library before
Thursday.

(A) to return
(B) returning
(C) be returned
(D) to be returned ( )

10. The new highway _____ by the end of next year.

(A) had been completed
(B) have been completed
(C) will has been completed
(D) will have been completed ( )

TEST 13 詳解

1. (**B**) He spent thirty minutes <u>waiting</u> for his girlfriend.

他花了三十分鐘等他女朋友。

spend「花費」的用法為：

$$人 + spend + \left\{ \begin{array}{l} 時間 \\ 金錢 \end{array} \right\} + \left\{ \begin{array}{l} (in) + V\text{-}ing \\ on + N. \end{array} \right.$$

wait for 等待

girlfriend〔'gɜl,frɛnd〕*n.* 女朋友

2. (**C**) Please <u>fill out</u> the form immediately.

請立刻填寫這張表格。

依句意，為祈使句，須用原形動詞，故選 (C) *fill out*「填寫」。

form〔fɔrm〕*n.* 表格

immediately〔ɪ'midɪɪtlɪ〕*adv.* 立刻

3. (**B**) When I was young, I <u>used to</u> play tennis quite well.

以前我年輕的時候，我網球打得相當好。

$$\left\{ \begin{array}{l} \textbf{\textit{used to}} + 原形 \textit{V.} \ 從前～ \\ \textbf{\textit{be used to}} + \textit{V-ing} \ 習慣於～ \ (= \textit{get used to} + \textit{V-ing}) \end{array} \right.$$

tennis〔'tɛnɪs〕*n.* 網球   quite〔kwaɪt〕*adv.* 相當

4. (**D**) I have to mail the letter. 我必須寄信。

依句意，選 (D) I must mail the letter. (我必須寄信。)

have to 必須 (= *must*)

mail〔mel〕*v.* 郵寄   letter〔'lɛtɚ〕*n.* 信

5. (**D**) The man <u>who sits</u> at the corner is my grandfather.
坐在轉角的那個人，是我的祖父。

關係代名詞 ***who*** 引導形容詞子句，修飾 the man。
而 (A) whom 爲關係代名詞受格，(B) that 雖然可以
代替人，但 seat 須改爲 seated 才能選，(C) whose
爲關係代名詞所有格，故用法皆不合。

corner〔'kɔrnɚ〕*n.* 轉角
grandfather〔'grænd,fɑðɚ〕*n.* 祖父

6. (**B**) Michelle <u>is taking</u> a course in News English this
semester. 蜜雪兒這學期要修一門新聞英語的課。

主詞 Michelle 爲第三人稱單數，且「選修課程」爲主動，
故本題選 (B) ***is taking***，現在進行式可表「現在正在進行
的動作」或「不久的未來」。

course〔kors〕*n.* 課程 news〔njuz〕*n.* 新聞
semester〔sə'mɛstɚ〕*n.* 學期

7. (**B**) If you ask politely, Mother will probably <u>let you
have</u> a piece of cake.
如果你有禮貌地問，媽媽可能會讓你吃一塊蛋糕。

let〔lɛt〕讓 爲使役動詞，而 allow〔ə'lau〕允許
爲一般動詞，用法不同：
$$\begin{cases} \textit{let} + sb. + 原形 \textit{V}. & 讓某人～ \\ \textit{allow} + sb. + \textit{to V}. & 允許某人～ \end{cases}$$

politely〔pə'laɪtlɪ〕*adv.* 有禮貌地
probably〔'prɑbəblɪ〕*adv.* 可能
a piece of 一塊

8. (**C**)　Shakespeare arrived in London about 1586, <u>where</u> he became a player. 莎士比亞大約在一五八六年左右到倫敦，他在那裡成為演員。

> 表「地點」，關係副詞用 *where*，在此等於 in which，選 (C)。而 (A) how 表「方法」，(B) which 為關係代名詞，(D) why 表「理由」，均用法不合。
>
> Shakespeare〔'ʃek͵spɪr〕*n.* 莎士比亞
> arrive〔ə'raɪv〕*v.* 到達
> London〔'lʌndən〕*n.* 倫敦（英國首都）
> player〔'pleɚ〕*n.* 演員

9. (**C**)　This book *had better be* <u>returned</u> to the library before Thursday. 這本書最好在星期四以前還到圖書館。

> *had better* + 原形 *V.* 最好
> 又依句意，為被動，即「be 動詞 + 過去分詞」的形式，故選 (C) *be returned*。　　return〔rɪ'tɜn〕*v.* 歸還
> library〔'laɪ͵brɛrɪ〕*n.* 圖書館

10. (**D**)　The new highway <u>will have been completed</u> by the end of next year. 新的公路將在明年年底前完工。

> 由時間副詞 by the end of next year「明年年底之前」可知，須用「未來完成式」，表「在未來某時間之前，已經完成的動作」，其形式為「will have + 過去分詞」，又依句意為被動，故選 (D) *will have been completed*。
> complete〔kəm'plit〕*v.* 完成
> highway〔'haɪ͵we〕*n.* 公路　　by 表「在～之前」。
> end〔ɛnd〕*n.* 最後部分；末尾

TEST 14

Directions: *Of the four choices given after each sentence, choose the one most suitable for filling in the blank.*

1. I will write to you _____ I have leisure.
   - (A) wherever
   - (B) whatever
   - (C) whenever
   - (D) however　　　　　　　　　　　　　( )

2. The train _____ when you reach the train station.
   - (A) had left
   - (B) has left
   - (C) will have left
   - (D) has been left　　　　　　　　　　( )

3. How _____ is it from here to the shopping mall?
   - (A) long
   - (B) far
   - (C) distant
   - (D) near　　　　　　　　　　　　　　( )

4. We are looking forward _____ you again.
   - (A) to see
   - (B) to seeing
   - (C) at seeing
   - (D) seeing　　　　　　　　　　　　　( )

5. The heavy rain kept us _____ on a picnic on Sunday.
   - (A) from to go
   - (B) with going
   - (C) from going
   - (D) by going　　　　　　　　　　　　( )

6. I don't understand _____ people put up with the
   bad service in this restaurant.
   (A) who
   (B) why
   (C) when
   (D) where   (   )

7. The best way to make people like you is to show an
   active interest in _____ they say.
   (A) that
   (B) what
   (C) whom
   (D) where   (   )

8. When I called on him yesterday, he was busy
   _____ homework.
   (A) with him
   (B) with his
   (C) to doing
   (D) by his   (   )

9. The rules of polite conduct may be different
   _____ country to country.
   (A) from
   (B) beside
   (C) among
   (D) both   (   )

10. The telephone makes _____ possible to get in
    touch with people quickly.
    (A) he
    (B) his
    (C) its
    (D) it   (   )

TEST 14 詳解

1. (**C**) I will write to you <u>whenever</u> I have leisure.
    每當我有空的時候，我就會寫信給你。

    > 在此需要連接詞，引導表「時間」的副詞子句，
    > 故選 (C) *whenever*，表「每當～」。
    > *write to sb.* 寫信給某人
    > leisure〔ˈliʒɚ〕*n.* 空閒

2. (**C**) The train <u>will have left</u> when you reach the train
    station.　當你到達火車站時，火車將已經離開了。

    > 由 when 子句中用現在式可知，本句應為未來式，
    > 而表示在未來某個時刻之前，已經完成的動作，用
    > 「未來完成式」，故選 (C) *will have left*。

3. (**B**) How <u>far</u> is it from here to the shopping mall?
    從這裡到購物中心有多遠？

    > 問距離「多遠」，疑問詞要用 How *far*，而不用
    > distant 或 near，故選 (B)。
    > (A) How long 用於問時間「多久」，句意不合。
    > *shopping mall* 購物中心
    > distant〔ˈdɪstənt〕*adj.* 遙遠的

4. (**B**) We *are looking forward to* <u>seeing</u> you again.
    我們非常期待再次見到你。

    > *look forward to* + *N.* / *V-ing* 期待～

5. (**C**) The heavy rain *kept* us *from* going on a picnic on
Sunday. 大雨使我們星期天無法去野餐。

keep
stop   } + O. + *from* + N. / V-ing 使～無法…
prevent

heavy〔'hɛvɪ〕*adj.* 大量的   *go on a picnic* 去野餐

6. (**B**) I don't understand <u>why</u> people put up with the bad
service in this restaurant.

我不了解，這家餐廳服務這麼差，人們為何要忍受。

表示不了解這個「原因」，空格中原應填入 the reason
why，而先行詞 the reason 可省略，故選 (B) *why*。而
(A) who 為疑問關係代名詞，作「誰」解，(C) when 表
「時間」，(D) where 表「地點」，均不合。

put up with 忍受   service〔'sɝvɪs〕*n.* 服務
restaurant〔'rɛstərənt〕*n.* 餐廳

7. (**B**) The best way to make people like you is to show an
active interest in <u>what</u> they say.

要讓別人喜歡你，最好的方法就是，對於別人所說的
事情，主動表現興趣。

空格引導名詞子句，做 in 的受詞，而在名詞子句中，
亦作 say 的受詞，故本題選 (B) *what*，為複合關代，
相當於 the thing(s) that。

way〔we〕*n.* 方法   show〔ʃo〕*v.* 表現
active〔'æktɪv〕*adj.* 主動的；積極的
interest〔'ɪntrɪst〕*n.* 興趣

8. (**B**) When I called on him yesterday, he *was busy*
   with his homework.
   當我昨天去拜訪他時，他正忙著寫功課。

   $$be\ busy \begin{cases} with + N. \\ (in) + V\text{-ing} \end{cases} 忙於～$$

   call on sb. 拜訪某人　homework〔'hom,wɜk〕*n.* 功課

9. (**A**) The rules of polite conduct may be different <u>from</u>
   country to country.
   合乎禮儀的行為規則，可能每個國家都不同。

   be different *from* country to country 表示「每個國家
   都不同」，又如 be different from person to person
   「每個人都不同」、be different from place to place
   「每個地方都不同」，故本題選 (A)。

   rule〔rul〕*n.* 規則　　polite〔pə'laɪt〕*adj.* 有禮貌的
   conduct〔'kɑndʌkt〕*n.* 行為

10. (**D**) The telephone makes <u>it</u> possible to get in touch with
   people quickly.
   電話使得人們能快速取得聯繫。

   句本中的 to get…people quickly 為真正受詞，而空
   格中則填入虛受詞，選 (D) *it*。

   get in touch with sb. 和某人聯繫

TEST 15

Directions: Of the four choices given after each sentence, choose the one most suitable for filling in the blank.

1. Either you or I _____ correct.
   - (A) are
   - (B) is
   - (C) am
   - (D) be   (   )

2. He ate two _____ this morning.
   - (A) pieces of bread
   - (B) pieces of breads
   - (C) piece of breads
   - (D) breads   (   )

3. Helen enjoys boating, _____.
   - (A) and so does Bill, too
   - (B) and nor does Mary either
   - (C) but Bill doesn't
   - (D) and Mary doesn't either   (   )

4. The weather is _____ in the fall than in the summer.
   - (A) much drier
   - (B) the driest
   - (C) as dry
   - (D) more drier   (   )

5. _____ the weather like in Paris yesterday?
   - (A) What was
   - (B) What's
   - (C) How was
   - (D) How's   (   )

6. The clerk doesn't have time to help you, but I'd
   _____.

   (A) be to
   (B) be happy
   (C) be happy to
   (D) be to happy ( )

7. They will be visiting us again _____ next summer.

   (A) some times
   (B) sometimes
   (C) some time
   (D) sometime ( )

8. "Have you got anything to eat?" "Yes, _____
   plenty of food in the refrigerator."

   (A) there are
   (B) there is
   (C) it is
   (D) they are ( )

9. "Which of the hats do you prefer?" "I like _____
   that has the feather in it."

   (A) those
   (B) the one
   (C) the hats
   (D) that which ( )

10. If you study the important influences on a person's life,
    you must first consider _____.

    (A) the environment in which he grew up
    (B) the environment where did he grow up
    (C) where did he grow up in the environment
    (D) the environment which did he grow up ( )

TEST 15　詳解

1. (**C**)　Either you or I <u>am</u> correct.　不是你，就是我，是正確的。

　　　either A *or* B「不是 A 就是 B」做主詞時，動詞須
　　　視 B 決定。（詳見「文法寶典」p.474）
　　　correct〔kəˋrɛkt〕*adj.* 正確的

2. (**A**)　He ate two <u>pieces of bread</u> this morning.
　　　他今天早上吃了兩片麵包。

　　　bread（麵包）爲物質名詞，物質名詞爲不可數名詞，須
　　　用表「單位」的名詞來表示「數」的觀念。其公式爲：

數詞＋單位名詞＋of＋物質名詞

3. (**C**)　Helen enjoys boating, <u>but Bill doesn't</u>.
　　　海倫喜歡划船，但是比爾不喜歡。

　　　and 連接語氣相同的句子，but 連接語氣相反的句子，
　　　故選 (C)。而 (A) 須改爲 and so does Bill 或 and Bill
　　　does, too；(B) 須改爲 but Mary doesn't；(D) 須改爲
　　　and Mary does, too，才能選。
　　　boat〔bot〕*v.* 划船

4. (**A**)　The weather is <u>much drier</u> in the fall than in the
　　　summer.　秋天的天氣比夏天乾燥許多。

　　　從 than 得知，爲比較級的句型，dry〔draɪ〕*adj.* 乾燥的
　　　比較級爲 drier，又比較級前面可用副詞 much 加強語氣，
　　　故選 (A) *much drier*。
　　　fall〔fɔl〕*n.* 秋天

5. (**A**) <u>What was</u> the weather like in Paris yesterday?

昨天巴黎的天氣如何？

$\left\{ \begin{array}{l} \textit{\textbf{What is the weather like?}}\ 天氣如何？ \\ = \text{How is the weather?} \end{array} \right.$

依句意，yesterday 爲過去的時間，故 be 動詞用 *was*。

Paris〔'pærɪs〕*n.* 巴黎

6. (**C**) The clerk doesn't have time to help you, but I'd <u>be</u>
<u>happy to</u>.

那位店員沒有時間爲你服務，但是我很樂意爲你服務。

be happy to 是 be happy to help you 的省略。

clerk〔klɜk〕*n.* 店員

7. (**D**) They will be visiting us again <u>sometime</u> next summer.

他們將在明年夏天的某時，再度拜訪我們。

依句意，選 (D) ***sometime***〔'sʌm,taɪm〕*adv.* 在某時。

而 (A) some times「好幾次」(= *several times*)，

(B) sometimes〔'sʌm,taɪmz〕*adv.* 有時候；偶爾，

(C) some time「一些時間」，在此皆不合句意。

visit〔'vɪzɪt〕*v.* 拜訪

8. (**B**) "Have you got anything to eat?" "Yes, <u>there is</u>
plenty of food in the refrigerator."

「你有任何東西可以吃嗎？」「有，冰箱裡有很多食物。」

「there + be 動詞」表「有」，又 food 爲不可數名詞，

故 be 動詞用 *is*，選 (B)。

plenty of 許多的

refrigerator〔rɪ'frɪdʒə,retə〕*n.* 冰箱

9. (**B**)　"Which of the hats do you prefer?" "I like <u>the one</u> that has the feather in it."

「你比較喜歡哪一頂帽子？」

「我比較喜歡有羽毛的那一頂。」

從 has 得知，空格須爲單數名詞，又限定是「這些帽子其中的一頂」，故須用定冠詞 the，選 (B) *the one*。

hat〔hæt〕*n.* 帽子　　prefer〔prɪˈfɝ〕*v.* 比較喜歡

feather〔ˈfɛðɚ〕*n.* 羽毛

10. (**A**)　If you study the important influences on a person's life, you must first consider <u>the environment in which he grew up</u>.

如果你要研究對人一生的重要影響力，你一定要先考慮他成長的環境。

consider〔kənˈsɪdɚ〕*v.* 考慮到 後面接名詞 *the environment in which he grew up* 做受詞，其中的 in which he grew up 做形容詞子句，修飾先行詞 the environment。

$\begin{cases} \text{the environment } \textbf{\textit{in which}} \text{ he grew up} \\ = \text{the environment } \textbf{\textit{where}} \text{ he grew up} \end{cases}$

environment〔ɪnˈvaɪrənmənt〕*n.* 環境

grow up 長大

study〔ˈstʌdɪ〕*v.* 研究

influence〔ˈɪnfluəns〕*n.* 影響 *< on >*

TEST 16

Directions: *Of the four choices given after each sentence, choose the one most suitable for filling in the blank.*

1. The skeleton _____ the human body.
   - (A) supported
   - (B) support
   - (C) supports
   - (D) is supporting   ( )

2. The police officer put on his uniform.
   - (A) He hung it on the rack.
   - (B) He sent it to the cleaner.
   - (C) He wore it.
   - (D) He cleaned it with soap and water.   ( )

3. Would you mind _____ I copy your notes?
   - (A) when
   - (B) and
   - (C) although
   - (D) if   ( )

4. I haven't seen her _____ she was a little girl.
   - (A) since
   - (B) for
   - (C) as
   - (D) when   ( )

5. Have you _____ that movie yet?
   - (A) looked at
   - (B) looked
   - (C) observed
   - (D) seen   ( )

6. You can depend _____ the automobile for transportation.

   (A) in
   (B) at
   (C) on
   (D) by   ( )

7. I avoid _____ in expensive hotels when I travel.

   (A) stay
   (B) staying
   (C) to stay
   (D) be staying   ( )

8. There is a short circuit because a wire is broken. To repair it, the wire _____.

   (A) has soldered
   (B) must be soldered
   (C) will solder
   (D) have to solder   ( )

9. The teacher gave a detailed explanation to the student in order _____ her learn more efficiently.

   (A) to help
   (B) for helping
   (C) helping
   (D) help   ( )

10. The wind's effect on an airplane while it is on the ground is different _____ when it is flying.

   (A) so
   (B) to
   (C) from
   (D) as   ( )

TEST 16 詳解

1. (**C**) The skeleton <u>supports</u> the human body.

骨骼支撐人類的身體。

「骨骼支撐全身」是事實，用現在簡單式，且主詞
The skeleton 為單數，故動詞用 **supports**，選 (C)。

support〔sə'port〕v. 支撐

skeleton〔'skɛlətn̩〕n. 骨骼

human〔'hjumən〕adj. 人類的

2. (**C**) The police officer put on his uniform.

那位警官穿上他的制服。

依句意選 (C) He wore it. (他穿著制服。)

police officer 警官　　**put on** 穿上

uniform〔'junə,fɔrm〕n. 制服

wear〔wɛr〕v. 穿著 (三態變化為：wear-wore-worn)

hang〔hæŋ〕v. 懸掛　　rack〔ræk〕n. 架子

cleaner〔'klinɚ〕n. 乾洗店　　soap〔sop〕n. 肥皂

3. (**D**) Would you mind <u>if</u> I copy your notes?

如果我影印你的筆記，你會介意嗎？

依句意選 (D) **if**「如果」。

mind〔maɪnd〕v. 介意　　copy〔'kɑpɪ〕v. 影印

notes〔nots〕n. pl. 筆記

although〔ɔl'ðo〕conj. 雖然

4. (**A**)　I haven't seen her <u>since</u> she was a little girl.

　　從她小時候起，我就沒有見過她了。

　　　前後兩句均為完整句，故此處需要連接詞，且主要子句
　　　用完成式，故連接詞應用 *since*，選 (A)。而 (B) for 為
　　　介系詞，文法不合，(C)、(D) 則不與完成式連用。

5. (**D**)　Have you <u>seen</u> that movie yet?

　　你已經看過那部電影了嗎？

　　　表示現在已經完成的動作，要用「現在完成式」
　　　"have + p.p."，而「看」電影動詞要用 see，
　　　故本題選 (D) *seen*。而 (A) look at「注視」，
　　　(C) observe〔əbˋzɝv〕*v.* 觀察，不用於看電影。

　　　yet〔jɛt〕*adv.*（用於疑問句中）已經

6. (**C**)　You can ***depend*** ***<u>on</u>*** the automobile for transportation.

　　你可以仰賴汽車作為交通工具。

　　　depend on　依賴（ = *count on* = *rely on* ）

　　　automobile〔ˋɔtəməˏbil, ˏɔtəˋmobil〕*n.* 汽車

　　　transportation〔ˏtrænspɚˋteʃən〕*n.* 運輸；交通工具

7. (**B**)　I avoid <u>staying</u> in expensive hotels when I travel.

　　當我去旅行時，我會避免住昂貴的旅館。

　　　avoid 之後，要接名詞或動名詞做受詞，故選 (B) ***staying***。

　　　stay〔ste〕*v.* 暫住；住宿（旅館）

　　　avoid〔əˋvɔɪd〕*v.* 避免　　hotel〔hoˋtɛl〕*n.* 旅館

　　　travel〔ˋtrævḷ〕*v.* 旅行

8. (**B**) There is a short circuit because a wire is broken.
To repair it, the wire <u>must be soldered</u>.

因為有一條電線斷了，所以發生了短路的問題。想要
修復，必須把電線焊接好。

依句意，電線「必須被焊接」，應用被動，故本題
選 (B) **must be soldered**。　solder〔'sɑdɚ〕*v.* 焊接

circuit〔'sɝkɪt〕*n.* 電路

short circuit 短路

wire〔waɪr〕*n.* 電線

broken〔'brokən〕*adj.* 斷掉的

repair〔rɪ'pɛr〕*v.* 修理

9. (**A**) The teacher gave a detailed explanation to the
student in order <u>to help</u> her learn more efficiently.

老師對那名學生做詳細的解說，以幫助她更有效率地學習。

in order to V. 為了~

detailed〔dɪ'teld〕*adj.* 詳細的

explanation〔,ɛksplə'neʃən〕*n.* 解釋

efficiently〔ə'fɪʃəntlɪ〕*adv.* 有效率地

10. (**C**) The wind's effect on an airplane while it is on the
ground is different <u>from</u> when it is flying.

風對飛機的影響，在地面上和在飛行中時，是不同的。

be different from 和~不同

wind〔wɪnd〕*n.* 風　　effect〔ɪ'fɛkt〕*n.* 影響

airplane〔,ɛr'plen〕*n.* 飛機

ground〔graʊnd〕*n.* 地面　　fly〔flaɪ〕*v.* 飛

TEST 17

Directions: *Of the four choices given after each sentence, choose the one most suitable for filling in the blank.*

1. _____ Chinese is difficult for me.
   - (A) To reading
   - (B) For reading
   - (C) Reading
   - (D) Read   (   )

2. Your opinions were _____ from hers.
   - (A) different
   - (B) differing
   - (C) differ
   - (D) difference   (   )

3. Julian picked up his clothes at the laundry.
   - (A) He saw them.
   - (B) He got them.
   - (C) He left them there.
   - (D) He checked them in.   (   )

4. Why don't you sit here until the manager _____?
   - (A) come
   - (B) comes
   - (C) coming
   - (D) will come   (   )

5. The president told his staff _____ his company.
   - (A) why he was managed
   - (B) how he managed
   - (C) where did manage
   - (D) when was he managed   (   )

6. Megan is watching an informative program _____ animals in Antarctica.

    (A) telling
    (B) about
    (C) from
    (D) with   (   )

7. I would have drowned if you _____ me yesterday.

    (A) have not saved
    (B) had not saved
    (C) did not save
    (D) had not saving   (   )

8. Karen's _____ her pet dog affected her life a lot.

    (A) lost
    (B) was losing
    (C) was lost
    (D) losing   (   )

9. Please tell me _____.

    (A) where does he live
    (B) what I should do
    (C) why did they leave the army
    (D) when will they come   (   )

10. My brother _____ other kinds of automobiles before.

    (A) has driven
    (B) is driving
    (C) will drive
    (D) have driven   (   )

TEST 17 詳解

1. (**C**) <u>Reading</u> Chinese is difficult for me.

閱讀中文對我而言很困難。

動詞須以動名詞或不定詞的形式，才能做主詞，故選 (C)。

difficult〔'dɪfəˌkʌlt〕*adj.* 困難的

2. (**A**) Your opinions were <u>different</u> from hers.

你的意見和她的不同。

依句意，選 (A) *different*〔'dɪfrənt〕*adj.* 不同的
be different from 和～不同
而 (B) (C) differ〔'dɪfɚ〕*v.* 不同，(D) difference
〔'dɪfərəns〕*n.* 差異，均用法不合。

opinion〔ə'pɪnjən〕*n.* 意見

3. (**B**) Julian picked up his clothes at the laundry.

朱利安在洗衣店拿他的衣服

依句意，選 (B) He got them. (他拿到它們。)
pick up 拿取　　laundry〔'lɔndrɪ〕*n.* 洗衣店
leave〔liv〕*v.* 遺留　　***check～in*** 登記～；記錄～

4. (**B**) Why don't you sit here until the manager <u>comes</u>?

你為何不坐在這裡，等經理來呢？

連接詞 until (直到) 引導副詞子句，又在表時間或
條件的副詞子句中，須用現在式表示未來，不可用
will 表示未來，故選 (B) *comes*。

manager〔'mænɪdʒɚ〕*n.* 經理

5. (**B**) The president told his staff <u>how he managed</u> his
company. 總裁告訴他的員工，他是如何管理公司的。

依句意，填名詞子句做動詞 told 的直接受詞，即「疑問詞
＋主詞＋動詞」的形式，故選 (B) *how he managed*。

manage〔'mænɪdʒ〕*v.* 管理；經營

president〔'prɛzədənt〕*n.* 總裁

staff〔stæf〕*n.* 全體職員

company〔'kʌmpənɪ〕*n.* 公司

6. (**B**) Megan is watching an informative program <u>about</u>
animals in Antarctica. 梅根正在看一個富有知識性的
節目，內容是有關南極地區的動物。

依句意，選 (B) *about*「關於」。而 (A) 須改為
telling about 才能選。

informative〔ɪn'fɔrmətɪv〕*adj.* 有知識性的

program〔'progræm〕*n.* 節目

animal〔'ænəml̩〕*n.* 動物

Antarctica〔æn'tɑrktɪkə〕*n.* 南極地區

7. (**B**) I would have drowned if you <u>had not saved</u> me
yesterday.
昨天如果你沒有救我的話，我可能就淹死了。

由 would have drowned 可知，本句為「與過去事實
相反」的假設語氣，if子句中，須用過去完成式，即
「had＋過去分詞」，故選 (B) *had not saved*。

save〔sev〕*v.* 拯救

drown〔draun〕*v.* 淹死

8. (**D**)　Karen's <u>losing</u> her pet dog affected her life a lot.
凱倫失去她的寵物狗，大大地影響到她的生活。

> lose her pet dog 做主詞，且置於所有格之後，須用
> 動名詞，故選 (D) *losing*。　lose〔luz〕*v.* 失去
> pet〔pɛt〕*adj.* 寵物的　　affect〔əˋfɛkt〕*v.* 影響
> *a lot* 非常（= *very much*）

9. (**B**)　Please tell me <u>what I should do</u>.
請告訴我，我應該做什麼。

> 依句意，空格應填名詞子句，做動詞 tell 的直接受詞，
> 即「疑問詞＋主詞＋動詞」的形式，故選 (B) *what I*
> *should do*。而 (A) 須改為 where he lives，(C) 須改為
> why they left the army，(D) 須改為 when they will
> come，才能選。
> leave〔liv〕*v.* 離開　　army〔ˋɑrmɪ〕*n.* 軍隊

10. (**A**)　My brother <u>has driven</u> other kinds of automobiles
before.　我哥哥以前開過其他種類的汽車。

> 表示「從過去某時到現在的經驗」，用「現在完成式」，
> 即「have/has ＋ 過去分詞」的形式，又主詞 My brother
> 為第三人稱單數，故用單數動詞，選 (A) *has driven*。
> （詳見「文法寶典」p.335）
> kind〔kaɪnd〕*n.* 種類
> automobile〔ˋɔtəməˏbɪl〕*n.* 汽車

TEST 18

Directions: *Of the four choices given after each sentence, choose the one most suitable for filling in the blank.*

1. _____ the people in this area like to fish and hunt.
    - (A) Most
    - (B) Most of
    - (C) Almost
    - (D) Almost of   (   )

2. Don't lie to your parents, _____ you will be punished.
    - (A) and
    - (B) but
    - (C) or
    - (D) unless   (   )

3. Please finish this _____ three o'clock.
    - (A) by
    - (B) on
    - (C) to
    - (D) from   (   )

4. It is difficult to find an excellent researcher _____.
    - (A) which is a good teacher as well
    - (B) what is an efficient teacher as well
    - (C) who is also a competent teacher
    - (D) who teaches also very well   (   )

5. _____ he sat on the sofa, he fell asleep.
    - (A) On and on
    - (B) As soon as
    - (C) On and off
    - (D) As far as   (   )

6. I don't remember the name of the song, but it has a melody that _____ like this.
   - (A) went
   - (B) goes
   - (C) had gone
   - (D) will go   .(   )

7. If I _____ Mary, I _____ happy to tell her you're looking for her.
   - (A) will see; will be
   - (B) see; am
   - (C) will see; am
   - (D) see; will be   (   )

8. My grandfather has strongly suggested that we _____ into a bigger house.
   - (A) to move
   - (B) move
   - (C) moved
   - (D) must move   (   )

9. The wind _____ so hard that several trees were knocked over.
   - (A) blew
   - (B) blows
   - (C) was blown
   - (D) had been blown   (   )

10. My English is _____ to speak to him.
   - (A) enough not good
   - (B) not enough good
   - (C) good not enough
   - (D) not good enough   (   )

TEST 18 詳解

1. (**B**) Most of the people in this area like to fish and hunt.
   在這個地區的大多數人，喜歡釣魚和打獵。

   $\begin{cases} \textit{most of the people} \quad 大多數人（most 為代名詞）\\ = \textit{most people}（most 為形容詞）\end{cases}$

   而 almost〔'ɔl,most〕*adv.* 幾乎；差不多，則用法不合。

   area〔'ɛrɪə〕*n.* 地區　　fish〔fɪʃ〕*v.* 釣魚

   hunt〔hʌnt〕*v.* 打獵

2. (**C**) Don't lie to your parents, <u>or</u> you will be punished.
   不要對你的父母說謊，否則你會被處罰。

   $\begin{cases} 祈使句, \textit{or} + S.+V.（or 表「否則」）\\ 祈使句, \textit{and} + S.+V.（and 表「就會」）\end{cases}$

   本句也可說成：*If* you lie to your parents, you will be
   punished.

   lie〔laɪ〕*v.* 說謊　　punish〔'pʌnɪʃ〕*v.* 處罰

   unless〔ʌn'lɛs〕*conj.* 除非

3. (**A**) Please finish this <u>by</u> three o'clock.
   請在三點鐘以前將這個完成。

   介系詞 *by* 表「在…之前」。而 (B) on 表「日期、星期或
   特定日子的早、午、晚」，(C) to 表示時間的終點，作「至…；
   到…」解，(D) from 表示時間的起點，作「從…起」解，
   均用法不合。

   finish〔'fɪnɪʃ〕*v.* 結束；完成

4. (**C**) It is difficult to find an excellent researcher <u>who is</u>
<u>also a competent teacher</u>.

要找到一個出色的研究員，同時也是一個有能力的老師，
是很困難的事情。

> 修飾人，關係代名詞用 who 或 that，故 (A)(B) 不合，而
> (D) 須改為 who *also* teaches very well 或 who teaches
> very well, *too* 才能選，故選 (C) ***who is also a competent***
> ***teacher***「同時也是一個有能力的老師」。
>
> competent〔'kɑmpətənt〕*adj.* 有能力的
>
> excellent〔'ɛksḷənt〕*adj.* 出色的
>
> researcher〔rɪ'sɝtʃɚ〕*n.* 研究員　　***as well*** 也（= *too*）
>
> efficient〔ɪ'fɪʃənt〕*adj.* 有效率的

5. (**B**) <u>As soon as</u> he sat on the sofa, he fell asleep.

他一坐上沙發，就睡著了。

> ***as soon as*** 一…就～（連接詞片語）
>
> 而 (A) on and on「繼續不停地」，(C) on and off「斷斷
> 續續地」，(D) as far as「遠到…（某地）；就…的程度
> 而言」，則用法和句意均不合。
>
> sofa〔'sofə〕*n.* 沙發　　***fall asleep*** 睡著

6. (**B**) I don't remember the name of the song, but it has a
melody that <u>goes</u> like this.

我不記得那首歌的名字了，但是它的旋律是這樣唱的。

> 依句意為現在式，故選 (B) ***goes***。
>
> go〔go〕*v.*（歌曲等）唱著
>
> melody〔'mɛlədɪ〕*n.* 旋律

7. (**D**) If I <u>see</u> Mary, I <u>will be</u> happy to tell her you're looking for her. 如果我看到瑪麗，我會很樂意告訴她你在找她。

在表條件的副詞子句中，須用現在式表示未來，而主要
子句則須依句意用未來式，故選 (D) *see; will be*。

look for 尋找

8. (**B**) My grandfather has strongly suggested that we <u>move</u> into a bigger house.
我的祖父強烈地建議，我們要搬到比較大的房子。

suggest〔sə'dʒɛst〕*v.* 建議 為慾望動詞，後面接的 that
子句中，因省略助動詞 should，故動詞須用原形動詞，
選 (B) ***move***。 move〔muv〕*v.* 搬家
（詳見「文法寶典」p.372）

strongly〔'stɔŋlɪ〕*adv.* 強烈地

9. (**A**) The wind <u>blew</u> so hard that several trees were knocked over. 風吹得很大，所以有好幾棵樹被吹倒了。

依句意為過去式，又 blow〔blo〕*v.* (風) 吹，為不及
物動詞，限用主動，三態變化為：blow-blew-blown，
故選 (A) ***blew***。

so…that~ 如此…以致於~ hard〔hɑrd〕*adv.* 猛烈地
knock over 打翻；撞倒

10. (**D**) My English is <u>not good enough</u> to speak to him.
我的英文不夠好，無法跟他說話。

be 動詞 + *adj.* + ***enough*** + ***to V.*** 夠…，足以~

TEST 19

Directions: *Of the four choices given after each sentence, choose the one most suitable for filling in the blank.*

1. That old-fashioned hat reminded me _____.
   - (A) at my father
   - (B) to my father
   - (C) of my father
   - (D) my father   (   )

2. The officer made us _____ in his office.
   - (A) waited
   - (B) waiting
   - (C) wait
   - (D) to wait   (   )

3. This is the house _____ my sister lives in.
   - (A) where
   - (B) which
   - (C) in where
   - (D) in where   (   )

4. I asked Olivia _____ she could drive.
   - (A) that
   - (B) if
   - (C) what
   - (D) which   (   )

5. Your jacket is dirty. Why don't you _____?
   - (A) take it off
   - (B) take off it
   - (C) take jacket off
   - (D) take off   (   )

6. The newlyweds are planning _____ in Italy for a week.
   (A) to stay
   (B) staying
   (C) will stay
   (D) be staying   (   )

7. Professor Johnson warned his students _____ late for the examination.
   (A) not be
   (B) be not
   (C) not to be
   (D) to be not   (   )

8. Thomas Edison spent the early years of his boyhood _____ newspapers on a train.
   (A) sell
   (B) to sell
   (C) selling
   (D) sold   (   )

9. Linda usually goes to piano lessons on Sundays. _____ her cousin.
   (A) Either does
   (B) Neither does
   (C) So too
   (D) So does   (   )

10. "Was Simon feeding his dog when the earthquake happened?"
    (A) "Yes, he will."
    (B) "Yes, he was."
    (C) "No, he was."
    (D) "No, he is."   (   )

TEST 19 詳解

1. (**C**) That old-fashioned hat *reminded* me *of* my father.
那頂舊式的帽子,讓我想起我的父親。

> remind〔rɪ'maɪnd〕*v.* 提醒;使想起
> *remind sb. of~* 使某人想起~
> old-fashioned〔'old'fæʃənd〕*adj.* 舊式的
> hat〔hæt〕*n.* 帽子

2. (**C**) The officer made us <u>wait</u> in his office.
那名軍官要我們在他的辦公室等候。

> make 爲使役動詞,接受詞後,須接原形動詞,故選 (C)。
> officer〔'ɔfəsɚ〕*n.* 軍官　　office〔'ɔfɪs〕*n.* 辦公室

3. (**B**) This is the house <u>which</u> my sister lives in.
這是我姊姊住的房子。

> 關係代名詞用 *which* 代替先行詞 the house,引導
> 形容詞子句。
> $\left\{ \begin{array}{l} \cdots\text{the house } \textit{which} \text{ my sister lives } \textit{in.} \\ = \cdots\text{the house } \textit{in which} \text{ my sister lives.} \\ = \cdots\text{the house } \textit{where} \text{ my sister lives.} \end{array} \right.$

4. (**B**) I asked Olivia <u>if</u> she could drive.
我問奧莉維亞,她是否會開車。

> if 引導名詞子句,表「是否」,做 asked 的直接受詞。

5. (**A**) Your jacket is dirty. Why don't you <u>take it off</u>?

你的夾克髒了。你為什麼不把它脫掉呢?

> ***take off***「脫掉」,受詞為代名詞時,須置於中間,
> 受詞為一般名詞時,則可置於中間或置於片語後面,
> 故選 (A) ***take it off*** (= *take off the jacket* = *take*
> *the jacket off*) 。
>
> jacket 〔'dʒækɪt 〕 *n.* 夾克   dirty 〔'dɜtɪ 〕 *adj.* 髒的

6. (**A**) The newlyweds are planning <u>to stay</u> in Italy for a
week. 那對新婚夫婦正在計劃,要在義大利待一個星期。

> ***plan + to V.*** 計劃~
>
> newlyweds 〔'njulɪ,wɛdz 〕 *n. pl.* 新婚夫婦
> Italy 〔'ɪtlɪ 〕 *n.* 義大利

7. (**C**) Professor Johnson ***warned*** his students ***not to be*** late
for the examination.

強生教授警告他的學生,考試不要遲到。

> warn 〔 wɔrn 〕 *v.* 警告
>
> { ***warn sb. to V.*** 警告某人做~
> { ***warn sb. not to V.*** 警告某人不要做~
>
> 不定詞的否定,否定的字須放在不定詞前面。
>
> professor 〔 prə'fɛsɚ 〕 *n.* 教授
> late 〔 let 〕 *adj.* 遲到的
> examination 〔 ɪg,zæmə'neʃən 〕 *n.* 考試

8. (**C**) Thomas Edison spent the early years of his boyhood
<u>selling</u> newspapers on a train.

湯瑪斯‧愛迪生的少年時代早期，是在火車上賣報紙度過的。

spend「花費」的用法為：

$$人 + \textbf{\textit{spend}} + \left\{ \begin{array}{l} 時間 \\ 金錢 \end{array} \right\} + \left\{ \begin{array}{l} (\textit{in}) + \textit{V-ing} \\ \textit{on} + \textit{N.} \end{array} \right.$$

boyhood〔'bɔɪhʊd〕*n.* 少年時代
newspaper〔'njuz,pepɚ〕*n.* 報紙

9. (**D**) Linda usually goes to piano lessons on Sundays.
<u>So does</u> her cousin.

琳達通常在星期天去上鋼琴課。她表妹也是。

So does her cousin. 這句話是由 So does her cousin
usually go to piano lessons on Sundays. 省略而來。

cousin〔'kʌzn̩〕*n.* 堂（表）兄弟姐妹

10. (**B**) "Was Simon feeding his dog when the earthquake
happened?"

「地震發生的時候，賽門正在餵他的狗嗎？」

在答句中，「Yes＋肯定內容」，「No＋否定內容」，
依句意，選 (B) *"Yes, he was."*「是的，他是。」

feed〔fid〕*v.* 餵食　　earthquake〔'ɝθ,kwek〕*n.* 地震
happen〔'hæpən〕*v.* 發生

TEST 20

Directions: *Of the four choices given after each sentence, choose the one most suitable for filling in the blank.*

1. The man _____ today left this message for you.
   - (A) called
   - (B) has called
   - (C) who calls
   - (D) who called   (   )

2. Your tent was blown down, but theirs _____.
   - (A) didn't
   - (B) wasn't
   - (C) weren't
   - (D) hadn't   (   )

3. _____ is extremely dangerous.
   - (A) Cars at very high speeds driving
   - (B) At very high speeds driving cars
   - (C) Cars driving at very high speeds
   - (D) Driving cars at very high speeds   (   )

4. We _____ when Joe came early.
   - (A) had surprised
   - (B) were surprised
   - (C) surprised
   - (D) were surprising   (   )

5. Jamie _____ dinner when the phone rang.
   - (A) has had
   - (B) is having
   - (C) was having
   - (D) has   (   )

6. _____ members attended the meeting this week than last week.

 (A) Few
 (B) A few
 (C) Fewer
 (D) Lesser   (   )

7. It's getting quite late. We'd better _____ home soon.

 (A) going
 (B) to be going
 (C) go
 (D) to go   (   )

8. There will _____ no charge for the lecture in the auditorium.

 (A) to have
 (B) be
 (C) have
 (D) to be   (   )

9. Bill would have taken more photographs if he _____ more film.

 (A) had had
 (B) has had
 (C) should have
 (D) would   (   )

10. The book I bought yesterday is worth _____.

 (A) to read
 (B) reading
 (C) to be read
 (D) to be reading   (   )

TEST 20　詳解

1. (**D**)　The man who called today left this message for you.
   今天打電話來的那位先生，留下這個留言給你。

   空格引導形容詞子句，修飾 The man，先行詞為人，
   關代用 who，且依句意為過去式，選 (D) **who called**。

   message〔ˈmɛsɪdʒ〕*n.* 訊息；留言

2. (**B**)　Your tent was blown down, but theirs wasn't.
   你們的帳篷被吹倒了，但他們的沒有。

   由連接詞 but 可知，前後句意相反，前句為肯定句，
   則後句應為否定，theirs 為所有代名詞，相當於
   their tent，空格原應填入 **wasn't** blown down，
   省略重複部分，故選 (B)。

   tent〔tɛnt〕*n.* 帳篷
   blow down　吹倒 (blow 的三態變化為 blow-blew-blown)

3. (**D**)　Driving cars at very high speeds is extremely
   dangerous.　高速開車是非常危險的。

   由空格後動詞用單數 is 可知，本句主詞須為單數，
   選 (D) **Driving cars at very high speeds**，動名詞
   片語做主詞，視為單數。而 (C) 應改成 Cars (which
   are) **driven** at very high speeds，為複數，動詞
   應用 are，在此不合。　　**at high speeds** 以高速
   extremely〔ɪkˈstrimlɪ〕*adv.* 非常地
   dangerous〔ˈdendʒərəs〕*adj.* 危險的

4. (**B**) We <u>were surprised</u> when Joe came early.

喬很早就到了，令我們很驚訝。

surprise 為「使驚訝」之意，表示「某人感到很驚訝」，
應用 *sb.* + be / feel surprised，且依句意為過去式，故
選 (B) *were surprised*。

5. (**C**) Jamie <u>was having</u> dinner when the phone rang.

當電話鈴響時，潔咪正在吃晚餐。

表示過去某動作發生時，另一個動作正在進行，前者用
「過去簡單式」，後者則用「過去進行式」，在本句中，
「電話鈴響」用過去式，「正在吃晚餐」則應用過去進
行式，故選 (C) *was having*。   have〔hæv〕*v.* 吃
phone〔fon〕*n.* 電話   ring〔rɪŋ〕*v.*（鈴）響

6. (**C**) <u>Fewer</u> members attended the meeting this week
than last week. 本週來參加會議的成員比上週少。

由後半句 than last week 可知，空格應用比較級，
表示「比較少的」應用 *Fewer*，選 (C)。而 (A) few「少
到幾乎沒有」，(B) a few「一些」，(D) lesser「較小的；
較低的」，不與 than 連用，均不合。

member〔ˈmɛmbɚ〕*n.* 成員；會員
attend〔əˈtɛnd〕*v.* 參加   meeting〔ˈmitɪŋ〕*n.* 會議

7. (**C**) It's getting quite late. We'*d better* <u>*go*</u> home soon.

時間很晚了，我們最好趕快回家。

had better + *V.* 最好～
quite〔kwaɪt〕*adv.* 相當   late〔let〕*adj.* 晚的

8. (**B**) There will <u>be</u> no charge for the lecture in the
auditorium. 在禮堂裡舉行的這場演講，將不收費。

「There + be 動詞」表示「有～」之意，在此空格
置於助動詞 will 之後，應用原形動詞，故選 (B) *be*。

charge〔tʃɑrdʒ〕*n.* 費用　　lecture〔ˈlɛktʃɚ〕*n.* 演講
auditorium〔ˌɔdəˈtorɪəm〕*n.* 禮堂；演講廳

9. (**A**) Bill would have taken more photographs if he <u>had had</u>
more film. 如果比爾當時還有底片，他就會多照點照片。

由主要子句中的 would have taken 可知，本句為
「與過去事實相反的假設語氣」，公式為：

$$\text{If + S. + had + p.p.} \cdots, \text{S.} + \begin{Bmatrix} \text{would} \\ \text{could} \\ \text{should} \\ \text{might} \end{Bmatrix} + \text{have + p.p.} \cdots$$

if 子句應用過去完成式，選 (A) *had had*。

photograph〔ˈfotəˌgræf〕*n.* 照片　film〔fɪlm〕*n.* 底片

10. (**B**) The book I bought yesterday *is worth reading*.
我昨天買的那本書，很值得讀。

worth〔wɝθ〕*adj.* 值得的
be worth + *V-ing* 值得～

worth 是特殊用法的形容詞，作用近似介系詞，其後須
接動名詞，且用主動表被動，所以 *is worth reading*
「值得讀」，也就是「值得被讀」，但英文不可說成
is worth being read（誤）。

TEST 21

Directions: *Of the four choices given after each sentence, choose the one most suitable for filling in the blank.*

1. _____ a foreign language is sometimes difficult.
   (A) Learning
   (B) Learn
   (C) Learned
   (D) Having learned   (   )

2. My uncle will be a little late _____ the rain.
   (A) around
   (B) in order to
   (C) because of
   (D) because   (   )

3. Never _____ late for school, Kate.
   (A) is
   (B) be
   (C) being
   (D) to be   (   )

4. Some students are from America; _____ are Chinese.
   (A) another
   (B) the other
   (C) other
   (D) others   (   )

5. Alex _____ for an apartment since last month.
   (A) has been looking
   (B) looked
   (C) was looking
   (D) will have looked   (   )

6. _____ his term as president many important advances were made.

   (A) Since
   (B) As
   (C) During
   (D) While   (   )

7. The little girl, dressed in her mother's clothes, looks as if she _____ all grown-up.

   (A) is
   (B) was
   (C) were
   (D) would be   (   )

8. They visited the house _____ George Washington lived.

   (A) which
   (B) what
   (C) where
   (D) that   (   )

9. Soldier, you _____ to a new post. Here are your orders.

   (A) had been assigned
   (B) have been assigned
   (C) have been assigning
   (D) had been assigning   (   )

10. His father _____ is seventy-five years old, sometimes plays badminton with his grandson.

   (A) whom
   (B) who
   (C) , who
   (D) , that   (   )

TEST 21 詳解

1. (**A**) <u>Learning</u> a foreign language is sometimes difficult.
   學外語有時候很困難。

   > 動詞須以動名詞或不定詞的形式,才能做主詞,故 (B) (C)
   > 不合,又 (D) Having learned 為完成式的動名詞,表示
   > 動名詞和主要動詞的時間先後,在此用法不合,故選 (A)。
   > foreign〔ˈfɔrɪn〕*adj.* 外國的
   > language〔ˈlæŋgwɪdʒ〕*n.* 語言

2. (**C**) My uncle will be a little late <u>because of</u> the rain.
   我叔叔將因為下雨的關係,稍微遲到一下。

   > $\begin{cases} \textbf{\textit{because of}} + \textbf{\textit{N.}} \ \ 因為\sim \\ \textbf{\textit{because}} + 子句 \end{cases}$
   >
   > 而 (A) around〔əˈraʊnd〕*prep.* 環繞;在…附近,
   > (B) in order to + V.「為了~」,均不合句意。

3. (**B**) Never <u>be</u> late for school, Kate.
   凱特,上學絕對不要遲到。

   > 此為祈使句的否定,故空格須填原形動詞,選 (B) *be*。

4. (**D**) Some students are from America; <u>others</u> are Chinese.
   有些學生來自美國;有些是中國人。

   > 從空格後面的動詞 are 判斷,空格須為複數主詞,故 (A)
   > another「(三者以上)另一個」,(B) the other「(兩者
   > 之中)另一個」,(C) other「其他的」,均用法不合,選
   > (D) *others*,在此等於 other students。

5. (**A**) Alex <u>has been looking</u> for an apartment since last month.　亞力克斯從上個月以來，就一直在找一間公寓。

> 介系詞 since「自從」，須與現在完成式或現在完成進行式
> 的動詞搭配，故選 (A) ***has been looking***，表示「從過去某
> 時間開始一直持續到現在仍在進行的動作」。
>
> ***look for*** 尋找
>
> apartment〔ə'pɑrtmənt〕*n.* 公寓

6. (**C**) <u>During</u> his term as president many important advances were made.　在他擔任總統的期間，有很多重要的發展。

> 依句意，選 (C) ***During***「在…期間」。而 (A) since 為
> 介系詞，作「自從」解，(B) as 和 (D) while 為連接詞，
> 作「當…的時候」解，用法均不合。
>
> term〔tɝm〕*n.* 任期　　　as〔æz〕*prep.* 作為
> president〔'prɛzədənt〕*n.* 總統
> advance〔əd'væns〕*n.* 發展

7. (**C**) The little girl, dressed in her mother's clothes, looks as if she <u>were</u> all grown-up.
那位小女孩穿上她媽媽的衣服後，看起來好像她已經長大
成人了。

> ***as if***「好像」引導假設法的副詞子句，依句意為「與現在
> 事實相反的假設語氣」，故 be 動詞須用 ***were***。
> （詳見「文法寶典」p.371）
>
> ***be dressed in*** 穿著；打扮
> grown-up〔'gron͵ʌp〕*adj.* 成年的

8. (**C**) They visited the house <u>where</u> George Washington
lived. 他們參觀喬治・華盛頓所住的房子。

> 空格引導形容詞子句，修飾先行詞 the house，且形容詞
> 子句中需要地方副詞，故選 (C) ***where***，爲關係副詞，相當
> 於 in which。而 (A) which 和 (D) that 均爲關係代名詞，
> (B) what 爲複合關係代名詞，在此用法不合。
>
> visit〔'vɪzɪt〕*v.* 參觀

9. (**B**) Soldier, you <u>have been assigned</u> to a new post. Here
are your orders.

士兵，你被分發到新的部隊。這是給你的命令。

> 依句意爲被動，即「be 動詞＋過去分詞」的形式，又表
> 「過去某時發生的動作，其結果影響到現在，或其狀態
> 持續到現在」，須用現在完成式，故選 (B) ***have been
> assigned***。　assign〔ə'saɪn〕*v.* 分派
>
> soldier〔'soldʒɚ〕*n.* 士兵
> post〔post〕*n.*（軍隊的）駐紮部隊；兵營
> order〔'ɔrdɚ〕*n.* 命令；指示

10. (**C**) His father, <u>who</u> is seventy-five years old, sometimes
plays badminton with his grandson.

他爸爸今年七十五歲，偶爾會和孫子打羽毛球。

> 空格應填關係代名詞，又先行詞 His father 具有獨特性，
> 故用「補述用法」的形容詞子句，即關代之前須有逗點，故
> 選 (C), ***who***。而 (D) that 作爲關係代名詞，可以代替人，
> 但前面不能有逗點，所以不能用於補述用法的形容詞子句。
>
> badminton〔'bædmɪntən〕*n.* 羽毛球
> grandson〔'grænd,sʌn〕*n.* 孫子

TEST 22

Directions: *Of the four choices given after each sentence, choose the one most suitable for filling in the blank.*

1. Smiling every day _____ years to your life.
   - (A) add
   - (B) adds
   - (C) adding
   - (D) to add ( )

2. The mechanic can repair all the _____ cars.
   - (A) breaking
   - (B) broke
   - (C) broken
   - (D) break ( )

3. Select the correct sentence.
   - (A) An electric current is by wire conducted.
   - (B) Conducted by wire an electric current is.
   - (C) Current is an electric conducted by wire.
   - (D) An electric current is conducted by wire. ( )

4. My mother enjoys _____.
   - (A) singing
   - (B) sings
   - (C) sing
   - (D) to sing ( )

5. I proposed that he _____ chairman.
   - (A) electing
   - (B) elected
   - (C) elects
   - (D) be elected ( )

6. The flowers in the garden are more beautiful than
_____ in the park.
   (A) this
   (B) that
   (C) these
   (D) those   (   )

7. Mr. White told the students _____ they had to
study harder.
   (A) how
   (B) why
   (C) because
   (D) though   (   )

8. When someone is against an idea, he _____.
   (A) opposes it
   (B) agrees with it
   (C) is trying it
   (D) doesn't understand it   (   )

9. In the United States, conversation is _____ proper
during meals.
   (A) considers
   (B) consider
   (C) considered
   (D) considering   (   )

10. _____ his surprise and joy, he received over a
thousand replies.
   (A) With
   (B) On
   (C) As
   (D) To   (   )

TEST 22 詳解

1. (**B**) Smiling every day <u>adds</u> years to your life.
   每天微笑會延年益壽

   > 空格應填動詞，又動名詞片語當主詞，視為單數，須
   > 接單數動詞，故選 (B) *adds*。
   > add〔æd〕*v.* 增加 < *to* >

   smile〔smaɪl〕*v.* 微笑　　life〔laɪf〕*n.* 壽命

2. (**C**) The mechanic can repair all the <u>broken</u> cars.
   那個修理工人，會修理所有壞掉的車子。

   > ***broken***〔'brokən〕*adj.* 壞掉的

   mechanic〔mə'kænɪk〕*n.* 修理工；技工
   repair〔rɪ'pɛr〕*v.* 修理
   broken〔'brokən〕*adj.* 壞掉的

3. (**D**) Select the correct sentence.
   選出正確的句子。

   An electric current is conducted by wire.
   電流是由電線所傳導的。

   > electric〔ɪ'lɛktrɪk〕*adj.* 電的
   > current〔'kɝənt〕*n.* (電) 流
   > conduct〔kən'dʌkt〕*v.* 傳導
   > wire〔waɪr〕*n.* 電線

4. (**A**) My mother enjoys <u>singing</u>.

我媽媽喜歡唱歌。

enjoy + *V-ing* 喜歡~

5. (**D**) I proposed that he <u>be elected</u> chairman.

我提議選他為主席。

propose〔prə'poz〕v. 提議 為慾望動詞，須接 that 子句，
在子句中，須用「should＋原形 V.」，又 should 可省略，
故選 (D) *be elected*。
elect〔ɪ'lɛkt〕v. 選舉
chairman〔'tʃɛrmən〕n. 主席

6. (**D**) The flowers in the garden are more beautiful than <u>those</u> in the park.

花園裡的花，比那些在公園裡的漂亮。

為避免重複前面所提到的名詞，單數用 that 代替，
複數則用 *those* 代替，故選 (D)。
those 在此等於 the flowers。
garden〔'gɑrdn̩〕n. 花園

7. (**B**) Mr. White told the students <u>why</u> they had to study harder.

懷特先生告訴學生，他們為什麼必須再用功一點。

why 引導名詞子句，做 told 的直接受詞。

study hard 用功讀書

8. (**A**) When someone is against an idea, he <u>opposes it</u>.

   當某人不贊成某個想法時，就是在反對它。

   > 依句意，選 (A) *opposes it*。　oppose 〔 ə'poz 〕 *v.* 反對
   >
   > against 〔 ə'gɛnst 〕 *prep.* 反對　　idea 〔 aɪ'diə 〕 *n.* 想法
   >
   > agree 〔 ə'gri 〕 *v.* 同意　　try 〔 traɪ 〕 *v.* 嘗試
   >
   > understand 〔 ,ʌndɚ'stænd 〕 *v.* 了解

9. (**C**) In the United States, conversation is <u>considered</u> proper during meals.

   在美國，用餐的時候說話，被認爲是適當的。

   > **be considered** (*to be*) 被認爲是～
   >
   > **the United States** 美國 (= *the U.S.*)
   >
   > conversation 〔 ,kɑnvɚ'seʃən 〕 *n.* 談話
   >
   > consider 〔 kən'sɪdɚ 〕 *v.* 認爲
   >
   > proper 〔 'prɑpɚ 〕 *adj.* 適當的
   >
   > during 〔 'djʊrɪŋ 〕 *prep.* 在～期間
   >
   > meal 〔 mil 〕 *n.* 用餐時間

10. (**D**) <u>To</u> his surprise and joy, he received over a thousand replies. 令他又驚又喜的是，他收到一千多封回函。

   > **to** *one's* + 情緒名詞 令某人～的是
   >
   > **to** *one's* **surprise** 令某人驚訝的是
   >
   > **to** *one's* **joy** 令某人高興的是
   >
   > surprise 〔 sə'praɪz 〕 *n.* 驚訝　　joy 〔 dʒɔɪ 〕 *n.* 歡喜
   >
   > receive 〔 rɪ'siv 〕 *v.* 接受；收到
   >
   > over 〔 'ovɚ 〕 *prep.* 超過　　reply 〔 rɪ'plaɪ 〕 *n.* 回函

TEST 23

Directions: *Of the four choices given after each sentence, choose the one most suitable for filling in the blank.*

1. _____ there any mail this morning?
   - (A) Are
   - (B) Being
   - (C) Be
   - (D) Is   (   )

2. I don't like doing housework. _____
   - (A) She doesn't too.
   - (B) Neither does she.
   - (C) Either doesn't she.
   - (D) Neither do she.   (   )

3. Let's start right now, _____?
   - (A) shall we
   - (B) won't we
   - (C) do we
   - (D) don't we   (   )

4. I asked my friend _____.
   - (A) some help for
   - (B) help some for
   - (C) for some help
   - (D) some for help   (   )

5. Do you remember the time _____ we first met?
   - (A) when
   - (B) where
   - (C) there
   - (D) which   (   )

6. Because Adam was late again for work, his boss became
   _____.

   (A) angrily
   (B) very angry
   (C) much angry
   (D) very angrily   (   )

7. I _____ play football, but I was too skinny to
   play well.

   (A) used
   (B) used to
   (C) am used to
   (D) was used to   (   )

8. Select the correct sentence.

   (A) The man went quickly into the office at 9:30 a.m.
   (B) The man into the office went quickly at 9:30 a.m.
   (C) The man went quickly at 9:30 a.m. into the office.
   (D) Into the office the man went quickly at 9:30 a.m.

                                                       (   )

9. When I walked out of the room, I heard the phone
   _____.

   (A) ring
   (B) rang
   (C) ringing
   (D) was rang   (   )

10. The young man still looks optimistic _____
    the bad luck he had yesterday.

    (A) in case
    (B) in spite of
    (C) until
    (D) whether   (   )

TEST 23 詳解

1. (**D**) <u>Is</u> there any mail this morning?

　　今天早上有信嗎？

　　　「*there* + *be* 動詞」表示「有～」，又 mail（信件）
　　　為單數名詞，故 be 動詞用 *Is*，選 (D)。

2. (**B**) I don't like doing housework. <u>Neither does she.</u>

　　我不喜歡做家事。她也不喜歡。

　　　這句話是由 Neither does she *like doing housework.* 的
　　　省略。*Neither does she.* 可改寫成 *She doesn't, either.*
　　　neither（ˈniðɚ）*adv.* 也不
　　　housework（ˈhaʊs,wɝk）*n.* 家事

3. (**A**) Let's start right now, <u>shall we?</u>

　　我們現在就開始，好嗎？

　　　Let's 開頭的句子，附加問句須用 *shall we?*，是
　　　shall we *start right now?* 的省略，選 (A)。
　　　start（start）*v.* 開始　　　*right now* 現在；立刻

4. (**C**) I asked my friend <u>for some help.</u>

　　我向我的朋友尋求一些幫忙。

　　　ask sb. for sb. 向某人請求某物
　　　而形容詞 some「一些」，修飾名詞 help。

5. (**A**) Do you remember the time <u>when</u> we first met?
你還記得我們初次見面是什麼時候嗎？

> 表「時間」，關係副詞用 ***when***，選 (A)。而 (B) where
> 表「地點」，(C) there「在那裡」為副詞，(D) which
> 為關係代名詞，均不合。
>
> meet〔mit〕*v.* 遇見

6. (**B**) Because Adam was late again for work, his boss
became <u>very angry</u>.
因為亞當上班又遲到了，他的老闆非常生氣。

> become（變成）為連綴動詞，後面接形容詞，故 (A)
> (D)不合，又 much 用於修飾比較級形容詞，在此不合，
> 故選 (B) ***very angry***。　angry〔'æŋgrɪ〕*adj.* 生氣的
> late〔let〕*adj.* 遲到的　angrily〔'æŋgrɪlɪ〕*adv.* 生氣地

7. (**B**) I <u>used to</u> play football, but I was too skinny to play
well. 我以前打橄欖球，但是我太瘦了，所以打得不好。

> ⎰ ***used to*** + 原形 *V.* 從前（在此 used 唸成〔just〕）
> ⎱ ***be used to*** + ***V-ing*** 習慣於（在此 used 唸成〔juzd〕）
>
> football〔'fut‚bɔl〕*n.* 美式足球；橄欖球
> skinny〔'skɪnɪ〕*adj.* 皮包骨的；極瘦的

8. (**A**) Select the correct sentence. 選出正確的句子。
The man went quickly into the office at 9:30 a.m.
那位男士在早上九點半的時候，迅速進入辦公室。

> office〔'ɔfɪs〕*n.* 辦公室　　***a.m.*** 早上（↔ ***p.m.*** 下午）

9. (**C**) When I walked out of the room, I heard the phone
   <u>ringing</u>. 當我走出房間時,我聽見電話鈴響。

   hear 為感官動詞,其用法為:

   hear + 受詞 + $\begin{cases} 原形 V. (表主動) \\ 現在分詞 (表主動進行) \\ p.p. (表被動) \end{cases}$

   依句意,電話「鈴響」為主動,又「無意中聽見」用現在
   分詞;「刻意聽見」用原形動詞,故選 (C) *ringing*。

   ring〔rɪŋ〕*v.*(鈴)響

   【比較】

   $\begin{cases} \text{I like to hear her } \textbf{\textit{sing}}. (正) \\ \text{I like to hear her } \textit{singing}. (誤) \end{cases}$

   我喜歡聽她唱歌。(詳見文法寶典 p.420)

   phone〔fon〕*n.* 電話

10. (**B**) The young man still looks optimistic <u>in spite of</u>
    the bad luck he had yesterday.

    儘管昨天運氣不好,那名年輕人看起來仍然很樂觀。

    空格應填可接名詞的介系詞片語,選 (B) *in spite of*
    「儘管」。而 (A) in case「以防萬一」,(C) until「直到」,
    (D) whether「不論」,均為連接詞片語,後面須引導
    子句,故用法不合。

    optimistic〔ˌɑptəˈmɪstɪk〕*adj.* 樂觀的
    luck〔lʌk〕*n.* 運氣

TEST 24

Directions*: Of the four choices given after each sentence, choose the one most suitable for filling in the blank.*

1. Dick works all the time. He _____.
   - (A) never relaxes
   - (B) often relaxes
   - (C) relaxes never
   - (D) relaxes sometimes   (   )

2. Adam is sure of his _____.
   - (A) succeed
   - (B) successful
   - (C) success
   - (D) successfully   (   )

3. I had my classmate _____ my book to the library.
   - (A) to return
   - (B) returned
   - (C) returning
   - (D) return   (   )

4. Mike went to school instead of _____ at home.
   - (A) to stay
   - (B) stay
   - (C) staying
   - (D) stayed   (   )

5. Why _____ volleyball tonight?
   - (A) about playing
   - (B) not playing
   - (C) don't we play
   - (D) we don't play   (   )

6. The couple has been watching TV _____.
   - (A) since three hours
   - (B) before yesterday
   - (C) for three o'clock
   - (D) for two hours ( )

7. We'd better find out _____ the lecture has started.
   - (A) does
   - (B) has
   - (C) did
   - (D) if ( )

8. She _____ in Taipei since her father went to the U.S.
   - (A) was living
   - (B) is living
   - (C) has been living
   - (D) had lived ( )

9. Because of _____ ability to "think," it is sometimes called an "electronic brain."
   - (A) his
   - (B) it's
   - (C) its
   - (D) her ( )

10. It's necessary that you _____ smoking.
    - (A) quitting
    - (B) quitted
    - (C) to quit
    - (D) quit ( )

TEST 24 詳解

1. (**A**) Dick works all the time. He <u>never relaxes</u>.
   迪克總是一直工作。他從來不休息。

   > 頻率副詞 never「從不」，often「經常」，sometimes
   > 「有時候」，須置於一般動詞之前，故選 (A) ***never relaxes***。
   > relax〔rɪ'læks〕v. 放鬆
   > ***all the time*** 總是；一直

2. (**C**) Adam is sure of his <u>success</u>.
   亞當確定他會成功。

   > 所有格 his 之後須接名詞，故選 (C) ***success***〔sək'sɛs〕n.
   > 成功。而 (A) succeed〔sək'sid〕v. 成功，(B) successful
   > 〔sək'sɛsfəl〕adj. 成功的，(D) successfully〔sək'sɛsfəlɪ〕
   > adv. 成功地，均用法不合。
   > ***be sure of*** 確定

3. (**D**) I had my classmate <u>return</u> my book to the library.
   我要我同學，把我的書還給圖書館。

   > have 為使役動詞，接受詞後，可接原形動詞表主動，
   > 過去分詞表被動，依句意，同學去還書是「主動」，
   > 故用原形動詞，選 (D) ***return***〔rɪ'tɜn〕v. 歸還。
   > classmate〔'klæs,met〕n. 同班同學
   > library〔'laɪ,brɛrɪ〕n. 圖書館

4. (**C**) Mike went to school instead of <u>staying</u> at home.

麥克去上學，而不是待在家中。

instead of「而不是」爲介系詞片語，其後須接名詞
或動名詞，故選 (C) ***staying***。　　stay〔ste〕*v.* 停留

5. (**C**) Why <u>don't we play</u> volleyball tonight?

我們今晚何不去打排球？

Why don't we + ***V.*** ~？ 我們何不～？
(= ***Why not*** + ***V.*** ~？)

volleyball〔'vɑlɪˏbɔl〕*n.* 排球

6. (**D**) The couple has been watching TV <u>for two hours</u>.

那對夫妻已經看了兩個小時的電視了。

「for + 一段時間」須與完成式連用，故選 (D) ***for two
hours***。而 (A) since 須接一個時間點，表「自從～」，
(B) 在昨天之前，須與過去式連用，均用法不合。

couple〔'kʌpl̩〕*n.* 夫妻；情侶

7. (**D**) We'd better find out <u>if</u> the lecture has started.

我們最好查一查，演講是否開始了。

if「是否」引導名詞子句，做 find out 的受詞。
had better + ***V.*** 最好～
find out 查出；發現
lecture〔'lɛktʃɚ〕*n.* 演講　　start〔stɑrt〕*v.* 開始

8. (**C**) She <u>has been living</u> in Taipei since her father went to the U.S.

自從她爸爸去美國之後，她就一直住在台北。

since 引導副詞子句，其主要子句須用現在完成式，
或現在完成進行式，故選 (C) ***has been living***。

the U.S. 美國 (= *the United States*)

9. (**C**) Because of <u>its</u> ability to "think," it is sometimes called an "electronic brain."

因爲它的「思考」能力，所以它有時又叫做「電腦。」

依句意，因爲「它的」思考能力，故選 (C) ***its***。
而 (A) 他的，(B) 它是，(D) 她的，均用法不合。

because of + ***N.*** 因爲～　　ability〔ə'bɪlətɪ〕*n.* 能力
sometimes〔'sʌm,taɪmz〕*adv.* 有時候
be called～ 叫做～
electronic〔ɪ,lɛk'trɑnɪk〕*adj.* 電子的
brain〔bren〕*n.* 腦

10. (**D**) It's necessary that you <u>quit</u> smoking.

戒菸是必要的。

It's necessary + ***that*** + ***S.*** + (***should***) + 原形動詞
～是必要的 (詳見「文法寶典」p.374)
quit + ***V-ing*** 戒除～
necessary〔'nɛsə,sɛrɪ〕*adj.* 必要的
smoke〔smok〕*v.* 抽煙

TEST 25

Directions: *Of the four choices given after each sentence, choose the one most suitable for filling in the blank.*

1. Morgan is never late for school, _____?
   - (A) isn't he
   - (B) did he
   - (C) didn't he
   - (D) is he   (   )

2. I insist that I _____ this time.
   - (A) pay
   - (B) paid
   - (C) pays
   - (D) paying   (   )

3. I can't find my scarf. Would you lend me _____?
   - (A) your
   - (B) yous
   - (C) yours
   - (D) you's   (   )

4. Carl shows me his love _____ singing love songs.
   - (A) about
   - (B) in
   - (C) with
   - (D) by   (   )

5. One of my hands is dirty, but _____ isn't.
   - (A) the other
   - (B) another
   - (C) each other
   - (D) other   (   )

6. The first three of these twenty questions are very difficult, but _____ are easy.

(A) others
(B) the other
(C) the others
(D) another   (　)

7. _____ the hard work is over, I'm going to take a rest for a few days.

(A) Now that
(B) That
(C) Because of
(D) Even if   (　)

8. He practiced very hard. It's not _____ that he came first in the contest.

(A) to the surprise
(B) surprising
(C) surprised
(D) surprise   (　)

9. Tracy was so lost in _____ that she couldn't even try to stop the man who took her money.

(A) amazement
(B) to amaze
(C) amazed
(D) amaze   (　)

10. Matt enjoys _____ a walk in the local park after dinner.

(A) have taken
(B) to taking
(C) take
(D) taking   (　)

TEST 25 詳解

1. (**D**) Morgan is never late for school, <u>is he</u>?

摩根上學從不遲到，不是嗎？

never（從不）為否定副詞，故附加問句要用肯定，且
主要句的動詞是 is，故附加問句的動詞用 is，代名詞
用 he 代替 Morgan，選 (D)。*is he?* 就是 is he *never
late for school?* 的省略疑問句。

2. (**A**) I insist that I <u>pay</u> this time.

我堅持這次我付錢。

insist〔ɪn'sɪst〕*v.* 堅持 為慾望動詞，其用法為：
S. + *insist* + *that* + *S.* + (*should*) + 原形動詞
（詳見文法寶典 p.372）
pay〔pe〕*v.* 付錢　　***this time*** 這一次

3. (**C**) I can't find my scarf. Would you lend me <u>yours</u>?

我找不到我的圍巾。你可以借我你的嗎？

所有代名詞代替前面提到的東西，就等於「所有格 +
名詞」。*yours* 在此等於 your scarf。
scarf〔skɑrf〕*n.* 圍巾　　lend〔lɛnd〕*v.* 借（出）

4. (**D**) Carl shows me his love <u>by</u> singing love songs.

卡爾藉由唱情歌，向我表示他的愛。

表示「藉由～（方法）」，介系詞用 *by*。
show〔ʃo〕*v.* 表示　　***love song*** 情歌

5. (**A**) One of my hands is dirty, but <u>the other</u> isn't.
我的一隻手是髒的，但另外一隻不是。

　　只有兩者的情況，一個用 one，另一個用 ***the other***。而 (B) another「（三者以上）另一個」，(C) each other「互相」，(D) other「其他的」，均不合句意。

　　dirty〔'dɜtɪ〕*adj.* 髒的

6. (**C**) The first three of these twenty questions are very difficult, but <u>the others</u> are easy.
這二十個問題的前三題很難，但其他的都很簡單。

　　有限定指這二十個問題時，用 ***the others*** 表示「剩下的其餘部分」。本句中，the others 等於 the other questions。而 (A) others 用於「some…others～」的句型，表「有些…有些～」，(B) the other「（兩者中）另一個」，(D) another「（三者以上）另一個」，均不合句意。

7. (**A**) <u>Now that</u> the hard work is over, I'm going to take a rest for a few days.
既然困難的工作已經結束了，我將要休息幾天。

　　空格應填引導子句的連接詞片語，依句意，選 (A) ***Now that***「既然」。而 (B) that 引導名詞子句，只能做句子的主詞、受詞或補語，(C) because of「因為」為介系詞片語，後面接名詞，(D) even if「儘管」，均不合。

　　hard〔hɑrd〕*adj.* 困難的；辛苦的
　　over〔'ovɚ〕*adj.* 結束的　　***take a rest*** 休息

8. (**B**) He practiced very hard. It's not <u>surprising</u> that he
came first in the contest.

他非常努力練習。他比賽得第一名,這並不令人驚訝。

> surprise〔səˈpraɪz〕v. 使驚訝 是情感動詞,「非人」
> 做主詞,須用現在分詞 surprising 修飾,「人」做主詞,
> 則用過去分詞 surprised 修飾。It 為虛主詞,代替後面
> 的 that 子句,故為「非人」,空格須用 **surprising**
> 〔səˈpraɪzɪŋ〕*adj.* 令人驚訝的。而 (C) surprised
> 「(人)感到驚訝的」,則不合句意。

> practice〔ˈpræktɪs〕v. 練習   hard〔hɑrd〕*adv.* 努力地
> ***come first*** 得第一名   contest〔ˈkɑntɛst〕*n.* 比賽

9. (**A**) Tracy was so lost in <u>amazement</u> that she couldn't
even try to stop the man who took her money.

崔西太驚訝了,驚訝到失神,所以甚至沒有試圖去攔下
拿她錢的人。

> 介系詞 in 後面須接名詞,故選 (A) ***amazement***
> 〔əˈmezmənt〕*n.* 驚訝。
> ***in amazement*** 驚訝地
> ***so…that～*** 如此…以致於～   lost〔lɔst〕*adj.* 迷惑的
> stop〔stɑp〕v. 攔下   amaze〔əˈmez〕v. 使驚訝
> amazed〔əˈmezd〕*adj.*(人)吃驚的

10. (**D**) Matt enjoys <u>taking</u> a walk in the local park after
dinner. 麥特喜歡在晚餐後,到當地的公園散步。

> ***enjoy + V-ing*** 喜歡   ***take a walk*** 散步
> local〔ˈlokḷ〕*adj.* 當地的

TEST 26

Directions: *Of the four choices given after each sentence, choose the one most suitable for filling in the blank.*

1. Robert _____ a lot of progress since September.
   - (A) have made
   - (B) has made
   - (C) does make
   - (D) makes   ( )

2. My cat caught rats but _____ didn't.
   - (A) you
   - (B) yours
   - (C) your
   - (D) you're   ( )

3. Nobel Prize winners are _____ of admiration.
   - (A) worth
   - (B) worthiness
   - (C) worthy
   - (D) worthily   ( )

4. We wish you _____ change the subject.
   - (A) would
   - (B) must
   - (C) have
   - (D) shall   ( )

5. Johnson won't go with you, and _____.
   - (A) nor do I
   - (B) nor can I
   - (C) neither will I
   - (D) I won't, too   ( )

6. There were hardly any books in the classroom,
_____?
   (A) weren't they
   (B) weren't there
   (C) were there
   (D) were they   (   )

7. Select the correct sentence.
   (A) Where from my country this I can check cash?
   (B) My check where cash can this country from I?
   (C) Can my country from where I cash this check?
   (D) Where can I cash this check from my country?

8. The student _____ work got the prize is the
youngest in my class.
   (A) who
   (B) whose
   (C) which
   (D) whom   (   )

9. One of his ambitions _____ to be an astronaut.
   (A) be
   (B) is
   (C) are
   (D) being   (   )

10. Why did those girls insist on _____ everything?
   (A) doing
   (B) to doing
   (C) to do
   (D) do   (   )

TEST 26 詳解

1. (**B**) Robert <u>has made</u> a lot of progress since September.
   自從九月以來，羅伯特已經進步很多了。

   > 由表時間的副詞片語 since September（自從九月以來）
   > 可知，動作由過去持續到現在，須用「現在完成式」，即
   > 「have / has + p.p.」的形式，又 Robert 是第三人稱單數，
   > 故選 (B) *has made*。
   >
   > progress〔'prɑgrɛs〕*n.* 進步
   > *make a lot of progress* 進步很多

2. (**B**) My cat caught rats but <u>yours</u> didn't.
   我的貓抓到老鼠了，但是你的沒有。

   > 依句意，我的貓抓到老鼠，但是「你的貓」沒有，須填
   > 所有代名詞，故選 (B) *yours*（ = *your cat*）。
   >
   > catch〔kætʃ〕*v.* 抓（三態變化為：catch-caught-caught）
   > rat〔ræt〕*n.* 老鼠

3. (**C**) Nobel Prize winners *are* ***worthy*** *of* admiration.
   諾貝爾獎的得主值得讚賞。

   > worthy〔'wɝðɪ〕*adj.* 值得的
   > *be worthy of N. / V-ing* 值得～
   > (A) worth 的用法是：be worth + N. / V-ing，在此不合。
   >
   > Nobel〔no'bɛl〕*n.* 諾貝爾　　*Nobel Prize* 諾貝爾獎
   > winner〔'wɪnɚ〕*n.* 獲勝者；得獎者
   > admiration〔,ædmə'reʃən〕*n.* 讚賞

4. (**A**) We wish you <u>would</u> change the subject.
我們希望你會改變話題。

> wish 作「希望」解時，其後接假設語氣，依句意為「與現
> 在事實相反的假設」，故其後的子句須用「S. + should /
> would / could / might + V. …」，故選 (A) ***would***。

> change〔tʃendʒ〕*v.* 改變　　subject〔'sʌbdʒɪkt〕*n.* 話題

5. (**C**) Johnson won't go with you, and <u>neither will I</u>.
強森將不會跟你一起去，而我也不會。

> 空格前有連接詞 and，且依句意為未來式，故選
> (C) ***neither will I***。　neither〔'niðɚ〕*adv.* 也不。
> 而 (A)、(B)當中的 nor 是連接詞，不可和 and 連用，且
> 助動詞也與時態不合，(D) too 則須改為 either 才能選。

6. (**C**) There were ***hardly*** any books in the classroom,
<u>were there</u>? 教室裡幾乎沒有任何書了，不是嗎？

> 形成附加問句，須前後主詞一致，且須用代名詞（there），
> 又 hardly「幾乎不」為否定字，故前句應視為否定句，附
> 加問句則須用肯定，選 (C) ***were there***。

> hardly〔'hardlɪ〕*adv.* 幾乎不
> classroom〔'klæs,rum〕*n.* 教室

7. (**D**) Select the correct sentence. 選出正確的句子。
Where can I cash this check from my country?
我可以在哪裡，把這張我們國家的支票兌現？

> cash〔kæʃ〕*v.* 把（支票）兌現
> check〔tʃɛk〕*n.* 支票　　country〔'kʌntrɪ〕*n.* 國家

8. (**B**) The student <u>whose</u> work got the prize is the youngest in my class.

那位作品得獎的學生，是我們班上年紀最小的。

依句意，「該學生的」作品得獎，過空格應填關係代名詞所有格，故選 (B) *whose*。

work〔wɜk〕*n.* 作品　　prize〔praɪz〕*n.* 獎

9. (**B**) One of his ambitions <u>is</u> to be an astronaut.

當一名太空人，是他的抱負之一。

本句缺少動詞，又「One of＋複數名詞」當主詞時，視為單數，故須用單數動詞，選 (B) *is*。

ambition〔æmˈbɪʃən〕*n.* 抱負
astronaut〔ˈæstrə‚nɔt〕*n.* 太空人

10. (**A**) Why did those girls insist on <u>doing</u> everything?

那些女孩為什麼堅持做每一件事？

insist〔ɪnˈsɪst〕*v.* 堅持
insist on＋*N./V-ing*　堅持～

TEST 27

***Directions**: Of the four choices given after each sentence, choose the one most suitable for filling in the blank.*

1. There's _____ on the phone for you.
   - (A) anyone
   - (B) anybody
   - (C) somebody
   - (D) everyone   ( )

2. I _____ do a lot of exercise, but now I'm too busy.
   - (A) am used to
   - (B) was used to
   - (C) used to
   - (D) get used to   ( )

3. If my brother doesn't go, I won't _____.
   - (A) neither
   - (B) too
   - (C) also
   - (D) either   ( )

4. _____ the students in the class passed the exam.
   - (A) Each
   - (B) All
   - (C) Other
   - (D) Every   ( )

5. _____ when he started criticizing bitterly.
   - (A) Barely did she arrive
   - (B) Hardly had she arrived
   - (C) No sooner had she arrived
   - (D) Scarcely did she arrive   ( )

6. Charlie was sorry about _____ coffee on Ellen's new dress.

    (A) to spilling
    (B) spill
    (C) to spill
    (D) spilling   (   )

7. Susan has to walk to work because she _____ drive yet.

    (A) can't
    (B) doesn't have to
    (C) wouldn't
    (D) might not   (   )

8. "How long have you been in the Navy?"
"By next month I _____ in the Navy for 22 years."

    (A) will be
    (B) have been
    (C) am
    (D) will have been   (   )

9. My friends would like to have a party for my birthday, but I _____.

    (A) prefer to not
    (B) not prefer
    (C) not prefer to
    (D) prefer not to   (   )

10. Jane could afford the time to go over her answer sheet before submitting _____ to the teacher.

    (A) one
    (B) it
    (C) its
    (D) them   (   )

TEST 27 詳解

1. (**C**) There's <u>somebody</u> on the phone for you.

   有人打電話找你。

   > 依句意為肯定句，故選 (C) ***somebody*** (= *someone*)。
   > 而 (A) anyone、(B) anybody 則用於疑問句或否定句，
   > (D) everyone「每個人」，則不合句意。

2. (**C**) I <u>used to</u> do a lot of exercise, but now I'm too busy.

   我以前常做運動，但是現在我太忙了。

   > $\begin{cases} \textbf{\textit{used to}} + 原形\ \textbf{\textit{V.}}\ 從前\text{\textasciitilde} \\ \textbf{\textit{be used to}} + \textbf{\textit{V-ing}}\ 習慣於\text{\textasciitilde}\ (= \textit{get used to} + \textit{V-ing}) \end{cases}$
   >
   > exercise〔'ɛksɚ͵saɪz〕*n.* 運動

3. (**D**) If my brother doesn't go, I won't <u>either</u>.

   如果我哥哥不去，我也不去。

   > 肯定句的「也」，用 too，而否定句的「也」，則用
   > ***either***，故選 (D)。而 (A) neither〔'niðɚ〕*adv.* 也不，
   > 須置於句首，且其後的主詞與動詞須倒裝，(C) also 也
   > 作「也」解，須用於肯定句，故用法皆不合。

4. (**B**) <u>All</u> the students in the class passed the exam.

   班上所有的學生都通過考試。

   > 依句意選 (B) ***All***「所有的；全部的」，置於複數名詞之前。
   > 而 (A) each「每個」、(D) every「每個」，修飾單數名詞，
   > (C) other「其他的」，用法與句意皆不合。
   >
   > pass〔pæs〕*v.* 通過 (考試)

5. (**B**) <u>Hardly had she arrived</u> when he started criticizing bitterly. 她一到，他就開始嚴厲批評。

> $\begin{cases} \textbf{\textit{barely / hardly / scarcely}}\cdots\textbf{\textit{when}}\sim & 一\cdots就\sim \\ \textbf{\textit{no sooner}}\cdots\textbf{\textit{than}}\sim & (=\textit{as soon as}\cdots) \end{cases}$

在此種句型中，主要子句的動詞通常用過去完成式，即「had + 過去分詞」的形式，而副詞子句的動詞通常為過去式。過去完成式表示比過去某個動作先發生，但加上否定副詞 barely〔'bɛrlɪ〕、hardly〔'hɑrdlɪ〕、scarcely〔'skɛrslɪ〕「幾乎不」或 no sooner，表示「幾乎沒有比…先發生」，也就是「一…就～」，加強語氣時，可將 barely、hardly、scarcely 或 no sooner 放在句首，形成倒裝句，故選 (B) *Hardly had she arrived*。

arrive〔ə'raɪv〕*v.* 到達（詳見「文法寶典」p.496）

criticize〔'krɪtə,saɪz〕*v.* 批評

bitterly〔'bɪtəlɪ〕*adv.* 嚴厲地；激烈地

6. (**D**) Charlie was sorry about <u>spilling</u> coffee on Ellen's new dress. 查理把咖啡灑到艾倫的新洋裝上，他感到很抱歉。

> *be sorry about* + *V-ing* 為…感到抱歉

spill〔spɪl〕*v.* 使溢出；使灑出

dress〔drɛs〕*n.* 洋裝

7. (**A**) Susan has to walk to work because she <u>can't</u> drive yet. 蘇珊必須走路去上班，因為她還不會開車。

助動詞 can 表示能力，故選 (A) *can't*。而 (B) doesn't have to「不必」，(C) wouldn't「將不」，(D) might not「可能不」，均不合句意。

yet〔jɛt〕*adv.* 還（沒）

8. (**D**)　"How long have you been in the Navy?"
"By next month I <u>will have been</u> in the Navy for 22 years."

「你在海軍待多久了？」

「到下個月，我就在海軍待二十二年了。」

敘述某事繼續到未來某時為止已經有若干時間，用「未來完成式」表達，即「will have＋過去分詞」的形式，故選 (D) ***will have been***。

Navy〔'nevɪ〕*n.* 海軍　　by 表「在～之前」。

9. (**D**)　My friends would like to have a party for my birthday, but I <u>prefer not to</u>.

我的朋友想為我舉辦生日派對，但是我寧可不要。

prefer〔prɪ'fɝ〕*v.* 寧可；比較喜歡
prefer 後面接不定詞，而不定詞的否定，否定字須置於不定詞之前，故選 (D) ***prefer not to***，是 prefer not to have a party for my birthday 的省略。

would like to V. 想要～

10. (**B**)　Jane could afford the time to go over her answer sheet before submitting <u>it</u> to the teacher.

珍在交答案卷給老師之前，有足夠的時間檢查一遍。

依句意，珍繳交「她的答案卷」，空格填一單數受詞，故選 (B) ***it***。而 (A) one 代替前面提到的非特定的名詞，(C) its 為所有格，(D) them 為複數受詞，用法均不合。

afford〔ə'ford〕*v.* 有足夠的…（去做～）
sheet〔ʃit〕*n.*（紙等的）一張　　***answer sheet*** 答案卷
submit〔sʌb'mɪt〕*v.* 繳交＜to＞

TEST 28

Directions: *Of the four choices given after each sentence, choose the one most suitable for filling in the blank.*

1. Rice is a widely _____ crop in Asia.

    (A) grow
    (B) growing
    (C) grown
    (D) growth   (   )

2. The living room is not large, _____ it's quite pleasant.

    (A) and
    (B) where
    (C) but
    (D) nor   (   )

3. I have to finish this work before I can go home.

    (A) I might finish the work.
    (B) I must finish the work.
    (C) I want to finish the work.
    (D) I should finish the work.   (   )

4. Richard is about to _____ his bedroom.

    (A) paint
    (B) be painted
    (C) have paint
    (D) painting   (   )

5. Rebecca glanced at my watch and realized _____.

    (A) it was that time for class
    (B) it that time was for class
    (C) that it was time for class
    (D) for that time it was class   (   )

6. We saw your younger sister a _____ times at the theater.

    (A) many
    (B) lots
    (C) some
    (D) few   ( )

7. Nicholas doesn't mind doing the dishes. He doesn't

  _____.

    (A) object to it
    (B) like to
    (C) want to
    (D) pay attention to it   ( )

8. Do you know _____?

    (A) when will he leave
    (B) what it is
    (C) why does she go
    (D) where may he be   ( )

9. Did you read all the lessons that Ms. Smith _____?

    (A) assigned
    (B) will assign
    (C) assigns
    (D) were assigned   ( )

10. Tom finds _____ difficult to cross the river.

    (A) there
    (B) one
    (C) that
    (D) it   ( )

TEST 28 詳解

1. (**C**) Rice is a widely <u>grown</u> crop in Asia.
   稻米在亞洲，是一種被廣泛種植的農作物。

   > 依句意，農作物是「被種植的」，故選 (C) *grown*。
   > grow〔gro〕*v.* 種植
   > rice〔raɪs〕*n.* 稻米
   > widely〔'waɪdlɪ〕*adv.* 廣泛地
   > crop〔krɑp〕*n.* 農作物
   > Asia〔'eʒə, 'eʃə〕*n.* 亞洲

2. (**C**) The living room is not large, <u>but</u> it's quite pleasant.
   這個客廳不大，但是卻相當舒適。

   > 依句意，選 (C) *but*「但是」。
   > *living room* 客廳　　large〔lɑrdʒ〕*adj.* 大的
   > quite〔kwaɪt〕*adv.* 相當
   > pleasant〔'plɛznt〕*adj.* 舒適的

3. (**B**) I have to finish this work before I can go home.
   我必須在回家之前，做完這個工作。

   > 依句意，選 (B) I must finish the work. (我必須要做
   > 完工作。)　　must〔mʌst〕*aux.* 必須
   > *have to* 必須　　finish〔'fɪnɪʃ〕*v.* 完成
   > might〔maɪt〕*aux.* 可能

4. (**A**) Richard *is about to* <u>paint</u> his bedroom.
理察將要油漆他的臥室。

> *be about to* + *V.* 將要～
>
> paint〔pent〕*v.* 油漆
> bedroom〔'bɛd,rum〕*n.* 臥室

5. (**C**) Rebecca glanced at my watch and realized <u>that it was time for class</u>.
麗貝卡看了一下我的手錶，知道上課的時間到了。

> that 引導名詞子句，做 realize 的受詞，其寫法是：
> 「that + 主詞 + 動詞…」，故選 (C) *that it was time for class*。 *it's time for* + *N.* ～的時間到了
> glance〔glæns〕*v.* 看一眼 realize〔'riə,laɪz〕*v.* 知道

6. (**D**) We saw your younger sister a <u>few</u> times at the theater.
我們在那家戲院，看過你妹妹幾次。

> *a few* + 可數名詞 一些～
> *younger sister* 妹妹 time〔taɪm〕*n.* 次數
> theater〔'θiətɚ〕*n.* 戲院

7. (**A**) Nicholas doesn't mind doing the dishes. He doesn't <u>object to it</u>. 尼可拉斯不介意洗碗。他並沒有反對。

> object〔əb'dʒɛkt〕*v.* 反對
> *object to* + *N.* 反對～
> mind〔maɪnd〕*v.* 介意 *do the dishes* 洗碗
> *pay attention to* 注意

8. (**B**) Do you know <u>what it is</u>?

你知道這是什麼嗎？

空格須填名詞子句，做 know 的受詞，名詞子句須寫成
間接問句的形式，主詞與動詞不須倒裝，即「疑問詞＋
主詞＋動詞」，故選 (B) ***what it is***。

而 (A) 須改爲 when he will leave，(C) 須改爲 why she
goes，(D) 須改爲 where he may be。

leave〔liv〕*v.* 離開

9. (**A**) Did you read all the lessons that Ms. Smith <u>assigned</u>?

史密斯女士指派的功課，你都唸完了嗎？

依句意爲過去式，又依句意，作業是史密斯女士「指派」的，
爲主動語態，故選 (A) ***assigned***。

assign〔ə'saɪn〕*v.* 指派

lessons〔'lɛsn̩z〕*n. pl.* 課業；功課

10. (**D**) Tom finds <u>it</u> difficult to cross the river.

湯姆覺得，要過這條河很困難。

空格須填虛受詞 *it*，代替真正受詞 to cross the river，
故選 (D)。

find〔faɪnd〕*v.* 發現；覺得

difficult〔'dɪfəˌkʌlt〕*adj.* 困難的

cross〔krɔs〕*v.* 越過　　river〔'rɪvɚ〕*n.* 河

TEST 29

Directions: *Of the four choices given after each sentence, choose the one most suitable for filling in the blank.*

1. My favorite recreation is _____.
   - (A) read
   - (B) reading
   - (C) on reading
   - (D) for reading   (   )

2. Don't light a match. The gas fumes _____ explode.
   - (A) ought to
   - (B) have to
   - (C) must
   - (D) will   (   )

3. I feel like having _____ soup.
   - (A) many
   - (B) few
   - (C) some
   - (D) any   (   )

4. My father had his hands _____.
   - (A) burn
   - (B) burned
   - (C) to burn
   - (D) be burned   (   )

5. Albert _____ to sign up for the field trip.
   - (A) could like
   - (B) had like
   - (C) is liking
   - (D) would like   (   )

6. Today frozen food is sold all over America, but it is not _____ as fresh food.
   - (A) more popular
   - (B) popular
   - (C) much popular
   - (D) as popular ( )

7. _____ me some cigarettes if you stop at the grocery store.
   - (A) Buy
   - (B) Will buy
   - (C) Would buy
   - (D) Should have bought ( )

8. As the weather became worse, we found that we _____ our work.
   - (A) not longer would continue
   - (B) not longer could continue
   - (C) could continue no longer
   - (D) could no longer continue ( )

9. I have been fixing the computer _____.
   - (A) for four hours
   - (B) since four hours
   - (C) for three o'clock
   - (D) before the day before yesterday ( )

10. It was dark, _____ Vivian couldn't see what was going on.
   - (A) because
   - (B) so
   - (C) or
   - (D) but ( )

TEST 29 詳解

1. (**B**) My favorite recreation is <u>reading</u>.

我最喜歡的消遣是閱讀。

依句意，空格須填名詞，做 is 的補語，故選 (B) *reading*。

favorite〔'fevərɪt〕*adj.* 最喜愛的

recreation〔ˌrɛkrɪ'eʃən〕*n.* 消遣

2. (**D**) Don't light a match. The gas fumes <u>will</u> explode.

不要點火柴。瓦斯氣體可能會爆炸。

依句意，選 (D) *will*「將會；可能」。而 (A) ought to「應該」，(B) have to「必須」，(C) must「必須」，均不合句意。

light〔laɪt〕*v.* 點燃　　match〔mætʃ〕*n.* 火柴

gas〔gæs〕*n.* 瓦斯

fume〔fjum〕*n.*（有害、濃烈、或難聞的）煙；氣

explode〔ɪk'splod〕*v.* 爆炸

3. (**C**) I feel like having <u>some</u> soup.

我想喝些湯。

soup〔sup〕*n.* 湯　為不可數名詞，依句意為肯定，故選 (C) *some*「一些」，用於肯定句，且可數及不可數名詞均可使用。而 (A) many「很多的」、(B) few「很少的」，修飾可數名詞，(D) any 用於否定句或疑問句，均用法不合。

feel like + *V-ing* 想要～　　have〔hæv〕*v.* 喝

4. (**B**) My father had his hands <u>burned</u>. 爸爸的手燙傷了。

> have「使」的用法為：
>
> $\begin{cases} \textbf{\textit{have}} + 人 + 原形動詞（表主動）\\ \textbf{\textit{have}} + 物 + 過去分詞（表被動） \end{cases}$
>
> 受詞為 his hands，故接 burn 的過去分詞 **burned**。
>
> burn〔bɜn〕*v.* 燙傷

5. (**D**) Albert <u>would like</u> to sign up for the field trip.
艾伯特想要報名參加校外教學。

> **would like to V.** 想要～（= *want to V.*）
>
> **sign up for** 報名參加　　**field trip** 校外教學

6. (**D**) Today frozen food is sold all over America, but it is
not <u>as popular</u> as fresh food. 現在全美國都有賣冷凍
食品，但還是沒有新鮮食品受歡迎。

> **as** + 原級形容詞 + **as**… 像…一樣～
>
> popular〔'pɑpjələ〕*adj.* 受歡迎的
>
> frozen〔'frozn̩〕*adj.* 冷凍的　　**all over** 遍及
>
> fresh〔frɛʃ〕*adj.* 新鮮的

7. (**A**) <u>Buy</u> me some cigarettes if you stop at the grocery
store. 如果你有停在雜貨店，那就幫我買些煙。

> 依句意，幫我買香煙，是祈使句，故空格應填原形
> 動詞，選 (A) **Buy**。　　**buy sb. sth.** 買某物給某人
>
> cigarette〔'sɪɡə,rɛt〕*n.* 香煙
>
> grocery〔'grosərɪ〕*n.* 食品雜貨
>
> **grocery store** 雜貨店

8. (**D**)　As the weather became worse, we found that we
　　　　 <u>could no longer continue</u> our work.

　　　　因為天氣越來越糟，我們發現無法再繼續我們的工作。

　　　　　副詞片語 ***no longer***「不再」須置於助動詞後面，一般
　　　　　動詞前面，故選 (D) ***could no longer continue***，在此
　　　　　等於 could not continue any longer。

　　　　　continue〔kən'tɪnjʊ〕*v.* 繼續

　　　　　weather〔'wɛðə〕*n.* 天氣

　　　　　worse〔wɝs〕*adj.* 更糟的（bad 的比較級）

9. (**A**)　I have been fixing the computer <u>for four hours</u>.

　　　　我已經修這台電腦修四個小時了。

　　　　　have been fixing the computer 為「現在完成進行式」，
　　　　　表示「從過去某時間開始，一直繼續到現在仍在進行的
　　　　　動作」，常與「for ＋一段時間」的時間片語搭配，表
　　　　　「持續（多久）」，故選 (A) ***for four hours***。而 (B)
　　　　　since「自從」，後面須接過去的一個特定時間，而不
　　　　　是一段時間，(D) 前天之前，用法皆不合。

　　　　　fix〔fɪks〕*v.* 修理　　　computer〔kəm'pjutə〕*n.* 電腦

　　　　　the day before yesterday 前天

10. (**B**)　It was dark, <u>so</u> Vivian couldn't see what was going on.

　　　　天色昏暗，所以薇薇安看不見發生了什麼事。

　　　　　依句意，用連接詞 ***so***「所以」，選 (B)。而 (A) because
　　　　　「因為」，(C) or「或是；否則」，(D) but「但是」，
　　　　　則不合句意。本句也可說成：***Because*** it was dark,
　　　　　Vivian couldn't see what was going on.

　　　　　dark〔dɑrk〕*adj.* 暗的　　　***go on*** 發生（＝ *happen*）

TEST 30

Directions: *Of the four choices given after each sentence, choose the one most suitable for filling in the blank.*

1. You haven't finished your work, _____ you?
   - (A) haven't
   - (B) have
   - (C) do
   - (D) don't   (   )

2. Michael and Dora are planning _____ next year.
   - (A) marrying
   - (B) be marrying
   - (C) to marry
   - (D) will marry   (   )

3. Cattle _____ grass.
   - (A) feeds at
   - (B) feeds on
   - (C) feed at
   - (D) feed on   (   )

4. May my sister _____ to the party with me next Friday?
   - (A) come
   - (B) comes
   - (C) to come
   - (D) coming   (   )

5. She _____ shopping tomorrow. Will you go, too?
   - (A) went
   - (B) will go
   - (C) would go
   - (D) often goes   (   )

6. I wonder _____.

   (A) who our new teacher is

   (B) who is our new teacher

   (C) where is our new teacher

   (D) where is our new teacher going   (   )

7. You may give the book to _____ you like.

   (A) whomever

   (B) whoever

   (C) whose

   (D) who   (   )

8. If you _____ a headache, you should take an aspirin.

   (A) had

   (B) have

   (C) are having

   (D) will have   (   )

9. A young man was seen _____ the park.

   (A) enter

   (B) to enter

   (C) to be entered

   (D) to entering   (   )

10. We'll be late unless we _____ now.

   (A) have left

   (B) had left

   (C) will leave

   (D) leave   (   )

TEST 30 詳解

1. (**B**) You haven't finished your work, <u>have</u> you?
   你還沒做完你的工作，不是嗎？

   > 形成附加問句須前後主詞相同，且須用代名詞（you），又
   > 前有否定字 haven't，附加問句須用肯定，故選(A) *have*。
   > have you，是由 have you *finished your work* 省略而來。
   > finish〔'fɪnɪʃ〕*v.* 完成

2. (**C**) Michael and Dora are planning <u>to marry</u> next year.
   麥可和朵拉打算明年結婚。

   > *plan to* + *V.* 打算~
   > marry〔'mærɪ〕*v.* 結婚

3. (**D**) Cattle <u>feed on</u> grass.
   牛以牧草爲主食。

   > *feed on* 以~爲食
   > cattle〔'kætl̩〕*n.* 牛（爲集合名詞，視爲複數形）
   > grass〔græs〕*n.* 草

4. (**A**) May my sister <u>come</u> to the party with me next Friday?
   下個星期五，我姊姊可以和我一起去參加宴會嗎？

   > May「可以」，爲助動詞，後面須用原形動詞，故選
   > (A) *come*。

5. (**B**) She <u>will go</u> shopping tomorrow. Will you go, too?
她明天將會去逛街購物。你也會去嗎？

依句意為未來式，故選 (B) *will go*。

go shopping 去逛街購物

6. (**A**) I wonder <u>who our new teacher is</u>.
我想知道誰是我們的新老師。

空格須填名詞子句，做 wonder 的受詞，名詞子句須寫成間接問句的形式，主詞與動詞不須倒裝，即「疑問詞＋主詞＋動詞」，故選 (A) *who our new teacher is*。
而 (C) 須改為 where our new teacher is，(D) 須改為 where our new teacher is going。

wonder〔'wʌdə〕*v.* 想知道

7. (**A**) You may give the book to <u>whomever</u> you like.
你可以把書給任何一個你喜歡的人。

依句意，把書給「任何一個」你喜歡的人，選受格 (A) *whomever*。而 (B) 為主格，(C) 為所有格，(D) 為主格，均用法不合。

8. (**B**) If you <u>have</u> a headache, you should take an aspirin.
如果你頭痛，你應該吃阿斯匹靈。

本句並非假設語氣，而是直說法的條件句。而 If 引導的條件句，須用現在式代替未來式，故選 (B) *have*。

headache〔'hɛd,ek〕*n.* 頭痛　　take〔tek〕*v.* 吃（藥）
aspirin〔'æspərɪn〕*n.* 阿斯匹靈

9. (**B**) A young man was seen <u>to enter</u> the park.

一個年輕人被人看見進入了公園。

> 感官動詞的被動語態，其後不定詞的 to 不可省略，
> 故選 (B) *to enter*。　 enter〔'ɛntɚ〕*v.* 進入
> *be seen to V.* 被看見～

10. (**D**) We'll be late unless we <u>leave</u> now.

除非我們現在離開，否則我們會遲到。

> 依句意，現在「離開」，須用現在式，又主詞 We
> 為第一人稱複數，故選 (D) *leave*。
>
> late〔let〕*adj.* 遲到的
> unless〔ən'lɛs〕*conj.* 除非
> leave〔liv〕*v.* 離開

TEST 31

Directions: *Of the four choices given after each sentence, choose the one most suitable for filling in the blank.*

1. Mr. Stewart _____ for that company for fifteen years.
    - (A) is being worked
    - (B) has been working
    - (C) been working
    - (D) is working   (   )

2. If you're going out in this drizzle, you'd better _____.
    - (A) fill the gas tank
    - (B) put on a raincoat
    - (C) turn off the lights
    - (D) open the windows   (   )

3. At noon the sun is right _____ our heads.
    - (A) by
    - (B) over
    - (C) under
    - (D) before   (   )

4. _____ you mind closing the door?
    - (A) Could
    - (B) Should
    - (C) Might
    - (D) Would   (   )

5. Ask Miss White _____ me back later.
    - (A) to call
    - (B) calls
    - (C) calling
    - (D) called   (   )

6. Jennifer and I don't eat dinner at that fast-food restaurant
   _____.

   (A) almost
   (B) since
   (C) already
   (D) any more   ( )

7. Sandy : Do you understand English well yet?
   Carl : No, but I'm trying _____ more.

   (A) of learning
   (B) for learning
   (C) for learn
   (D) to learn   ( )

8. All children need love from their parents. Not only do
   _____ need it, but _____ also deserve it.

   (A) it, it
   (B) she, they
   (C) they, they
   (D) we, he   ( )

9. After _____ for three hours, she finally understood
   the lesson.

   (A) to study
   (B) studies
   (C) studied
   (D) studying   ( )

10. I'm tired _____ watching TV. Let's go for a walk.

    (A) to
    (B) of
    (C) by
    (D) for   ( )

TEST 31 詳解

1. (**B**) Mr. Stewart <u>has been working</u> for that company for fifteen years. 史都華先生已經在那家公司工作十五年了。

「*for* + 一段時間」表「持續 (多久)」，常與「現在完成進行式」搭配，即「have / has + 現在分詞」的形式，表示從過去某時間開始，一直持續到現在，而且還在進行的動作。

company〔'kʌmpənɪ〕*n.* 公司

2. (**B**) If you're going out in this drizzle, you'd better <u>put on a raincoat</u>.
現在在下毛毛雨，如果你要出門的話，最好穿上雨衣。

這條題目是考句意，外面在下毛毛雨，所以最好「穿上雨衣」，選 (B) *put on a raincoat*。而 (A) 把油箱加滿，(C) 把燈關掉，(D) 打開窗戶，則不合句意。

drizzle〔'drɪzḷ〕*n.* 毛毛雨　　*had better V.* 最好
fill〔fɪl〕*v.* 裝滿　　gas〔gæs〕*n.* 汽油
tank〔tæŋk〕*n.* (油) 箱　　*turn off* 關掉 (電器)
light〔laɪt〕*n.* 燈

3. (**B**) At noon the sun is right <u>over</u> our heads.
正午的時候，太陽在我們頭頂的正上方。

介系詞 *over* 表「在…的上方」。而 (A) by「在…旁邊」，(C) under「在…的下面」，(D) before「在…之前」，則不合句意。

noon〔nun〕*n.* 正午　　right〔raɪt〕*adv.* 正好

4. (**D**) <u>Would</u> you mind closing the door?
   你介不介意把門關上呢？

   > ***Would you mind + V-ing?*** 你介不介意～？
   >
   > （表示委婉的請求）
   >
   > mind〔maɪnd〕*v.* 介意

5. (**A**) Ask Miss White <u>to call</u> me back later.
   請懷特小姐待會回電話給我。

   > ***ask*** *sb.* ***to V.*** 請求某人做～
   >
   > ***call*** *sb.* ***back*** 回電話給某人
   >
   > later〔'letə〕*adv.* 待會；稍後

6. (**D**) Jennifer and I do***n't*** eat dinner at that fast-food
   restaurant ***any more***.
   珍妮佛和我已不再到那家速食店吃晚餐了。

   > ***not···any more*** 不再（= *not···anymore*）
   >
   > ***fast-food restaurant*** 速食店

7. (**D**) Sandy : Do you understand English well yet?
   Carl   : No, but I'm trying <u>to learn</u> more.
   珊蒂：你已經能完全了解英文了嗎？
   卡爾：還不行，但是我正在努力想多學一點。

   > ***try to V.*** 試圖～；努力～
   >
   > understand〔ˌʌndə'stænd〕*v.* 理解
   >
   > yet〔jɛt〕*adv.*（用於疑問句）現在；已經

8. (**C**) *All children* need love from their parents. Not only do *they* need it, but *they* also deserve it.

所有的小孩都需要父母的愛。他們不僅需要愛，而且也應該得到愛。

> 這條題目考代名詞，children 爲複數名詞，故代名詞用 *they*。
>
> *not only…but also~*　不僅…而且~
> deserve〔dɪˋzɝv〕v. 應得

9. (**D**) After <u>studying</u> for three hours, she finally understood the lesson.

研讀了三個小時之後，她終於了解這一課了。

> After 在此爲介系詞，後面須接動名詞，故選 (D) *studying*。
> After studying for three hours 在這裡等於 After having studied for three hours，因爲 After 已說明時間先後。
>
> finally〔ˋfaɪnḷɪ〕*adv.* 最後；終於
> lesson〔ˋlɛsṇ〕*n.* 課

10. (**B**) I *'m tired of* watching TV. Let's go for a walk.

我看電視看煩了。咱們去散步吧。

> *be tired of*　對~感到厭煩
> *go for a walk*　去散步

TEST 32

Directions*: Of the four choices given after each sentence, choose the one most suitable for filling in the blank.*

1. I remember the place _____ I first saw my wife.
   - (A) when
   - (B) which
   - (C) how
   - (D) where   (   )

2. Edward is not the kind of man _____ work.
   - (A) avoids
   - (B) to avoid
   - (C) avoiding
   - (D) avoided   (   )

3. George is seven feet tall. His brother is six feet tall. George is _____ his brother.
   - (A) tallest of
   - (B) as tall as
   - (C) taller than
   - (D) more tall   (   )

4. Don't _____ to the concert tonight.
   - (A) going
   - (B) went
   - (C) to go
   - (D) go   (   )

5. Do you want me _____ the letter?
   - (A) do mail
   - (B) for mail
   - (C) mailing
   - (D) to mail   (   )

6. I don't remember that name, but I _____ have heard it before.

   (A) can
   (B) will
   (C) might
   (D) would   (   )

7. This notebook is similar _____ mine.

   (A) as
   (B) from
   (C) than
   (D) to   (   )

8. If I had enough money, I _____ a computer.

   (A) have bought
   (B) had bought
   (C) will buy
   (D) would buy   (   )

9. Why don't you wait here until she _____?

   (A) come
   (B) comes
   (C) will come
   (D) is going to come   (   )

10. The teacher was _____ her lunch.

   (A) eaten
   (B) eat
   (C) ate
   (D) eating   (   )

TEST 32 詳解

1. (**D**) I remember the place <u>where</u> I first saw my wife.
我記得第一次見到我太太的那個地方。

> 表「地點」，關係副詞用 *where*，在此等於 in which，選 (D)。
> 而 (A) when 表「時間」，(C) how 表「方法」，(B) which
> 爲關係代名詞，用法皆不合。
>
> remember〔rɪ'mɛmbɚ〕v. 記得　　wife〔waɪf〕n. 妻子

2. (**B**) Edward is not the kind of man <u>to avoid</u> work.
愛德華不是那種會逃避工作的人。

> avoid〔ə'vɔɪd〕v. 避免
> (A) 須改爲 who avoids，(C) 須改爲 known for avoiding，
> (D) 須改爲 who avoids，才能選。
> 這條題目是考不定詞片語當形容詞片語用。
>
> Edward is not the kind of man *to avoid work*. (正)
>
> Edward is not the kind of man *who avoids work*. (正)
> (愛德華不是那種會逃避工作的人。)
>
> Edward is not the kind of man *avoiding work*. (誤)
>
> 這句話錯的原因是句意上的問題，因爲分詞有表示「進行」
> 的意味，不能說「愛德華是正在逃避工作的人。」我們只能
> 說「愛德華不是那種會逃避工作的人。」所以後面只能接不
> 定詞片語，不能接分詞片語。
>
> kind〔kaɪnd〕n. 種類

3. (**C**) George is seven feet tall. His brother is six feet tall.
George is <u>taller than</u> his brother.

喬治有七英呎高。他弟弟是六英呎高。喬治比他弟弟高。

依句意,「喬治比他弟弟高」,爲比較級,且 tall 的比較
級是 taller,故選 (C) *taller than*。
feet〔fit〕*n.pl.* 英呎(單數是 foot〔fut〕)
tall〔tɔl〕*adj.* 高

4. (**D**) Don't <u>go</u> to the concert tonight.

今天晚上不要去參加演唱會。

助動詞後,須接原形動詞,故選 (D) *go*。
concert〔'kɑnsɝt〕*n.* 演唱會;音樂會

5. (**D**) Do you want me <u>to mail</u> the letter?
你要我去寄這封信嗎?

want「想要」爲一般動詞,接受詞後,須接不定詞,
故選 (D) *to mail*。   mail〔mel〕*v.* 郵寄
letter〔'lɛtɚ〕*n.* 信

6. (**C**) I don't remember that name, but I ***might have heard***
it before.

我不記得那個名字,但我以前可能曾經聽過。

may 和 might 都可用來表現在或未來的推測,但 may 的
可能性大一點,might 的可能性小一點。
⎰ ***might* + *V.*** 可能~(表對現在的推測)
⎱ ***might have* + *V-ing*** 以前可能~(表現在對過去的推測)
remember〔rɪ'mɛmbɚ〕*v.* 記得

7. (**D**) This notebook *is similar to* mine.

這本筆記本和我的很類似。

similar〔'sɪmələ 〕*adj.* 類似的

be similar to 和～類似

（不要和 be familiar with「對～熟悉」搞混。）

notebook〔'not,bʊk 〕*n.* 筆記本

8. (**D**) If I *had* enough money, I ***would buy*** a computer.

如果我有足夠的錢，我就會買電腦。

表「與現在事實相反的假設」，其用法為：

$$\text{If} + \text{S.} + \left\{ \begin{array}{l} \text{were} \\ \text{過去式動詞} \end{array} \right\} \cdots, \text{S.} + \left\{ \begin{array}{l} \text{should} \\ \text{would} \\ \text{could} \\ \text{might} \end{array} \right\} + \text{V.}$$

computer〔kəm'pjutə 〕*n.* 電腦

9. (**B**) Why don't you wait here until she <u>comes</u>?

你何不在這裡等到她來？

在表時間的副詞子句中，須用現在簡單式表示未來，

不可用 shall、will，或 be going to 表示未來，

故選 (B) ***comes***。

Why don't you + *V.?* 你何不～？

(= *Why not* + *V.?*)

10. (**D**) The teacher was <u>eating</u> her lunch.

那位老師正在吃她的午餐。

依句意為過去進行式，即「was 或 were + V-ing」，

且為主動，故選 (D) ***eating***。

TEST 33

Directions: *Of the four choices given after each sentence, choose the one most suitable for filling in the blank.*

1. He'd be a good speaker if he _____ not so nervous.
   - (A) was
   - (B) were
   - (C) is
   - (D) will be   (   )

2. By this same time next year he _____ already.
   - (A) will graduate
   - (B) graduate
   - (C) will have graduated
   - (D) is graduating   (   )

3. His idea of a good father _____ yours, isn't it?
   - (A) is different from
   - (B) differ with
   - (C) has difference between
   - (D) is differential from   (   )

4. Pete wanted to call Paul, but he was _____.
   - (A) afraid to
   - (B) to afraid
   - (C) afraid of call
   - (D) afraid call to   (   )

5. The man _____ is feeding carps is my uncle.
   - (A) what
   - (B) which
   - (C) who
   - (D) whose   (   )

6. The sergeant and his friend write to _____ about once a month.
   - (A) each one
   - (B) another one
   - (C) one another
   - (D) the other   (   )

7. It _____ happened recently, or I would have remembered it.
   - (A) not must have
   - (B) must have not
   - (C) must not have
   - (D) not have must   (   )

8. Greg doesn't let me _____ his answers to the questions, because he thinks it's wrong.
   - (A) to see
   - (B) see
   - (C) seeing
   - (D) saw   (   )

9. He'll be allowed to enter the university _____ he passes the exam.
   - (A) providing
   - (B) in case
   - (C) unless
   - (D) although   (   )

10. "What does Sam do in his spare time?"
    "He spends most of his time _____."
    - (A) to study
    - (B) studying
    - (C) be studied
    - (D) studied   (   )

TEST 33 詳解

1. (**B**) He'd be a good speaker if he <u>were</u> not so nervous.
如果他沒那麼緊張，他會是一位很好的演講者。

> 從主要子句中的 'd be (即 would be) 可知，本句為
> 「與現在事實相反的假設語氣」，故 if 子句中的 be
> 動詞須用 *were*。
>
> speaker〔'spikə〕*n.* 演講者
> nervous〔'nɜvəs〕*adj.* 緊張的

2. (**C**) By this same time next year he <u>will have graduated</u>
already. 明年的這個時候，他將已經畢業了。

> 表示「未來某時間之前，已經完成的動作」，用「未來完成
> 式」表達，即「will have + 過去分詞」的形式，故選 (C)
> *will have graduated*。   graduate〔'grædʒu,et〕*v.* 畢業
> already〔ɔl'rɛdɪ〕*adv.* 已經

3. (**A**) His idea of a good father <u>is different from</u> yours,
isn't it? 他對於好爸爸的想法和你不一樣，不是嗎？

> 依句意，選 (A) *is different from*「和~不同」。
> different〔'dɪfrənt〕*adj.* 不同的
> 而若選 (B) differ〔'dɪfə〕*v.* 不同，須改為 His idea of a
> good father *differs from yours*…或 His idea of a good
> father *differs with you*…，(C) difference〔'dɪfərəns〕
> *n.* 差異 用於「have difference between A and B」的
> 句型，表「A 和 B 兩者之間有差異」，(D) differential
> 〔,dɪfə'rɛnʃəl〕*adj.* 差別的 *n.* 差別，均用法不合。

4. (**A**) Pete wanted to call Paul, but he was <u>afraid to</u>.
彼特想打電話給保羅，但是他害怕打給他。

> **be afraid + to V.** 害怕~ (= *be afraid + of V-ing*)
> **was afraid to** 是 was afraid to call Paul 的省略。

5. (**C**) The man <u>who</u> is feeding carps is my uncle.
正在餵食鯉魚的那個男人，是我叔叔。

> 空格引導形容詞子句，修飾先行詞 The man，故選 (C)
> **who**，修飾人的先行詞。而 (A) what 為複合關係代名詞，
> (B) which 為修飾事物的關係代名詞，(D) whose 為關係
> 代名詞所有格，均用法不合。
>
> feed〔fid〕*v.* 餵　　carp〔kɑrp〕*n.* 鯉魚

6. (**C**) The sergeant and his friend write to <u>one another</u>
about once a month.
陸軍中士和他的朋友，彼此大約每個月通信一次。

> **one another** 彼此 (= *each other*)
> sergeant〔'sɑrdʒənt〕*n.* 陸軍中士
> **write to sb.** 寫信給某人

7. (**C**) It <u>must not have</u> happened recently, or I would have
remembered it. 那絕對不是最近發生的，不然我會記得。

> 從 would have remembered 可知，此為「與過去事實相
> 反的假設語氣」，實際上是「我不記得」，故空格用「must
> have + p.p.」的形式，表示「對過去肯定的推測」，且依
> 句意為否定，故選 (C) **must not have**。
>
> recently〔'risn̩tlɪ〕*adv.* 最近
> or〔ɔr〕*conj.* 否則；要不然

8. (**B**) Greg doesn't let me <u>see</u> his answers to the questions, because he thinks it's wrong. 葛瑞格不讓我看他回答問題的答案，因為他認為這樣做不對。

　　let〔lɛt〕v. 讓 為使役動詞，接受詞後，須接原形動詞，故選 (B) *see*。

9. (**A**) He'll be allowed to enter the university <u>providing</u> he passes the exam.
如果他通過考試，他將可以進入大學就讀。

　　依句意，選 (A) *providing*〔prə'vaɪdɪŋ〕*conj.* 如果 (= *if*)。而 (B) in case「以防萬一」，(C) unless「除非」，(D) although「雖然」，均不合句意。

　　allow〔ə'laʊ〕v. 准許　　enter〔'ɛntɚ〕v. 進入
　　university〔͵junə'vɝsətɪ〕n. 大學
　　pass〔pæs〕v. 通過

10. (**B**) "What does Sam do in his spare time?"
"He spends most of his time <u>studying</u>."
「山姆有空的時候，都做些什麼？」
「他大部分的時間都花在唸書上。」

　　spend「花費」的用法為：

$$人 + spend + \begin{cases} 時間 \\ 金錢 \end{cases} + \begin{cases} (in) + V\text{-}ing \\ on + N. \end{cases}$$

　　spare〔spɛr〕*adj.* 空閒的
　　spare time 空閒時間 (= *free time*)

TEST 34

Directions: *Of the four choices given after each sentence, choose the one most suitable for filling in the blank.*

1. Ask John _____ for me for a moment.
   - (A) waits
   - (B) waiting
   - (C) waited
   - (D) to wait   (   )

2. The clerk tried to sell _____ another pair of trousers.
   - (A) her
   - (B) hers
   - (C) she
   - (D) his   (   )

3. The sunshine feels wonderful _____ me.
   - (A) for
   - (B) to
   - (C) with
   - (D) into   (   )

4. Would you mind _____ the eraser to me?
   - (A) lending
   - (B) lent
   - (C) lend
   - (D) to have lent   (   )

5. Samuel was tired of _____ to so many complaints.
   - (A) to listen
   - (B) listen
   - (C) listened
   - (D) listening   (   )

6. Judy wasn't in class this morning. Bob wasn't there,
   _____.

   (A) too
   (B) either
   (C) both
   (D) neither   (   )

7. Have you _____ been to New York?

   (A) can
   (B) how
   (C) ever
   (D) never   (   )

8. It's against regulations _____ in your dorm.

   (A) to smoked
   (B) to smoke
   (C) to smoking
   (D) smoke   (   )

9. In any physical fitness program, self-discipline must be
   _____.

   (A) underscored
   (B) to underscore
   (C) underscore
   (D) underscoring   (   )

10. Select the correct sentence.

    (A) May likes on Christmas to visit her grandparents.
    (B) On Christmas to visit her grandparents May likes.
    (C) May likes to visit her grandparents on Christmas.
    (D) May likes her grandparents on Christmas to visit.
                                                   (   )

TEST 34 詳解

1. (**D**) Ask John <u>to wait</u> for me for a moment.
請約翰等我一下。

> ***ask sb. to V.*** 請求某人～
> ***wait for*** 等待
> moment〔'momənt〕*n.* 片刻
> ***for a moment*** 一下子；一會兒

2. (**A**) The clerk tried to sell <u>her</u> another pair of trousers.
那名店員企圖要賣另一條褲子給她。

> sell 爲及物動詞，其後須接受詞，故須用受格，
> 選 (A) ***her***。而 (B) hers 爲所有代名詞，(C) she 爲
> 主格，(D) his 爲所有格，皆用法不合。
> clerk〔klɜk〕*n.* 店員　　***try to V.*** 試圖
> pair〔pɛr〕*n.* (一)條
> trousers〔'trauzəz〕*n. pl.* 褲子

3. (**B**) The sunshine feels wonderful <u>to</u> me.
我覺得陽光很棒。

> ***sth. feels wonderful to sb.*** 某人覺得某物很棒
> sunshine〔'sʌn͵ʃaɪn〕*n.* 陽光
> feel〔fil〕*v.* 令人覺得
> wonderful〔'wʌndəfəl〕*adj.* 很棒的

4. (**A**) Would you mind <u>lending</u> the eraser to me?

你介不介意把橡皮擦借給我？

> 動詞 mind 的後面須接動名詞，故選 (A) *lending*。
>
> *mind + V-ing* 介意～   lend〔lɛnd〕*v.* 借（出）
>
> *lend sth. to sb.* 把某物借給某人
>
> eraser〔ɪˈresɚ〕*n.* 橡皮擦

5. (**D**) Samuel ***was tired of*** <u>listening</u> to so many complaints.

聽到這麼多的抱怨，使山謬覺得很厭煩。

> be tired of 表「對～厭倦」，of 是介系詞，其後須接動
>
> 名詞，故選 (D) *listening*。   *listen to* 聽
>
> complaint〔kəmˈplent〕*n.* 抱怨

6. (**B**) Judy wasn't in class this morning. Bob wasn't
there, <u>either</u>.

茱蒂今天早上沒來上課。鮑伯也沒有。

> 肯定句的「也」，用 too，否定句的「也」，則
>
> 用 *either*，故選 (B)。
>
> *be in class* 上課

7. (**C**) Have you <u>ever</u> been to New York?

你有沒有去過紐約？

> 依句意，選 (C) *ever*「曾經」。
>
> *have ever been to*～ 曾經去過～
>
> New York〔ˌnjuˈjɔrk〕*n.* 紐約

8. (**B**) It's against regulations <u>to smoke</u> in your dorm.
在宿舍裡抽煙是違反規定的。

> It 是虛主詞，故選 (B) *to smoke* in your dorm，做句
> 子的眞正主詞。 smoke〔smok〕*v.* 抽煙
>
> against〔ə'gɛnst〕*prep.* 違反
> regulation〔,rɛgjə'leʃən〕*n.* 規定
> dorm〔dɔrm〕*n.* 宿舍（= *dormitory*）

9. (**A**) In any physical fitness program, self-discipline must
be <u>underscored</u>.
在任何的體能訓練課程中，一定都要強調自我訓練。

> 依句意爲被動語態，即「be 動詞＋ p.p.」，故空格應
> 填過去分詞，選 (A) *underscored*。
> underscore〔'ʌndə,skɔr, ,ʌndə'skɔr〕*v.* 強調
> physical〔'fɪzɪkl̩〕*adj.* 身體的
> fitness〔'fɪtnɪs〕*n.* 健康
> program〔'progræm〕*n.* 課程
> self-discipline〔'sɛlf'dɪsəplɪn〕*n.* 自律；自我訓練

10. (**C**) Select the correct sentence.
選出正確的句子。

> May likes to visit her grandparents on Christmas.
> （梅喜歡在聖誕節時，去探望她的祖父母。）
> visit〔'vɪzɪt〕*v.* 探望；拜訪
> grandparents〔'grænd,pɛrənts〕*n.pl.* 祖父母

TEST 35

Directions: *Of the four choices given after each sentence, choose the one most suitable for filling in the blank.*

1. When did you last hear _____ your father-in-law?
   - (A) by
   - (B) concerning
   - (C) from
   - (D) since   (   )

2. Students who _____ are good learners.
   - (A) are interested
   - (B) interesting
   - (C) be interested
   - (D) have interested   (   )

3. The number of whooping cranes _____ decreasing.
   - (A) being
   - (B) are
   - (C) is
   - (D) were   (   )

4. Do you enjoy _____ action movies?
   - (A) watched
   - (B) watching
   - (C) watch
   - (D) to watch   (   )

5. Are you _____ to visit your uncle tomorrow?
   - (A) come
   - (B) coming
   - (C) came
   - (D) comes   (   )

6. Paul always sits in _____ favorite chair.
   - (A) him
   - (B) his
   - (C) yours
   - (D) mine   (   )

7. The NCO expects his men _____ the proper uniform.
   - (A) wear
   - (B) to wear
   - (C) be wearing
   - (D) are wearing   (   )

8. I _____ home by 10 o'clock last night.
   - (A) will go
   - (B) am going
   - (C) had gone
   - (D) go   (   )

9. "Do you ever eat in a French restaurant?"
   - (A) "No, I eat in a French restaurant never."
   - (B) "No, in a French restaurant I eat never."
   - (C) "No, I never eat in a French restaurant."
   - (D) "No, never I eat in a French restaurant."   (   )

10. Do you _____ the time?
    - (A) has
    - (B) have
    - (C) had
    - (D) having   (   )

TEST 35 詳解

1. (**C**) When did you last ***hear from*** your father-in-law?

你上一次收到你岳父的信，是什麼時候？

依句意，「收到岳父的信」，選 (C) ***hear from*** *sb.*「收到某人的信；得知某人的消息」。

而 (A) by「藉由」，(B) concerning〔kən'sɜnɪŋ〕*prep.* 關於，(D) since「自從」，皆不合句意。

last〔læst〕*adv.* 上次

father-in-law〔'faðəɪn͵lɔ〕*n.* 公公；岳父

2. (**A**) Students who <u>are interested</u> are good learners.

有興趣的學生，會學得很好。

who 引導形容詞子句，修飾先行詞 Students，子句中須有動詞，依句意，選 (A) ***are interested***。

interested〔'ɪntrɪstɪd〕*adj.* 有興趣的

learner〔'lɜnə〕*n.* 學習者

3. (**C**) The number of whooping cranes <u>is</u> decreasing.

巨大的起重機的數量，正在減少中。

空格應填動詞，且主詞是 The number，為第三人稱單數，故選 (C) ***is***。

number〔'nʌmbə〕*n.* 數量

whooping〔'hupɪŋ〕*adj.* 巨大的

crane〔kren〕*n.* 起重機

decrease〔dɪ'kris〕*v.* 減少

4. (**B**) Do you enjoy <u>watching</u> action movies?
　　　你喜歡看動作片嗎？

　　　　　enjoy + *V-ing* 喜歡～

　　　　　action〔'ækʃən〕*n.* 動作
　　　　　action movie 動作片

5. (**B**) Are you <u>coming</u> to visit your uncle tomorrow?
　　　你明天會來探望你的叔叔嗎？

　　　　　「現在進行式」可表「不久的未來」，故選 (B) *coming*。

　　　　　visit〔'vɪzɪt〕*v.* 拜訪；探望
　　　　　uncle〔'ʌŋkḷ〕*n.* 叔叔；舅舅；伯父

6. (**B**) Paul always sits in <u>his</u> favorite chair.
　　　保羅總是坐在他最喜歡的椅子上。

　　　　　空格應填所有格，故選 (B) *his*。而 (A) him 是受格，
　　　　　(C) yours 是所有代名詞，(D) mine 也是所有代名詞，
　　　　　均用法不合。

　　　　　favorite〔'fevərɪt〕*adj.* 最喜歡的

7. (**B**) The NCO *expects* his men *to wear* the proper uniform.
　　　那位士官希望他的士兵們，都能穿著適當的制服。

　　　　　expect〔ɪk'spɛkt〕*v.* 期待
　　　　　expect sb. *to V.* 期待某人～

　　　　　NCO 軍士；士官（= *noncommissioned officer*）
　　　　　men〔mɛn〕*n. pl.* 士兵　　proper〔'prɑpɚ〕*adj.* 適當的
　　　　　uniform〔'junə,fɔrm〕*n.* 制服

8. (**C**) I <u>had gone</u> home by 10 o'clock last night.

　　我昨天晚上十點前，就已經回到家了。

> 表過去某特定時刻之前，已發生的動作，須用「過去
> 完成式」，即「had + p.p.」，故選 (C) ***had gone***。
> 介系詞 by，表「在～之前」。

9. (**C**) "Do you ever eat in a French restaurant?"
　　<u>"No, I never eat in a French restaurant."</u>

　　「你曾在法國餐廳吃過飯嗎？」
　　「不，我從未在法國餐廳吃過飯。」

> ever〔ˋɛvɚ〕*adv.* 曾經
> French〔frɛntʃ〕*adj.* 法國的
> restaurant〔ˋrɛstərənt〕*n.* 餐廳

10. (**B**) Do you <u>have</u> the time?

　　你知道現在幾點嗎？

> 前有助動詞 Do，故空格應填原形動詞，選 (B) ***have***。
>
> 問別人「現在幾點」的說法有：
>
> Do you have ***the*** time?
> Have you got ***the*** time?（你知道現在幾點嗎？）
> What time is it?（現在幾點？）
> Do you know what time it is?（你知道現在幾點嗎？）
>
> 【比較】
> ⎰ Do you have ***the*** time?（你知道現在幾點嗎？）
> ⎱ Do you have time?（你有時間嗎？；你有空嗎？）

TEST 36

Directions: *Of the four choices given after each sentence, choose the one most suitable for filling in the blank.*

1. The students had trouble _____ the instruction.
   - (A) understood
   - (B) to understand
   - (C) to be understood
   - (D) understanding ( )

2. The manager insists that I _____ responsibility.
   - (A) take
   - (B) has taken
   - (C) taking
   - (D) took ( )

3. There is _____ ice on the roads.
   - (A) a large number of
   - (B) lot of
   - (C) a great deal of
   - (D) many ( )

4. I don't know _____ she's coming _____ not.
   - (A) neither ; nor
   - (B) whether ; or
   - (C) either ; or
   - (D) rather ; than ( )

5. So far, she _____ writing the book.
   - (A) hasn't finished
   - (B) didn't finish
   - (C) doesn't finish
   - (D) isn't finished ( )

6. Donald's family _____ in Chicago from 1980 to 1989, and then they moved to New York.
   (A) lived
   (B) is living
   (C) have lived
   (D) has been living   (   )

7. She _____ named president of the organization tomorrow.
   (A) is to be
   (B) is to being
   (C) was to being
   (D) have to be   (   )

8. My wife thinks _____ would look very nice in the dining room.
   (A) a large furniture
   (B) a large piece of furniture
   (C) a large pieces of furnitures
   (D) large furnitures   (   )

9. I need to get _____, but I'm so busy that I don't have enough time to go to the beauty salon now!
   (A) done my hair
   (B) my hair doing
   (C) my hair done
   (D) my hair to do   (   )

10. Never ask personal questions, like how much money _____.
    (A) does he make
    (B) do he have
    (C) he have
    (D) he makes   (   )

TEST 36 詳解

1. (**D**) The students had trouble <u>understanding</u> the
   instruction. 學生在了解授課內容方面有困難。

   > trouble〔'trʌbl̩〕*n.* 困難
   >
   > $have + \begin{cases} \textit{\textbf{trouble}} \\ \textit{\textbf{difficulty}} \\ \textit{\textbf{problem}} \end{cases} + \textit{\textbf{(in)}} + \textit{\textbf{V-ing}}$ 做…有困難
   >
   > understand〔͵ʌndə'stænd〕*v.* 了解
   >
   > instruction〔ɪn'strʌkʃən〕*n.* 教學；講授

2. (**A**) The manager insists that I <u>take</u> responsibility.
   經理堅持我要負責任。

   > insist〔ɪn'sɪst〕*v.* 堅持 爲慾望動詞，後面接的 that 子句
   > 中，因省略助動詞 should，故動詞須用原形動詞，選 (A)
   > *take*。（詳見「文法寶典」p.372）
   >
   > manager〔'mænɪdʒɚ〕*n.* 經理
   >
   > responsibility〔rɪ͵spɑnsə'bɪlətɪ〕*n.* 責任

3. (**C**) There is <u>a great deal of</u> ice on the roads.
   路上有非常多的冰。

   > ice〔aɪs〕*n.* 冰 爲不可數名詞，故選 (C) *a great deal of*
   > 「大量的」。而 (A) a large number of「很多的」修飾可
   > 數名詞，(B) 須改爲 lots of 或 a lot of 才能選，作「很多的」
   > 解，可接可數或不可數名詞，(D) many「很多的」修飾可
   > 數名詞，故用法皆不合。

4. (**B**)　I don't know <u>whether</u> she's coming <u>or</u> not.

　　　　我不知道她是否會來。

> ***whether…or not***　是否～（引導名詞子句）
>
> 而 (A) neither A nor B「既不 A 也不 B」，(C) either
> A or B「不是 A 就是 B」，(D) rather than「而不是」，
> 句意與用法皆不合。

5. (**A**)　So far, she <u>hasn't finished</u> writing the book.

　　　　到目前為止，她還沒把書寫完。

> so far「到目前為止」通常與「現在完成式」搭配，表示
> 「從過去持續到現在的動作或狀態」，故選 (A) ***hasn't***
> ***finished***。　　finish〔ˈfɪnɪʃ〕*v.* 完成

6. (**A**)　Donald's family <u>lived</u> in Chicago from 1980 to 1989,
　　　　and then they moved to New York.　唐納德的家人從一
　　　　九八〇年到一九八九年都住在芝加哥，然後就搬到紐約。

> 從一九八〇年到一九八九年，為過去的時間，故動詞用
> 過去式動詞，選 (A) ***lived***。
>
> Chicago〔ʃɪˈkago〕*n.* 芝加哥（美國城市名）
> move〔muv〕*v.* 搬家

7. (**A**)　She <u>is to be</u> named president of the organization
　　　　tomorrow.　她明天會被任命為該機構的總裁。

> 「be 動詞 + to V.」表「預定」，又依句意為被動，故須
> 用「be 動詞 + to be p.p.」的形式，故選 (A) ***is to be***。
>
> name〔nem〕*v.* 任命　　president〔ˈprɛzədənt〕*n.* 總裁
> organization〔ˌɔrgənəˈzeʃən〕*n.* 組織；機構

8. (**B**) My wife thinks <u>a large piece of furniture</u> would look very nice in the dining room.

我太太認爲在餐廳裡有個大型傢俱,看起來會很不錯。

furniture (ˈfɜnɪtʃə) *n.* 傢俱 表示「所有傢俱的總稱」, 意義上爲集合名詞,但文法上爲物質名詞,即不可數名詞, 須用表「單位」的名詞來表示「數」的觀念。其公式爲:

> 數詞＋單位名詞＋of＋物質名詞

如:a piece of furniture「一件傢俱」,several pieces of furniture「好幾件傢俱」。

dining room 餐廳;飯廳

9. (**C**) I need to get <u>my hair done</u>, but I'm so busy that I don't have enough time to go to the beauty salon now!

我需要去做頭髮,但是我太忙了,所以現在沒有足夠的 時間去美容院。

$$\textbf{\textit{get}} + \textbf{\textit{O}}. + \begin{cases} \textbf{\textit{to V}}. \text{ (表主動) 使～} \\ \textbf{\textit{p.p.}} \text{ (表被動)} \end{cases}$$

依句意,我的頭髮被別人做,是「被動」,故用過去分詞, 選 (C) ***my hair done***。 ***do one's hair*** 做頭髮;梳理頭髮 ***so…that～*** 如此…以致於～ ***beauty salon*** 美容院

10. (**D**) Never ask personal questions, like how much money <u>he makes</u>. 絕對不要問私人的問題,像是他賺多少錢。

依句意爲名詞子句,即「疑問詞＋主詞＋動詞」的形式, 故選 (D) ***he makes***。而 (C) 須改爲 he has 才能選。

personal (ˈpɜsn̩l) *adj.* 私人的

TEST 37

Directions: *Of the four choices given after each sentence, choose the one most suitable for filling in the blank.*

1. At that moment I didn't realize _____ to say that.
   - (A) how foolish it is
   - (B) how foolish is it
   - (C) how foolish it was
   - (D) how it was foolish   (   )

2. _____, I was told that I passed the test.
   - (A) Happily
   - (B) Happy
   - (C) For happiness
   - (D) Happiness   (   )

3. If the room is dark, _____ on the light.
   - (A) to turn
   - (B) turning
   - (C) turns
   - (D) turn   (   )

4. _____ something to eat is better than nothing.
   - (A) Have
   - (B) Had
   - (C) Has
   - (D) Having   (   )

5. _____ well is always our major concern.
   - (A) How the job done
   - (B) How doing the job
   - (C) How to do the job
   - (D) How do the job   (   )

6. We must be patient enough until _____ a satisfactory result.

    (A) we have to get
    (B) we are getting
    (C) we got
    (D) we get   (   )

7. He was so _____ that he couldn't hold the pen tight.

    (A) a drunk
    (B) a drinking
    (C) drunk
    (D) drunken   (   )

8. This is the boy _____ I have been waiting.

    (A) for whom
    (B) and whom
    (C) whom
    (D) and who   (   )

9. The tail of a fox is longer than _____ of a hare.

    (A) this
    (B) that
    (C) those
    (D) it   (   )

10. Dave came _____ than all the others.

    (A) later
    (B) latest
    (C) latter
    (D) last   (   )

TEST 37 詳解

1. (**C**) At that moment I didn't realize <u>how foolish it was</u> to say that. 在那時我並不明白，那麼說有多麼愚蠢。

> how 在此作「多麼」解，引導名詞子句，做 realize 的受詞，名詞子句的結構為：「how + 形容詞 + S. + V.」，且從前面助動詞 didn't 可知，此處應用過去式，故選 (C) ***how foolish it was***。　foolish〔'fulɪʃ〕*adj.* 愚蠢的
> moment〔'momənt〕*n.* 瞬間；片刻
> realize〔'riə,laɪz〕*v.* 了解

2. (**A**) <u>Happily</u>, I was told that I passed the test. 幸好，我收到通知，我通過測驗了。

> 修飾全句，應用副詞 ***Happily***，在此作「幸運地；幸好」解，選 (A)。
> pass〔pæs〕*v.* 通過

3. (**D**) If the room is dark, <u>turn</u> on the light. 如果房間裡很暗，就把電燈打開。

> 依句意，是「你」把電燈打開，但因句意明顯，而把主詞「你」省略，用祈使句，故本題選 (D) ***turn***。
> ***turn on*** 打開（電器）
> dark〔dɑrk〕*adj.* 黑暗的　　light〔laɪt〕*n.* 燈

4. (**D**) <u>Having</u> something to eat is better than nothing. 有東西吃總比沒有好。

> 此處應用動名詞做主詞，選 (D) ***Having***。

5. (**C**) <u>How to do the job</u> well is always our major concern.

如何把工作做好，一向都是我們最關心的事。

「疑問詞 + to V.」形成名詞片語，可做整句話的主詞，
故本題選 (C) *How to do the job*。

major〔ˋmedʒɚ〕 *adj.* 主要的
concern〔kənˋsɝn〕 *n.* 關心之事

6. (**D**) We must be patient enough until <u>we get</u> a satisfactory result.

我們必須有足夠的耐心，直到得到令人滿意的結果爲止。

依句意，「直到我們得到結果」，但其實尚未得到，
應是未來式，但是在表「時間」的副詞子句中，要用
現在式表示未來，故選 (D) *we get*。

patient〔ˋpeʃənt〕 *adj.* 有耐心的
satisfactory〔͵sætɪsˋfæktərɪ〕 *adj.* 令人滿意的
result〔rɪˋzʌlt〕 *n.* 結果

7. (**C**) He was so <u>drunk</u> that he couldn't hold the pen tight.

他喝得非常醉，連筆都握不緊。

so ~ that… 如此 ~ 以致於…
drunk〔drʌŋk〕 *adj.* 喝醉的（不置於名詞前）
drunken〔ˋdrʌŋkən〕 *adj.* 喝醉的（置於名詞前）
hold〔hold〕 *v.* 握著
tight〔taɪt〕 *adv.* 緊緊地

8. (**A**) This is the boy <u>for whom</u> I have been waiting.
這就是我一直在等的那個男孩。

> 空格引導形容詞子句，修飾先行詞 the boy，關代
> whom 做動詞片語 waiting for 的受詞，可將介系詞
> 移至關代前面，故選 (A) *for whom*。

9. (**B**) The tail of a fox is longer than <u>that</u> of a hare.
狐狸的尾巴比野兔的長。

> 在英文中，同類的事物才能相比，空格裡原本應填
> 入 <u>the tail</u> of a hare，但為了避免重複，而用單數
> 代名詞 *that* 代替，選 (B)。（詳見「文法寶典」p.122）
>
> tail〔tel〕*n.* 尾巴　　fox〔fɑks〕*n.* 狐狸
> hare〔hɛr〕*n.* 野兔

10. (**A**) Dave came <u>later</u> than all the others.
戴夫比其他人都晚來。

> 由空格後的 than 可知，此處為比較級，且依句意應為
> 時間上的比較，故選 (A) *later*，作「較遲；較晚」解。
>
> 【比較】
> { late-later-latest（表「時間」的先後）
> { late-latter-last（表「順序」的先後）
>
> later〔'letɚ〕*adj., adv.*（時間上）較晚；稍後
> latest〔'letɪst〕*adj., adv.*（時間上）最遲；最新的
> latter〔'lætɚ〕*adj.*（順序上）後者的
> last〔læst〕*adj.*（順序上）最後的

TEST 38

Directions: *Of the four choices given after each sentence, choose the one most suitable for filling in the blank.*

1. Our teacher didn't come so we _____ to go home.
   - (A) told
   - (B) were told
   - (C) were telling
   - (D) tell   (   )

2. My boss had the telephone _____ out of the office.
   - (A) take
   - (B) took
   - (C) taken
   - (D) taking   (   )

3. They're planning _____ for New York next week.
   - (A) to leave
   - (B) be leaving
   - (C) leaving
   - (D) and leave   (   )

4. I cannot drive farther _____ I'm almost out of gas.
   - (A) or
   - (B) so
   - (C) although
   - (D) because   (   )

5. They _____ there for three months.
   - (A) are living
   - (B) were living
   - (C) have been living
   - (D) live   (   )

6. Select the correct sentence.
    (A) How to operate this machine tell me can you?
    (B) How to operate this machine can you tell me?
    (C) Can you tell me this machine how to operate?
    (D) Can you tell me how to operate this machine?
    (   )

7. I _____ have gone out last night. Now I'm really worried about my test today.
    (A) couldn't
    (B) won't
    (C) shouldn't
    (D) can't   (   )

8. I'm awfully sorry _____ with you.
    (A) not to be able to go
    (B) to not be able to go
    (C) being not able to go
    (D) for going not   (   )

9. We will call on them today because we have not _____ them for four months.
    (A) saw
    (B) seen
    (C) see
    (D) to see   (   )

10. There is _____ how long the dog will live.
    (A) not knowing
    (B) not to know
    (C) no knowing
    (D) for knowing   (   )

TEST 38 詳解

1. (**B**) Our teacher didn't come so we <u>were told</u> to go home.
我們老師沒有來，所以我們被通知回家。

> 依句意，我們「被告知」回家，爲被動語態，故
> 選 (B) *were told*。

2. (**C**) My boss had the telephone <u>taken</u> out of the office.
老闆要人把電話移出辦公室。

> have 爲使役動詞，接受詞後，可接原形動詞或過去
> 分詞，做受詞補語，在此，電話「被移走」爲被動，
> 故受詞補語須用過去分詞，選 (C) *taken*。

3. (**A**) They're planning <u>to leave</u> for New York next week.
他們正在計劃，下週動身前往紐約。

> 表示「計劃做某事」，應用 plan to V.，故本題
> 選 (A) *to leave*。
>
> *leave for* 動身前往

4. (**D**) I cannot drive farther <u>because</u> I'm almost out of gas.
我沒辦法再往前開了，因爲我幾乎沒油了。

> 依句意，「因爲」沒油，所以不能再開了，連接詞用
> *because*，選 (D)。而 (A) or「或者」，(B) so「所以」，
> (C) although「雖然」，均不合句意。
>
> farther〔ˈfɑrðɚ〕adv.（距離）再往前地；更遠地
> *be out of* 用完　　 gas〔gæs〕n. 汽油

5. (**C**) They <u>have been living</u> there for three months.
他們已經住在那裡三個月了。

> 表示「動作從過去某時持續到現在」，並暗示該
> 動作將繼續進行下去，用「現在完成進行式」，
> 選 (C) *have been living*。

6. (**D**) Select the correct sentence. 選出正確的句子。
Can you tell me how to operate this machine?
你可不可以告訴我，如何操作這台機器？

> how to operate this machine 在此為名詞片語，
> 做 tell 的直接受詞，選 (D)。 operate〔'ɑpəˌret〕*v.* 操作
> machine〔mə'ʃin〕*n.* 機器

7. (**C**) I *shouldn't have gone out* last night. Now I'm really
worried about my test today.
我昨晚不應該出去的。現在我真擔心我今天的考試。

> 由句意可知，此處表示「過去不該做而已做」，應用
> *shouldn't* have + p.p.，故選 (C)。
>
> *be worried about* 擔心

8. (**A**) I'm awfully sorry <u>not to be able to go</u> with you.
我非常抱歉，不能和你一起去。

> 表示「因～感到抱歉」，可用 be sorry for + N. / V-ing
> 或 be sorry to + V.，而不定詞的否定用法中，not 要置
> 於 to 之前，故本題選 (A) *not to be able to go*。
> *be able to V.* 能夠
>
> awfully〔'ɔflɪ〕*adv.* 非常地

9. (**B**) We will call on them today because we have not seen them for four months.

我們今天將去拜訪他們，因為我們已經四個月沒有見到他們了。

> 表示「動作從過去某時持續到現在」，應用現在完成式，寫成「have + p.p」.，故選 (C) *seen*。
>
> *call on sb.* 拜訪某人 (= *visit sb.*)

10. (**C**) There is <u>no knowing</u> how long the dog will live.

我們不可能知道，那隻狗能活多久。

> $\begin{cases} \textbf{\textit{There is no}} + \textbf{\textit{V-ing}} \ \ 不可能\sim \\ = \text{It is impossible to} + \text{V.} \end{cases}$
>
> （詳見「文法寶典」p.439）
>
> *how long* 多久

TEST 39

Directions: *Of the four choices given after each sentence, choose the one most suitable for filling in the blank.*

1. Why _____ when you saw me?
   - (A) weren't you stopping
   - (B) didn't you stop
   - (C) you don't stop
   - (D) haven't you stopped   (   )

2. Please _____ the glasses with water.
   - (A) have filled up
   - (B) filling up
   - (C) fill up
   - (D) will fill   (   )

3. Robert speaks English _____ than Becky.
   - (A) good
   - (B) well
   - (C) better
   - (D) best   (   )

4. I have to see the doctor.
   - (A) I should see him.
   - (B) I won't see him.
   - (C) I have seen him.
   - (D) I must see him.   (   )

5. The diligent student _____ to the library every week.
   - (A) goes
   - (B) is going
   - (C) will go
   - (D) has gone   (   )

6. Michael _____ a course in Chinese history this semester.
   - (A) may be taken
   - (B) is taken
   - (C) is taking
   - (D) have taken   (   )

7. As soon as I entered his bedroom, I saw him _____ on the sofa.
   - (A) lying
   - (B) laying
   - (C) laid
   - (D) lain   (   )

8. Last night, unluckily, the team forfeited the game because they _____ begin without their coach.
   - (A) mustn't
   - (B) shouldn't
   - (C) wouldn't
   - (D) can't   (   )

9. Chinese and English are the two languages that _____ in all the high schools here.
   - (A) are teaching
   - (B) are taught
   - (C) will be teaching
   - (D) will teach   (   )

10. My new instructor, Mr. Brown, gave me a booklet _____.
    - (A) read
    - (B) to read
    - (C) reading
    - (D) to reading   (   )

TEST 39 詳解

1. (**B**) Why <u>didn't you stop</u> when you saw me?

    當你看到我時，為什麼不停下來呢？

    > 疑問句中，主詞和助動詞須倒裝，而 when 子句為過去
    > 式，故主要子句亦用過去式，選 (B) *didn't you stop*。

2. (**C**) Please <u>fill up</u> the glasses with water.

    請將這些玻璃杯裝滿水。

    > 本句以 Please 起首，而且沒有主詞，為祈使句，應用
    > 原形動詞，故選 (C) *fill up*「裝滿」。

    > glass〔glæs〕*n.* 玻璃杯

3. (**C**) Robert speaks English <u>better</u> than Becky.

    羅伯特英文說得比貝琪好。

    > 形容動詞「說英文」，應用副詞，且在此用比較級，
    > 故選 (C) *better*。

4. (**D**) I have to the see the doctor.

    我必須去看醫生。

    > 依句意，選 (D) I must see him. (我必須去看他。)

    > ***have to*** 必須 (= *must*)

5. (**A**) The diligent student <u>goes</u> to the library every week.
這個勤勉的學生，每週都去圖書館。

由副詞片語 every week 可知，這名學生去圖書館
是固定的習慣，用現在簡單式，故選 (A) *goes*。

diligent〔'dɪlədʒənt〕*adj.* 勤勉的
library〔'laɪˌbrɛrɪ〕*n.* 圖書館

6. (**C**) Michael <u>is taking</u> a course in Chinese history this
semester. 麥克這個學期要修一門中國歷史的課。

主詞 Michael 為第三人稱單數，且「選修課程」為
主動，故本題選 (C) *is taking*，用現在進行式可表示
「現在正在進行的動作」或「計劃未來要做的事」。

course〔kors〕*n.* 課程　　*take a course* 修一門課
history〔'hɪstrɪ〕*n.* 歷史
semester〔sə'mɛstə〕*n.* 學期

7. (**A**) As soon as I entered his bedroom, I saw him <u>lying</u> on
the sofa. 我一走進他的臥室，就看到他躺在沙發上。

感官動詞 see 接受詞後，可接現在分詞做受詞補語，
強調受詞的動作正在進行，而 lie「躺」的三態變化
為：lie-lay-lain，現在分詞為 *lying*，故選 (A)。
lay 作原形動詞時，作「產（卵）；放置」解，三態變
化為：lay-laid-laid，現在分詞為 laying，在此不合。

as soon as 一～就⋯　　enter〔'ɛntə〕*v.* 進入
bedroom〔'bɛdˌrum〕*n.* 臥室　　sofa〔'sofə〕*n.* 沙發

8. (**C**)　Last night, unluckily, the team forfeited the game because they <u>wouldn't</u> begin without their coach.

昨天晚上，該隊很不幸地喪失比賽資格，因為他們沒有教練在場，不願意開始比賽。

> 由時間副詞 Last night 可知，事情發生在過去，他們「不願意」開始，選 (C) ***wouldn't***。
>
> unluckily〔ʌnˈlʌkɪlɪ〕*adv.* 不幸地
> forfeit〔ˈfɔrfɪt〕*v.* 喪失（權利、資格等）
> coach〔kotʃ〕*n.* 教練

9. (**B**)　Chinese and English are the two languages that <u>are taught</u> in all the high schools here.

國文和英文，是本地所有的高中，都要教授的兩種語言。

> that 在此為關代，引導形容詞子句，修飾先行詞 languages，而語言應是「被教授」，要用被動，故選 (B) ***are taught***。
>
> language〔ˈlæŋgwɪdʒ〕*n.* 語言
> ***high school*** 高中

10. (**B**)　My new instructor, Mr. Brown, gave me a booklet <u>to read</u>.

我的新老師，布朗先生，給我一本小冊子要我讀。

> 不定詞可做形容詞用，放在所修飾的名詞之後，故選 (B) ***to read***。
>
> instructor〔ɪnˈstrʌktɚ〕*n.* 教師；教官；講師
> booklet〔ˈbuklɪt〕*n.* 小冊子

TEST 40

Directions: *Of the four choices given after each sentence, choose the one most suitable for filling in the blank.*

1. Select the correct sentence.
    - (A) I'll later have coffee, please.
    - (B) I'll have coffee later, please.
    - (C) I'll have later coffee, please.
    - (D) Please, coffee later I'll have. ( )

2. Ted _____ to go to the photo shop before noon.
    - (A) is liking
    - (B) could like
    - (C) would like
    - (D) had like ( )

3. Edward felt that he should help his friends.
    - (A) Edward felt that he had an obligation to help them.
    - (B) Edward felt that he would help them.
    - (C) He had a certain way of helping them.
    - (D) He had a special time to help them. ( )

4. My favorite sport is _____.
    - (A) swim
    - (B) swimming
    - (C) on swimming
    - (D) for swimming ( )

5. Maybe I will eat _____ salad.
    - (A) any
    - (B) few
    - (C) many
    - (D) some ( )

6. Paula's _____ her job affected her family's life
   tremendously.
   (A) lost
   (B) losing
   (C) was lost
   (D) was losing   (   )

7. You must _____ drive a car without fastening
   your seat belt.
   (A) always
   (B) usually
   (C) never
   (D) perhaps   (   )

8. I'm reading an interesting magazine about animals
   and the places _____ they live.
   (A) at that
   (B) that
   (C) which
   (D) where   (   )

9. The boys used to _____ when they were little.
   (A) play together
   (B) playing together
   (C) be playing together
   (D) be played together   (   )

10. I _____ other kinds of jets before.
    (A) have flown
    (B) am flying
    (C) will fly
    (D) flown   (   )

TEST 40 詳解

1. (**B**) Select the correct sentence. 選出正確的句子。
   I'll have coffee later, please.
   我待會再喝咖啡,謝謝。

   > later「稍後;待會」爲時間副詞,應置於句尾,
   > 最後再加上 please,表示客氣,選 (B)。
   >
   > please 用於禮貌性徵求對方的意見,或接受對方的
   > 邀請,作「好嗎;行嗎;謝謝」解。
   >
   > have〔hæv〕v. 吃;喝

2. (**C**) Ted <u>would like</u> to go to the photo shop before noon.
   泰德想要中午以前到照相館去。

   > ***would like to V.*** 表「想要~」,其他選項無此用法,
   > 故選 (C)。
   >
   > photo〔'foto〕n. 照片 (= *photograph*)
   > ***photo shop*** 照相館　　noon〔nun〕n. 正午

3. (**A**) Edward felt that he should help his friends.
   愛德華覺得,他應該幫助他的朋友。

   > 依句意,should「應該」,即是「有義務、有責任」,故
   > 選 (A) Edward felt that he had an obligation to help
   > them. (愛德華覺得,他有義務要幫助他們。)
   >
   > obligation〔,ɑblə'geʃən〕n. 義務;責任
   > certain〔'sɝtṇ〕adj. 特定的;某種

4. (**B**) My favorite sport is <u>swimming</u>.

我最喜歡的運動是游泳。

此處應用動名詞，做 is 的補語，故選 (B) *swimming*。

favorite (ˈfevərɪt) *adj.* 最喜歡的

5. (**D**) Maybe I will eat <u>some</u> salad.   也許我會吃點沙拉。

some「一點；一些」用於肯定句，且可數及不可數
名詞均可使用，故選 (D)。

any 用於否定句和疑問句；few「幾乎沒有」，爲否定
用法，many「很多」爲肯定，均用於可數複數名詞；
salad 爲不可數名詞，故 (A)、(B)、(C) 均不合。

salad (ˈsæləd) *n.* 沙拉

6. (**B**) Paula's <u>losing</u> her job affected her family's life
tremendously.

寶拉失業，大大地影響到她家裡的生活。

lose *one's* job「失業」做主詞，且置於所有格之後，
應用動名詞，故選 (B) *losing*。　　lose (luz) *v.* 失去

affect (əˈfɛkt) *v.* 影響
tremendously (trɪˈmɛndəslɪ) *adv.* 大大地

7. (**C**) You must ***never*** drive a car ***without*** fastening your
seat belt.   你開車絕不可以不繫上安全帶。

表示「絕不可以不…」，爲雙重否定，用 ***never*** ~
without…，故選 (C)。

fasten (ˈfæsn̩) *v.* 繫上　　 ***seat belt*** 安全帶

8. (**D**) I'm reading an interesting magazine about animals and the places <u>where</u> they live.

我正在讀一本有趣的雜誌，有關動物與牠們居住的地方。

> 空格引導形容詞子句，修飾先行詞 places，且形容詞
> 子句中需要地方副詞，故本題選 (D) *where*，為關係
> 副詞，相當於 in which。that 和 which 均為關代，
> 在此用法不合。

9. (**A**) The boys used to <u>play together</u> when they were little.

這些男孩小時候常常一起玩耍。

> 【比較】
> $\begin{cases} \textit{used to} + \textit{V.} & \text{以前常常；以前曾經} \\ \textit{be used to} + \textit{N. / V-ing} & \text{習慣於} \sim \\ \textit{be used to} + \textit{V.} & \text{被用來} \sim \end{cases}$
>
> 依句意，選 (A) *play together*。

10. (**A**) I <u>have flown</u> other kinds of jets before.

我以前開過其他種類的噴射機。

> 表示從過去某時到現在的經驗，用「現在完成式」，
> 表示過去的經驗，也可用「過去簡單式」，故選
> (A) *have flown*。
>
> fly〔flaɪ〕*v.* 搭飛機；開（飛機）
> （fly 的三態變化為 fly-flew-flown）
> kind〔kaɪnd〕*n.* 種類
> jet〔dʒɛt〕*n.* 噴射機（= *jet plane*）

TEST 41

Directions: *Of the four choices given after each sentence, choose the one most suitable for filling in the blank.*

1. Select the correct sentence.
   - (A) Three years ago with my parents lived I.
   - (B) Three years ago with my parents I lived.
   - (C) Three years ago I with my parents lived.
   - (D) Three years ago I lived with my parents. (   )

2. _____ fine today, we are going for an excursion.
   - (A) Owing to
   - (B) It is
   - (C) It being
   - (D) Because of it is   (   )

3. I believe _____ necessary to work hard.
   - (A) that
   - (B) that it
   - (C) it
   - (D) this   (   )

4. Do you mind if I take Linda home?
   - (A) Do you want to take Linda home?
   - (B) Do you have any objections if I take Linda home?
   - (C) Do you care to take Linda home?
   - (D) Does Linda want to go home with you? (   )

5. Do you mind _____ me your telephone number?
   - (A) tell
   - (B) to tell
   - (C) tells
   - (D) telling   (   )

6. My history teacher, Mr. Smith, lives _____ 1211 Jefferson Street.

    (A) in
    (B) on
    (C) at
    (D) to   (　　)

7. The movie is <u>over</u> at ten o'clock.

    (A) started
    (B) through
    (C) running
    (D) on   (　　)

8. You will get to the museum _____ if you go by bus.

    (A) more fastly
    (B) more faster
    (C) the fast
    (D) faster   (　　)

9. My car is parked _____ the garage.

    (A) of
    (B) in
    (C) to
    (D) for   (　　)

10. Luke speaks English very _____.

    (A) good
    (B) well
    (C) nice
    (D) beautiful   (　　)

TEST 41 詳解

1. (**D**) Select the correct sentence. 選出正確的句子。

Three years ago I lived with my parents.

三年前，我和我的父母住在一起。

parents〔'pɛrənts〕*n. pl.* 父母

2. (**C**) It being fine today, we are going for an excursion.

因為今天天氣晴朗，我們打算要去遠足。

> 本句是由 Because it is fine today, we are going for
> an excursion. 轉化而來。
>
> 副詞子句簡化為分詞構句的步驟有三：
>
> ① 去連接詞（Because）。
>
> ② 前後主詞一致，可省略，不一致，則保留。（it 和 we
> 不一致，所以保留）。
>
> ③ 動詞改為現在分詞（is→being）。
>
> fine〔faɪn〕*adj.* 晴朗的
>
> excursion〔ɪk'skɝʒən〕*n.* 短途旅行；遠足
>
> ***owing to*** + ***N.*** 由於～（= *because of* + *N.*)

3. (**C**) I believe it necessary to work hard.

我認為努力工作是必要的。

> 空格應填虛受詞 *it*，代替真正受詞 to work hard，故選 (C)。
>
> believe〔bɪ'liv〕*v.* 認為
>
> necessary〔'nɛsə,sɛrɪ〕*adj.* 必要的
>
> ***work hard*** 努力工作

4. (**B**) Do you mind if I take Linda home?

你介意我帶琳達回家嗎？

依句意，選 (B) Do you have any objections if I take Linda home? (如果我帶琳達回家，你會反對嗎？)

> mind〔maɪnd〕*v.* 介意　　take〔tek〕*v.* 帶
> objection〔əb'dʒɛkʃən〕*n.* 反對
> *care to V.* 喜歡；想要

5. (**D**) Do you mind <u>telling</u> me your telephone number?

你介意告訴我，你的電話號碼嗎？

> *mind + V-ing* 介意～
> telephone〔'tɛlə,fon〕*n.* 電話
> number〔'nʌmbɚ〕*n.* 號碼

6. (**C**) My history teacher, Mr. Smith, lives <u>at</u> 1211 Jefferson Street.

我的歷史老師史密斯先生，住在傑佛遜街 1211 號。

依句意，住「在」傑佛遜街 1211 號，介系詞須用 *at*，故選 (C)。

> history〔'hɪstrɪ〕*n.* 歷史

7. (**B**) The movie is <u>over</u> at ten o'clock.

那部電影十點結束。

> 依句意，選 (B) *be through* 結束；終了。
> through〔θru〕*adv.* 終了
> over〔'ovɚ〕*adj.* 結束的

8. (**D**) You will get to the museum <u>faster</u> if you go by bus.

如果你搭公車，會比較快到達博物館。

副詞 fast 的比較級為 *faster*，故選 (D)。

get to 到達　　museum〔mju'ziəm〕*n.* 博物館

by bus 搭公車

9. (**B**) My car is parked <u>in</u> the garage.

我的車停在車庫裡。

介系詞 *in* 表「在～裡面」，故選 (B)。

park〔pɑrk〕*v.* 停（車）

garage〔gə'rɑʒ〕*n.* 車庫

10. (**B**) Luke speaks English very <u>well</u>.

盧克英文說得很好。

修飾動詞 speaks 須用副詞，故選 (B)。

speak English very well 英文說得很好

= speak very good English

= speak English very fluently　英文說得很流利

TEST 42

Directions: *Of the four choices given after each sentence, choose the one most suitable for filling in the blank.*

1. Philip runs _____ to be the champion.
   - (A) fast enough
   - (B) fastly enough
   - (C) enough fast
   - (D) enough fastly   (   )

2. Many changes _____ since then.
   - (A) have taken place
   - (B) has taken place
   - (C) were taking place
   - (D) will take place   (   )

3. Your teacher would like you _____.
   - (A) learn Japanese
   - (B) to arrive on time
   - (C) buy a dictionary
   - (D) teaching English   (   )

4. Do you know _____ to Peggy?
   - (A) what happened
   - (B) what's happened
   - (C) what it happens
   - (D) what did it happen   (   )

5. I didn't come yesterday _____.
   - (A) because I am ill
   - (B) because of illness
   - (C) because of I was ill
   - (D) because I illed   (   )

6. As soon as I _____ Frank tomorrow, I'll tell him the plan.
   - (A) will see
   - (B) seen
   - (C) saw
   - (D) see   (   )

7. Tracy is three years junior _____. However, she is taller than I.
   - (A) to I
   - (B) to me
   - (C) than I
   - (D) than me   (   )

8. Allen : You'd better get to class on time.
   Kevin : You're right. I _____ go now.
   - (A) had
   - (B) may
   - (C) must
   - (D) ought   (   )

9. I recommended that she _____ her composition as soon as possible.
   - (A) finishes writing
   - (B) should finish the writing
   - (C) finish writing
   - (D) finished writing   (   )

10. _____ you please tell me your address?
   - (A) Do
   - (B) Have
   - (C) Shall
   - (D) Would   (   )

TEST 42 詳解

1. (**A**) Philip runs <u>fast enough</u> to be the champion.
   菲力浦跑得很快，快到足以獲得冠軍。

   > 修飾動詞 runs 須用副詞 *fast*，並沒有 fastly 這個字，又
   > 副詞 enough 須置於所修飾的副詞之後，形成「*adv.* +
   > enough + to V.」的句型，表「夠～，足以…」，故選 (A)。
   > champion〔'tʃæmpɪən〕*n.* 冠軍

2. (**A**) Many changes <u>have taken place</u> since then.
   自那時以來，發生了許多變化。

   > 介系詞 since「自從」須與「現在完成式」搭配使用，
   > 即「have/has + 過去分詞」的形式，表示「從過去持續
   > 到現在的動作或狀態」，主詞 Many changes 爲複數
   > 名詞，須用複數動詞，故選 (A) *have taken place*。
   > *take place* 發生 (= *happen*)
   > change〔 tʃendʒ 〕*n.* 改變；變化

3. (**B**) Your teacher would like you <u>to arrive on time</u>.
   你的老師希望你準時到。

   > $\begin{cases} \textbf{\textit{would like}} + \textbf{\textit{sb.}} + \textbf{\textit{to V.}} \text{ 希望某人～} \\ = \textbf{\textit{want}} + \textbf{\textit{sb.}} + \textbf{\textit{to V.}} \end{cases}$
   > arrive〔 ə'raɪv 〕*v.* 到達   *on time* 準時
   > Japanese〔ˌdʒæpə'niz〕*n.* 日語
   > dictionary〔'dɪkʃənˌɛrɪ〕*n.* 字典

4. (**A**) Do you know <u>what happened</u> to Peggy?

你知道佩姬發生了什麼事嗎？

happen〔ˈhæpən〕*v.* 發生 為不及物動詞，限用主動。

*sth. **happen to** sb.* 某人發生某事

5. (**B**) I didn't come yesterday <u>because of illness</u>.

我昨天沒來，因為我生病了。

$$\begin{cases} \textit{because} + 子句 \ \ 因為 \\ = \textit{because of} + N. \end{cases}$$

依句意為過去式，故 (A) 須改為 because I *was* ill，才能選。

illness〔ˈɪlnɪs〕*n.* 疾病　　ill〔ɪl〕*adj.* 生病的

6. (**D**) As soon as I <u>see</u> Frank tomorrow, I'll tell him the
plan.　我明天一看到法蘭克，就會告訴他這項計劃。

as soon as「一…，就～」引導副詞子句，且在表
時間或條件的副詞子句中，須用現在式表示未來，
不可用 will 表示未來，故選 (D) *see*。

plan〔plæn〕*n.* 計劃

7. (**B**) Tracy is three years junior <u>to me</u>. However, she is
taller than I.　崔西比我小三歲。但是她比我高。

$$\begin{cases} A \textit{ is junior to } B \ \ A 比 B 年紀小 \\ \ \ (= A \textit{ is younger than } B) \\ A \textit{ is senior to } B \ \ A 比 B 年紀大 (= A \textit{ is older than } B) \end{cases}$$

片語 be junior to「比～小」中，to 為介系詞，須接受
格，故選 (B)。　junior〔ˈdʒunjɚ〕*adj.* 較年輕的

however〔hauˈɛvɚ〕*adv.* 然而

8. (**C**) Allen : You'd better get to class on time.

Kevin: You're right.　I <u>must</u> go now.

艾倫：你最好準時去上課。

凱文：你說的對。我現在必須走了。

依句意，選 (C) *must*「必須」。而 (A) had 後面接過去分詞，形成「過去完成式」，故用法不合；(B) may「可能；可以」，均不合句意；(D) ought 須改為 ought to「應該」(= should)，才能選。

had better 最好

get to class 去上課 (= *go to class*)

on time 準時

9. (**C**) I recommended that she <u>finish writing</u> her composition as soon as possible.

我建議她，儘快寫完她的作文。

recommend〔͵rɛkə'mɛnd 〕*v.* 建議；勸告

為慾望動詞，其用法為：

S. + *recommend* + *that* + *S*. + (*should*) + 原形動詞

（詳見文法寶典 p.372）

finish* + *V-ing 做完~

composition〔͵kɑmpə'zɪʃən 〕*n.* 作文

as soon as possible 儘快

10. (**D**) <u>Would</u> you please tell me your address?

能不能請你告訴我你的地址？

***Would you please* + *V*.** 能不能請你~？（表委婉的請求）

address〔ə'drɛs 〕*n.* 地址

TEST 43

Directions: *Of the four choices given after each sentence, choose the one most suitable for filling in the blank.*

1. They _____ already seen that movie.
   - (A) were
   - (B) are
   - (C) had
   - (D) having   (   )

2. I see the pretty woman. Jack _____, too.
   - (A) see it
   - (B) sees her
   - (C) saw him
   - (D) seen me   (   )

3. The mailman didn't bring _____ packages today.
   - (A) none
   - (B) some
   - (C) any
   - (D) no   (   )

4. The students play _____ on the basketball court.
   - (A) good
   - (B) well
   - (C) slow
   - (D) careful   (   )

5. Exercise keeps our body _____.
   - (A) strong
   - (B) strength
   - (C) strongly
   - (D) strengthen   (   )

6. Studying rules _____ helpful, but until such rules are applied, they can be of no value to you.

   (A) are
   (B) were
   (C) have been
   (D) is   (   )

7. Both Mary's and Tim's houses _____ destroyed by fire last month.

   (A) is
   (B) was
   (C) are
   (D) were   (   )

8. Amanda often _____ on a diet, but it never lasts for long.

   (A) goes
   (B) go
   (C) went
   (D) going   (   )

9. Energy can be changed from one form into _____.

   (A) another
   (B) other
   (C) others
   (D) the rest   (   )

10. We enjoyed _____.

   (A) very much to the zoo our visit
   (B) to the zoo our visit very much
   (C) our visit to the zoo very much
   (D) our visit very much to the zoo   (   )

TEST 43 詳解

1. (**C**) They <u>had</u> already seen that movie.

他們已經看過那部電影了。

> 依句意，他們「已經」看過那部電影，須用完成式，選
> (C) **had**。
>
> already〔ɔl'rɛdɪ〕 *adv.* 已經

2. (**B**) I see the pretty woman. Jack <u>sees her</u>, too.

我看到那位漂亮的女士。傑克也看到她了。

> 依句意為現在式，又 Jack 是第三人稱單數，須接單數
> 動詞，故選 (B) **sees her**。
>
> pretty〔'prɪtɪ〕 *adj.* 漂亮的

3. (**C**) The mailman didn't bring <u>any</u> packages today.

郵差今天沒有帶來任何包裹。

> **any**「任何的」用於否定句或疑問句，故選 (C)。
>
> mailman〔'mel,mæn〕 *n.* 郵差
> package〔'pækɪdʒ〕 *n.* 包裹

4. (**B**) The students play <u>well</u> on the basketball court.

學生們在籃球場上，玩得很愉快。

> 修飾動詞 play，須用副詞，故選 (B) **well**「愉快地」。
>
> basketball〔'bæskɪt,bɔl〕 *n.* 籃球
> court〔kort〕 *n.* 球場

5. (**A**) Exercise keeps our body <u>strong</u>.
運動使我們的身體保持強壯。

> keep「使保持」接受詞之後，須接形容詞當受詞補語，
> 故選 (A) ***strong*** 〔 strɔŋ 〕 *adj.* 強壯的。而 (B) strength
> 〔 strɛŋθ 〕 *n.* 力量，(C) strongly 〔'strɔŋlɪ 〕 *adv.* 強壯地，
> (D) strengthen 〔'strɛŋθən 〕 *v.* 加強，均用法不合。

> exercise 〔'ɛksə͵saɪz 〕 *n.* 運動

6. (**D**) Studying rules <u>is</u> helpful, but until such rules are
applied, they can be of no value to you.
研究法規固然很有幫助，但是除非你會應用它們，否則
這些法規對你而言，一點價值都沒有。

> 動名詞當主詞視爲單數，須接單數動詞，又 helpful 爲形
> 容詞，前面須有 be 動詞，故選 (D) ***is***。

> study 〔'stʌdɪ 〕 *v.* 研究　　rule 〔 rul 〕 *n.* 法規
> helpful 〔'hɛlpfəl 〕 *adj.* 有幫助的
> until 〔 ən'tɪl 〕 *adv.* 除非　　apply 〔 ə'plaɪ 〕 *v.* 應用
> value 〔'vælju 〕 *n.* 價值　　***of no value*** 沒有價值的

7. (**D**) Both Mary's and Tim's houses <u>were</u> destroyed by fire
last month. 瑪麗和提姆的房子，都在上個月被火燒毀了。

> 依句意爲過去式，且房子被燒毀，爲被動語態，故選
> (D) ***were***。

> destroy 〔 dɪ'strɔɪ 〕 *v.* 毀壞
> fire 〔 faɪr 〕 *n.* 火

8. (**A**) Amanda often <u>goes</u> on a diet, but it never lasts for long. 阿曼達經常節食，但是從來不曾持久。

依句意為現在式，且 Amanda 為第三人稱單數，須接單數動詞，故選 (A) *goes*。 *go on a diet* 節食

last〔læst〕*v.* 持續

for long 長久地

9. (**A**) Energy can be changed from one form into <u>another</u>.
能量可以從某一種形式，轉變成為另一種形式。

another 表「（不特定的）另一個」，故選 (A)。在此，another 就等於 another form。而 (B) other「其他的」為形容詞，(C) others「其他的人或事物」」表複數，(D) the rest「其餘的部分」，均用法不合。

energy〔'ɛnədʒɪ〕*n.* 能量　　change〔tʃendʒ〕*v.* 改變

form〔fɔrm〕*n.* 形式

10. (**C**) We enjoyed <u>our visit to the zoo very much</u>.
我們去動物園玩得非常愉快。

enjoy 之後須接名詞 our visit，而 to the zoo 則為形容詞片語，修飾 visit，very much 為副詞片語，修飾 enjoyed，置於句尾，故選 (C)。

visit〔'vɪzɪt〕*n.* 參觀；遊覽

zoo〔zu〕*n.* 動物園

TEST 44

Directions: *Of the four choices given after each sentence, choose the one most suitable for filling in the blank.*

1. Zoe has been to Europe several times, _____?
   (A) isn't she
   (B) doesn't she
   (C) has she
   (D) hasn't she   ( )

2. Have you _____ that CD yet?
   (A) listened to
   (B) listen to
   (C) heard
   (D) hear   ( )

3. "Who is going to take care of the baby?"
   (A) "I am."
   (B) "I am going."
   (C) "I take."
   (D) "I do."   ( )

4. Let me _____ you a ride.
   (A) give
   (B) to give
   (C) giving
   (D) gave   ( )

5. I saw the car _____ into the telephone pole.
   (A) bumping
   (B) to bump
   (C) which bumping
   (D) have bumped   ( )

6. Jill wants to go to the show next week, but she can't make it.
   - (A) Jill is going to the show.
   - (B) Jill doesn't care about the show.
   - (C) Jill wants to go, but she is going to be busy.
   - (D) The show took place last week.   (   )

7. The maid quit because Mrs. Jones kept _____ her work.
   - (A) have criticized
   - (B) to criticize
   - (C) criticize
   - (D) criticizing   (   )

8. I bought the dress three years ago, but it still looks _____ now.
   - (A) beauty
   - (B) beautiful
   - (C) beautifully
   - (D) beautify   (   )

9. _____ my surprise, Catherine won the English speech contest for the third time.
   - (A) In
   - (B) Let
   - (C) To
   - (D) Under   (   )

10. When we were in high school, Jerry often helped me _____ my mathematics.
    - (A) with
    - (B) through
    - (C) by
    - (D) to   (   )

TEST 44 詳解

1. (**D**) Zoe has been to Europe several times, <u>hasn't she</u>?
柔依去過歐洲好幾次，不是嗎？

> ***have been to*** 表「曾經去過」，用現在完成式表過去
> 到現在的經驗。本句中的 has 做助動詞用，故附加問句
> 須用助動詞 has，且前面為肯定，附加問句須用否定，
> 選 (D)。而 ***hasn't she?*** 是 hasn't she *been to Europe*
> *several times*? 的省略疑問句。

> Europe〔'jurəp〕*n.* 歐洲
> several〔'sɛvərəl〕*adj.* 好幾個　　time〔taɪm〕*n.* 次數

2. (**A**) Have you <u>listened to</u> that CD yet?
你已經聽過那張 CD 了嗎？

> 「have/has + 過去分詞」為現在完成式，表「從過去
> 持續到現在的動作或狀態」，又「聽」音樂，須用
> ***listen to***，而 hear「聽到」，則表示自然本能。

> yet〔jɛt〕*adv.* (用於疑問句) 已經

3. (**A**) "Who is going to take care of the baby?"
「誰要照顧小嬰兒？」

> 依句意，選 (A) ***"I am."*** (「我。」)，從 I am *going*
> *to take care of the baby.* 簡化而來。而 (B) 須改為 I am
> going to. 才能選。

> ***take care of*** 照顧

4. (**A**)　Let me <u>give</u> you a ride.　讓我順便載你一程。

> let 為使役動詞，接受詞後，須接原形動詞，故選 (A)。
>
> ***give sb. a ride*** 順便載某人一程

5. (**A**)　I saw the car <u>bumping</u> into the telephone pole.
> 我看到那部車撞到電線桿。

> see 為感官動詞，其用法為：
>
> see + 受詞 +
> ⎧ 原形 V. (表主動)
> ⎨ 現在分詞 (表主動進行)
> ⎩ p.p. (表被動)
>
> 依句意，車子「撞到」電線桿，為主動，故選 (A) ***bumping***。
>
> ***bump into*** 撞到
>
> pole〔pol〕*n.* 柱子　　***telephone pole*** 電線桿

6. (**C**)　Jill wants to go to the show next week, but she can't
make it.　吉兒下星期想去看表演，但是她沒辦法去。

> 依句意，選 (C) Jill wants to go, but she is going to
> be busy. (吉兒想去，但是她將會很忙。)
>
> show〔ʃo〕*n.* 表演　　***make it*** 成功；辦到
> ***care about*** 在乎；關心　　***take place*** 發生；舉行

7. (**D**)　The maid quit because Mrs. Jones kept <u>criticizing</u> her
work.　那位女傭辭職了，因為瓊斯太太一直批評她的工作。

> ***keep + V-ing*** 一直～
>
> criticize〔'krɪtə,saɪz〕*v.* 批評
>
> maid〔med〕*n.* 女傭　　quit〔kwɪt〕*v.* 辭職（三態同形）

8. (**B**) I bought the dress three years ago, but it still looks <u>beautiful</u> now.

我三年前買了這件洋裝，但它現在看起來仍然很漂亮。

> look「看起來～」為連綴動詞，其用法為：
> $\begin{cases} \text{look} + adj. \\ \text{look like} + \text{N.} \end{cases}$
>
> 故空格應填入形容詞，選 (B) *beautiful*「漂亮的」。
>
> 而 (A) beauty〔'bjutɪ〕*n.* 美，(C) 漂亮地，是副詞，
> (D) beautify〔'bjutə,faɪ〕*v.* 美化，均用法不合。
>
> dress〔drɛs〕*n.* 洋裝

9. (**C**) <u>To</u> my surprise, Catherine won the English speech contest for the third time.

令我驚訝的是，凱薩琳第三次贏得英文演講比賽。

> ***to** one's **surprise*** 令某人驚訝的是
>
> win〔wɪn〕*v.* 贏得　　speech〔spitʃ〕*n.* 演講
> contest〔'kɑntɛst〕*n.* 比賽　　time〔taɪm〕*n.* 次數

10. (**A**) When we were in high school, Jerry often ***helped*** me ***with*** my mathematics.

我們在高中的時候，傑瑞經常在數學方面幫忙我。

> ***help***「幫助」的用法為：
> $\begin{cases} \textbf{\textit{help}} + 人 + \textbf{\textit{(to)}}\ \textbf{\textit{V.}} \\ \textbf{\textit{help}} + 人 + \textbf{\textit{with}} + \textbf{\textit{N.}} \end{cases}$
>
> ***high school*** 高中
> mathematics〔,mæθə'mætɪks〕*n.* 數學（= *math*）

TEST 45

Directions: *Of the four choices given after each sentence, choose the one most suitable for filling in the blank.*

1. The new textbook on the desk is _____.

    (A) us
    (B) them
    (C) ours
    (D) their   (   )

2. You can't ride a bicycle, _____?

    (A) can't you
    (B) don't you
    (C) do you
    (D) can you   (   )

3. Though Susan likes to swim, she is not a good swimmer.

    (A) Susan is a good swimmer and likes to swim.
    (B) Susan is a good swimmer, but doesn't like to swim.
    (C) Susan doesn't like to swim and she can't swim well.
    (D) Susan is not a good swimmer, but she likes to swim.

4. Could you talk _____? I'm trying to study.

    (A) more quietly
    (B) quieter than
    (C) more quiet
    (D) quiet   (   )

5. Select the correct sentence.

    (A) The car started after he checking the tires.
    (B) After checking the tires, he started the car.
    (C) The tires after checking he the car started.
    (D) He after checking the tires, the car started.

6. After the war, many soldiers _____ to their hometowns.

    (A) returns
    (B) had returned
    (C) has returned
    (D) returned   (   )

7. If it had not rained so hard yesterday, we _____ to Keelung.

    (A) should go
    (B) would go
    (C) would have gone
    (D) must have gone   (   )

8. I _____ better after I had taken an aspirin.

    (A) felt
    (B) had felt
    (C) will feel
    (D) can't   (   )

9. They built this temple 4,000 years ago. This must _____ a great civilization.

    (A) not have been
    (B) have been
    (C) has been
    (D) was   (   )

10. Everyone _____ with me.

    (A) agree
    (B) agrees
    (C) had been agreed
    (D) have agreed   (   )

TEST 45 詳解

1. (**C**) The new textbook on the desk is <u>ours</u>.
書桌上那本新的教科書是我們的。

> 依句意,書桌上那本新的教科書是「我們的教科書」,
> 須填所有代名詞,故選 (C) ***ours*** (= *our textbook*)。
>
> textbook〔'tɛkst,buk〕*n.* 教科書
> desk〔dɛsk〕*n.* 書桌

2. (**D**) You can't ride a bicycle, <u>can you</u>?
你不會騎腳踏車,是嗎?

> 形成附加問句的條件有三:
> ① 主詞須相同 (you)。
> ② 附加問句中的主詞須用代名詞 (you)。
> ③ 前句為否定句,後句則須用肯定 (can't→can),
> 反之亦然。
>
> can you 是由 can you *ride a bicycle* 省略而來。
>
> ride〔raɪd〕*v.* 騎   bicycle〔'baɪsɪkl̩〕*n.* 腳踏車

3. (**D**) Though Susan likes to swim, she is not a good swimmer.
雖然蘇珊很喜歡游泳,但她游得並不好。

> 依句意,選 (D) Susan is not a good swimmer, but she likes to swim. (蘇珊游泳游得不好,但是她很喜歡游泳。)
>
> though〔ðo〕*conj.* 雖然
> swimmer〔'swɪmɚ〕*n.* 游泳者   swim〔swɪm〕*v.* 游泳

4. (**A**) Could you talk <u>more quietly</u>? I'm trying to study.
你說話可以小聲一點嗎？我正在努力讀書。

> 修飾動詞 talk 須用副詞，而副詞 quietly 的比較級是
> ***more quietly***，故選 (A)。
> quietly〔'kwaɪətlɪ〕*adv.* 安靜地
>
> ***try to V.*** 試圖～；努力～   study〔'stʌdɪ〕*v.* 讀書

5. (**B**) Select the correct sentence. 選出正確的句子。
After checking the tires, he started the car.
檢查完輪胎之後，他發動車子。

> ***after + V-ing*** 在～之後   check〔tʃɛk〕*v.* 檢查
> tire〔taɪr〕*n.* 輪胎   start〔stɑrt〕*v.* 發動

6. (**D**) After the war, many soldiers <u>returned</u> to their
hometowns. 戰爭過後，很多士兵回到他們的故鄉。

> 依句意爲過去式，故選 (D) ***returned***。
> return〔rɪ'tɝn〕*v.* 返回。
>
> war〔wɔr〕*n.* 戰爭   soldier〔'soldʒɚ〕*n.* 士兵
> hometown〔'hom'taʊn〕*n.* 故鄉

7. (**C**) If it had not rained so hard yesterday, we <u>would have
gone</u> to Keelung.
如果昨天沒有下這麼大的雨，我們應該就會去基隆。

> 依句意爲「與過去事實相反的假設」，主要子句須用
> 「should / would / could / might + have + p.p.」，
> 故選 (C) ***would have gone***。
>
> hard〔hɑrd〕*adv.* 猛烈地   ***rain hard*** 下大雨

8. (**A**) I <u>felt</u> better after I had taken an aspirin.

吃過阿斯匹靈之後，我覺得好多了。

先兩個動作發生在過去，先發生的用「過去完成式」，

後發生的用「過去簡單式」，依句意，先吃了阿斯匹靈，

之後才覺得好多了，故空格應填過去式動詞，選 (A) *felt*。

feel〔fil〕*v.* 覺得 (三態變化為：feel-felt-felt)

take〔tek〕*v.* 吃 (藥)

aspirin〔'æspərɪn〕*n.* 阿斯匹靈

9. (**B**) They built this temple 4,000 years ago. This must <u>have been</u> a great civilization.

他們在四千年前建造這座廟。這一定是一項偉大的文明。

依句意，四千年前的這座廟「在當時一定是」偉大的文明，

表「對現在推測過去」，須用「must have + p.p.」，故

選 (B) *have been*。

build〔bɪld〕*v.* 建造 (三態變化為：build-built-built)

temple〔'tɛmpḷ〕*n.* 廟　　great〔gret〕*adj.* 偉大的

civilization〔,sɪvḷə'zeʃən〕*n.* 文明

10. (**B**) Everyone <u>agrees</u> with me.

每個人都和我意見一致。

Everyone 為第三人稱單數，故須接單數動詞，選 (B)

agrees。　agree〔ə'gri〕*v.* 意見一致

agree with sb. 與某人意見一致；同意某人的看法

TEST 46

Directions: *Of the four choices given after each sentence, choose the one most suitable for filling in the blank.*

1. Portable electric drills are used for _____ holes.
   - (A) boring
   - (B) bore
   - (C) to bore
   - (D) bored   ( )

2. _____ the rain the barbecue had to be put off.
   - (A) As if
   - (B) Because
   - (C) In case
   - (D) Owing to   ( )

3. Today men and women of all ages enjoy _____ music.
   - (A) listening
   - (B) listening to
   - (C) to listen
   - (D) to listen to   ( )

4. Would you mind _____ I sit here?
   - (A) if
   - (B) and
   - (C) or
   - (D) when   ( )

5. If I _____ wings, I would fly to you.
   - (A) had
   - (B) has
   - (C) have
   - (D) will have   ( )

6. My girlfriend agreed to cook the dinner.
   (A) She agreed that someone should cook the dinner.
   (B) She agreed that she had cooked the dinner.
   (C) She agreed that anyone could cook the dinner.
   (D) She agreed that she would cook the dinner.
                                                (　)

7. At first, Roger had trouble _____ English when he moved to the U.S.
   (A) to understanding
   (B) to understand
   (C) understanding
   (D) understand   (　)

8. Bob and his wife are no long living together. They have a _____ marriage.
   (A) break
   (B) broke
   (C) broken
   (D) breaking   (　)

9. Peter : I've never sent a telegram before.
   Jack　: I haven't, _____.
   (A) neither
   (B) too
   (C) also
   (D) either   (　)

10. It is essential that you _____ me all the information at your disposal.
    (A) give
    (B) gave
    (C) gives
    (D) to give   (　)

TEST 46 詳解

1. (**A**) Portable electric drills are used for <u>boring</u> holes.
   手提式的電鑽是用來鑽孔用的。

   > 表「被用來~」,說法有:
   > $\begin{cases} \textbf{\textit{be used to}} + \textbf{\textit{V.}} \\ \textbf{\textit{be used for}} + \textbf{\textit{V-ing}} \end{cases}$
   > 故選 (A) ***boring***。　bore〔bor〕*v.* 鑽孔
   >
   > portable〔'portəbḷ〕*adj.* 手提式的
   >
   > electric〔ɪ'lɛktrɪk〕*adj.* 電的
   >
   > drill〔drɪl〕*n.* 鑽洞機　　hole〔hol〕*n.* 洞

2. (**D**) <u>Owing to</u> the rain the barbecue had to be put off.
   由於下雨,烤肉必須延期。

   > 空格應填可接名詞的介系詞片語,選 (D) ***Owing to***
   > 「由於」。而 (A) as if「就好像」,(B) because「因為」,
   > (C) in case「以防萬一」,均為連接詞(片語),後面
   > 須接子句,均用法不合。
   >
   > barbecue〔'barbɪ,kju〕*n.* 烤肉　　***have to*** 必須
   > ***put off*** 延期

3. (**B**) Today men and women of all ages enjoy <u>listening to</u>
   music. 現今各年齡層的男男女女,都喜歡聽音樂。

   > ***enjoy*** + ***V-ing*** 喜歡
   > ***listen to*** 聽
   >
   > today〔tə'de〕*adv.* 現在　　age〔edʒ〕*n.* 年齡

4. (**A**) Would you mind <u>if</u> I sit here?

如果我坐這裡的話，你介不介意？

> ***Would you mind if*** + 子句? 如果～，你介不介意～？
> mind〔maɪnd〕*v.* 介意

5. (**A**) If I <u>had</u> wings, I would fly to you.

如果我有翅膀的話，我就會飛向你。

> 由 would 可知，本句為「與現在事實相反」的假設語氣，
> 其公式為：

$$\text{If} + \text{S.} + \begin{cases} \text{were} \\ \text{過去式動詞} \end{cases} \cdots, \text{S.} + \begin{cases} \text{should} \\ \text{would} \\ \text{could} \\ \text{might} \end{cases} + \text{V.}$$

> wing〔wɪŋ〕*n.* 翅膀　　fly〔flaɪ〕*v.* 飛

6. (**D**) My girlfriend agreed to cook the dinner.

我的女朋友同意做晚餐。

> 依句意，選 (D) She agreed that she would cook the
> dinner.（她同意她要做晚餐。）　agree〔əˈgri〕*v.* 同意

7. (**C**) At first, Roger had trouble <u>understanding</u> English
when he moved to the U.S.

起初，羅傑搬到美國的時候，在理解英文方面有困難。

> $$have \begin{cases} \textit{trouble} \\ \textit{problem} \\ \textit{difficulty} \end{cases} + (\textit{in}) + \textit{V-ing}\ \ 做～有困難$$
>
> ***at first*** 起初　　understand〔ˌʌndɚˈstænd〕*v.* 理解
> move〔muv〕*v.* 搬家

8. (**C**) Bob and his wife are no long living together. They have a <u>broken</u> marriage.

鮑伯和他太太不住在一起了。他們的婚姻破裂了。

> 修飾名詞 marriage，須用形容詞，依句意，選 (C)
> ***broken*** 〔'brokən 〕 *adj.* (婚姻) 破裂的 而 (A) break
> 〔 brek 〕 *v.* 打破，(B) broke 〔 brok 〕 *adj.* 沒錢的，
> (D) breaking 〔'brekɪŋ 〕 *n.* 破壞，均不合句意。
>
> ***no longer*** 不再　　marriage 〔'mærɪdʒ 〕 *n.* 婚姻

9. (**D**) Peter : I've never sent a telegram before.
Jack　: I haven't, <u>either</u>.

彼得：我以前從來沒發過電報。
傑克：我也沒有。

> 肯定句的「也」用 too，否定句的「也」用 ***either***，
> 依句意為否定，故選 (D)，本句可改寫成：Neither
> have I.。
>
> send 〔 sɛnd 〕 *v.* 發送
> telegram 〔'tɛlə‚græm 〕 *n.* 電報

10. (**A**) It is essential that you <u>give</u> me all the information at your disposal. 你給我所有你所掌握的資訊，是必要的。

> ***It's essential*** + ***that*** + ***S.*** + (***should***) + 原形動詞
> ～是必要的 (詳見文法寶典 p.374)
>
> essential 〔 ɪ'sɛnʃəl 〕 *adj.* 必要的
> information 〔‚ɪnfɚ'meʃən 〕 *n.* 資訊
> disposal 〔 dɪ'spozl̩ 〕 *n.* 處置
> ***at*** *one's* ***disposal*** 供某人使用；任某人支配

TEST 47

Directions: *Of the four choices given after each sentence, choose the one most suitable for filling in the blank.*

1. Mandy and I found _____ in a strange part of the city.
   - (A) ourselves
   - (B) our
   - (C) us
   - (D) we   (   )

2. It is important that you _____ drinking.
   - (A) stop
   - (B) stopped
   - (C) stopping
   - (D) to stop   (   )

3. Nick _____ to listen to the CD tonight.
   - (A) should
   - (B) will
   - (C) ought
   - (D) must   (   )

4. Eva will go to college after _____ from high school.
   - (A) graduates
   - (B) graduating
   - (C) graduated
   - (D) being graduated   (   )

5. You should have _____ slower.
   - (A) driving
   - (B) drove
   - (C) drive
   - (D) driven   (   )

6. We had been listening to the speaker before the bell
   _____.

   (A) rang
   (B) rings
   (C) is ringing
   (D) will ring   (   )

7. I drove Sam to the train station.

   (A) I chased him to the train station.
   (B) I took him to the train station in my car.
   (C) I used him to transport me there.
   (D) I compelled him to go to the train station. (   )

8. Tom and Tina come _____ different parts of the
   country.

   (A) in
   (B) from
   (C) along
   (D) of   (   )

9. You won't fail the test if _____.

   (A) you study hard tonight
   (B) hard you study tonight
   (C) hard study you tonight
   (D) you tonight study hard   (   )

10. I can't think of any reason _____ you should take
    all the blame.

    (A) whose
    (B) where
    (C) for whom
    (D) for which   (   )

TEST 47 詳解

1. (**A**) Mandy and I found <u>ourselves</u> in a strange part of the city.

曼蒂和我都發現我們自己，身處在這個都市當中，一個陌生的地方。

> 依句意，發現「我們自己」，身處在一個陌生的地方，選 (A) *ourselves*。

> strange〔strendʒ〕*adj.* 陌生的
> part〔part〕*n.* 部分；地方　city〔'sɪtɪ〕*n.* 城市

2. (**A**) It is important that you <u>stop</u> drinking.

戒酒是很重要的一件事。

> ***It's important*** + ***that*** + ***S.*** + (***should***) + 原形動詞
> ～是重要的
> 此句型常考的形容詞有：essential（必要的）、
> necessary（必須的），及 important（重要的）等。
> ***stop*** + ***V-ing*** 停止～；戒除～（ = ***quit*** + ***V-ing***）

> important〔ɪm'pɔrtn̩t〕*adj.* 重要的
> drink〔drɪŋk〕*v.* 喝酒

3. (**C**) Nick <u>ought</u> to listen to the CD tonight.

尼克今天晚上應該要聽 CD。

> ***ought to*** + ***V.*** 應該～（ = ***should*** + ***V.***）
> ***listen to*** 聽

4. (**B**) Eva will go to college after <u>graduating</u> from high school. 伊娃高中畢業之後，將要上大學。

> after 為介系詞，其後應接動名詞，且依句意為主動，故選 (B) *graduating*。 graduate〔'grædʒʊˌet〕*v.* 畢業
>
> college〔'kɑlɪdʒ〕*n.* 大學 *high school* 高中

5. (**D**) You should have <u>driven</u> slower. 你開車應該開慢一點。

> 「should + have + p.p.」作「早該」解，表「過去該做而未做」，故選 (D) *driven*。 drive〔draɪv〕*v.* 開車
>
> slow〔slo〕*adv.* 慢慢地

6. (**A**) We had been listening to the speaker before the bell <u>rang</u>. 鈴聲響之前，我們正在聽那位演說者演講。

> 先兩個動作發生在過去，先發生的用「過去完成式」，後發生的用「過去簡單式」，依句意，先聽演講者演講，鈴聲才響，故空格應填過去式動詞，選 (A) *rang*。
> ring〔rɪŋ〕*v.*（鈴）響（三態變化為：ring-rang-rung）
> speaker〔'spikɚ〕*n.* 演說者　　bell〔bɛl〕*n.* 鈴；鐘

7. (**B**) I drove Sam to the train station. 我開車載山姆去火車站。

> 依句意，選 (B) I took him to the train station in my car.
> （我開我的車帶他去火車站。）
>
> drive〔draɪv〕*v.* 開車載　　*train station* 火車站
> chase〔tʃes〕*v.* 追逐　 transport〔træns'port〕*v.* 運送
> compel〔kəm'pɛl〕*v.* 強迫

8. (**B**) Tom and Tina come <u>from</u> different parts of the country.

湯姆和蒂娜是從這個國家，不同的地方來的。

> ***come from*** 來自～
>
> different〔'dɪfrənt〕*adj.* 不同的

9. (**A**) You won't fail the test if <u>you study hard tonight</u>.

如果你今天晚上用功讀書，你就不會考試不及格。

> If 所引導的是條件句，不是假設語氣，須用現在式代替
> 未來式，故選 (A) ***you study hard tonight***。
>
> fail〔fel〕*v.* 不及格   test〔tɛst〕*n.* 考試

10. (**D**) I can't think of any reason <u>for which</u> you should take all the blame.

我想不出任何理由解釋，為什麼你該負責。

> 表原因或理由，關係副詞須用 why，就等於 ***for which***，
> 選 (D)。
>
> ***think of*** 想到   reason〔'rizn̩〕*n.* 理由；原因
> blame〔blem〕*n.* 責備；（對於過錯的）責任
> ***take the blame*** 負～的責任

TEST 48

Directions: *Of the four choices given after each sentence, choose the one most suitable for filling in the blank.*

1. If I need your assistance, I _____ you right away.
   - (A) will tell
   - (B) had told
   - (C) am telling
   - (D) going to tell   (   )

2. Would you mind _____ me a favor?
   - (A) to do
   - (B) do
   - (C) to doing
   - (D) doing   (   )

3. _____, the meeting didn't go well.
   - (A) Overall
   - (B) Provided
   - (C) In case of
   - (D) In spite of   (   )

4. Let's go out for dinner, _____?
   - (A) will we
   - (B) don't we
   - (C) shall we
   - (D) are we   (   )

5. Your ring is similar _____ mine.
   - (A) of
   - (B) as
   - (C) to
   - (D) from   (   )

6. How _____ is it from here to the airport?

    (A) tall

    (B) near

    (C) long

    (D) far   (   )

7. The mayor was so tired _____ right in front of the TV cameras.

    (A) that to doze off

    (B) that he dozed off

    (C) to doze off

    (D) to be dozing off   (   )

8. I am willing to work in Brazil, _____ that I have access to constant air-conditioning.

    (A) if

    (B) only

    (C) beyond

    (D) provided   (   )

9. The cost of the whole project was _____ one thousand dollars.

    (A) below

    (B) behind

    (C) after

    (D) before   (   )

10. Maria   : He's such a great acrobat!

    George : Never _____ that I know done anything like that.

    (A) can someone

    (B) will someone

    (C) has anyone

    (D) will anyone   (   )

TEST 48 詳解

1. (**A**) If I need your assistance, I <u>will tell</u> you right away.
   如果我需要你的協助，我會立刻告訴你。

   > 從 If 子句中，動詞 need 為現在式判斷，If 所引導的是
   > 直說法的條件句，並非假設語氣，故主要子句也要用
   > 直說法，依句意，選 (A) *will tell*。

   > assistance〔əˈsɪstəns〕*n.* 協助　　*right away* 立刻

2. (**D**) Would you mind <u>doing</u> me a favor?
   你介意幫我一個忙嗎？

   > mind〔maɪnd〕*v.* 介意
   > *Would you mind + V-ing?* 你介意～嗎？
   > favor〔ˈfevɚ〕*n.* 恩惠
   > *do sb. a favor* 幫某人一個忙

3. (**A**) <u>Overall</u>, the meeting didn't go well.
   大體而言，會議進行得不順利。

   > 空格應填一副詞，修飾整個句子，故選 (A) *overall*
   > 〔ˌovɚˈɔl〕*adv.* 大體而言。而 (B) provided〔prəˈvaɪdɪd〕
   > *conj.* 如果 引導子句；(C) in case of「如果」和 (D)
   > in spite of「儘管」為介系詞片語，後面須接名詞，
   > 故用法不合。

   > meeting〔ˈmitɪŋ〕*n.* 會議　　*go well* 進行順利

4. (**C**) Let's go out for dinner, <u>shall we</u>?

我們出去外面吃晚餐，好嗎？

Let's + V. 的附加問句，須用 ***shall we?***，選 (C)。

shall we? 就是 shall we *go out for dinner?*

的省略疑問句。

5. (**C**) Your ring ***is similar <u>to</u>*** mine.

你的戒指和我的戒指很類似。

similar〔'sɪmələ〕*adj.* 類似的

be similar to 和～類似

ring〔rɪŋ〕*n.* 戒指

6. (**D**) How <u>far</u> is it from here to the airport?

從這裡到機場有多遠？

問距離「多遠」，疑問詞要用 How ***far***，而不用 tall 或

near，(C) How long 則用於問「（時間）多久」，故選 (D)。

airport〔'ɛr,port〕*n.* 機場

7. (**B**) The mayor was so tired <u>that he dozed off</u> right in
front of the TV cameras.

市長非常累，所以他竟然在電視攝影機前面，就打起瞌睡了。

so + *adj.* + ***that*** 子句 如此…以致於～

that 後面接子句，須有主詞與動詞，故選 (B) ***that he***

dozed off。 ***doze off*** 打瞌睡

mayor〔'meə〕*n.* 市長   tired〔taɪrd〕*adj.* 疲累的

right〔raɪt〕*adv.* 正好   ***in front of*** 在…前面

camera〔'kæmərə〕*n.* 攝影機

8. (**D**) I'm willing to work in Brazil, <u>provided</u> that I have access to constant air-conditioning.

如果我可以持續有空調設備的話，我願意在巴西工作。

> 空格後有 that，故選 (D) ***provided that*** 如果（引導子句）
> (= *if*) 而 (B) only 沒有連接詞功能，(C) beyond「在…的
> 那一邊；超越（範圍）」為介系詞，均用法不合。
>
> ***be willing to V.*** 願意　　Brazil〔brə'zɪl〕*n.* 巴西
> access〔'æksɛs〕*n.* 使用權 < *to* >
> constant〔'kɑnstənt〕*adj.* 持續的
> air-conditioning〔'ɛr kən'dɪʃənɪŋ〕*n.* 空調設備

9. (**A**) The cost of the whole project was <u>below</u> one thousand dollars. 整個計劃案的全部費用，在一千元以下。

> 介系詞 ***below***〔bə'lo〕表「（指數量、程度等）在…以下」。
> 而 (B) behind〔bɪ'haɪnd〕「在…之後」，(C) after「在…
> 之後」，(D) before「在…之前」，均不合句意。
>
> cost〔kɔst〕*n.* 費用　　whole〔hol〕*adj.* 全部的
> project〔'prɑdʒɛkt〕*n.* 計劃；企劃

10. (**C**) Maria　: He's such a great acrobat!
George: Never <u>has anyone</u> that I know done anything like that.

瑪麗亞：他是一位非常棒的特技演員！

喬　　治：我所認識的人當中，從來沒有人會做像那樣的
　　　　　事情。

> 從 done 得知，助動詞須用 ***has***，故選 (C) ***has anyone***。
>
> great〔gret〕*adj.* 很棒的
> acrobat〔'ækrəbæt〕*n.* 特技演員

TEST 49

Directions: *Of the four choices given after each sentence, choose the one most suitable for filling in the blank.*

1. The ladder on _____ I was standing began to slip.

    (A) that
    (B) which
    (C) what
    (D) ✕   (   )

2. The man _____ is a general.

    (A) live next door
    (B) lives next door
    (C) who live next door
    (D) living next door   (   )

3. You need to get your shoes _____.

    (A) repair
    (B) repairing
    (C) repairs
    (D) repaired   (   )

4. Select the correct sentence.

    (A) His friend Paul to the club took.
    (B) Paul took his friend to the club.
    (C) Paul to the club his friend took.
    (D) Paul his friend took to the club.   (   )

5. This boy is capable _____ taught.

    (A) to be
    (B) of being
    (C) of to be
    (D) to have   (   )

6. Eddie　　: How long has Mr. Brown studied English?
   Thomas : He _____ it for a month.

   (A) studies
   (B) is studying
   (C) will study
   (D) has been studying　　　　　　　　　( )

7. My brother will go to graduate school _____
   university.

   (A) after
   (B) before
   (C) when
   (D) until　　　　　　　　　　　　　　( )

8. It's getting more _____ to find an inexpensive
   apartment.

   (A) hardly
   (B) and more difficult
   (C) the most difficult
   (D) and very difficult　　　　　　　　( )

9. The reporter suggested that the government _____
   a new committee.

   (A) to set up
   (B) to sit up
   (C) set up
   (D) sit up　　　　　　　　　　　　　( )

10. Children under five years old _____ swim without
    an adult. It's dangerous for them to swim alone.

    (A) don't have to
    (B) must not
    (C) are supposed to
    (D) have to　　　　　　　　　　　　( )

TEST 49 詳解

1.(**B**) The ladder on <u>which</u> I was standing began to slip.
    我所站的梯子，開始向下滑了。

> 空格應填關係代名詞，引導形容詞子句，在子句中，關代
> 又做 standing on 的受詞，又介系詞 on 可移至關代前，
> 又關代 that 關 that 不可與介系詞連用，故選 (B) *which*。
>
> ladder〔'lædɚ〕*n.* 梯子   *begin to* + *V.* 開始~
> slip〔slɪp〕*v.* 滑落

2.(**D**) The man <u>living next door</u> is a general.
    住在隔壁的那位男士是個將軍。

> 本句是由 The man *who lives next door* is a general.
> 轉化而來。形容詞子句改為分詞片語，有兩個步驟：
>
> ① 去關代（who）。
> ② 動詞改為現在分詞（lives → living）。
>
> *next door* 在隔壁   general〔'dʒɛnərəl〕*n.* 將軍

3.(**D**) You need to get your shoes <u>repaired</u>.
    你必須把你的鞋子拿去修理。

> get 作「使~」解時，其用法為：
>
> get + 受詞 + V-ing（表主動）
> get + 受詞 + p.p.（表被動）
>
> 依句意，鞋子是「被修理」，故選 (D) *repaired*。
> repair〔rɪ'pɛr〕*v.* 修理
>
> *need to* + *V.* 需要~   shoes〔ʃuz〕*n. pl.* 鞋子

4. (**B**) Select the correct sentence. 選出正確的句子。

Paul took his friend to the club.

保羅帶他的朋友去俱樂部。

> ***take sb. to~*** 帶某人去~
>
> club〔klʌb〕*n.* 俱樂部

5. (**B**) This boy is capable <u>of being</u> taught.

這個男孩可以教。

> capable〔'kepəbḷ〕*adj.* 有能力的
>
> { ***be capable of*** + ***V-ing*** 可以~；能夠~
>
> { = ***be able to*** + ***V.***

6. (**D**) Eddie ：How long has Mr. Brown studied English?

Thomas：He <u>has been studying</u> it for a month.

艾　迪：伯朗先生學英文學多久了？

湯瑪斯：他已經學一個月了。

> 「for + 一段時間」與現在完成式，或現在完成進行式
>
> 連用，故選 (D) ***has been studying***。
>
> ***how long*** 多久　　study〔'stʌdɪ〕*v.* 研讀；學習

7. (**A**) My brother will go to graduate school <u>after</u> university.

我哥哥大學畢業之後，將會上研究所。

> 依句意，大學畢業「之後」，要上研究所，故選 (A) ***after***。
>
> ***graduate school*** 研究所
>
> university〔ˌjunə'vɜsətɪ〕*n.* 大學

8. (**B**) It's getting more <u>and more difficult</u> to find an inexpensive apartment.

要找一間便宜的公寓，越來越困難。

> ***more and more~*** 越來越~
>
> inexpensive〔͵ɪnɪkˈspɛnsɪv〕*adj.* 不貴的；便宜的
>
> apartment〔əˈpɑrtmənt〕*n.* 公寓

9. (**C**) The reporter suggested that the government <u>set up</u> a new committee.

那位記者建議，政府應該設立一個新的委員會。

> suggest〔səˈdʒɛst〕*v.* 建議，為慾望動詞，其用法為：
> 「suggest + that + S. + (should) + V.」，故選 (C) ***set up***「設立」。而 (D) sit up「坐起來；熬夜」，則不合句意。
>
> reporter〔rɪˈportɚ〕*n.* 記者
> government〔ˈgʌvɚnmənt〕*n.* 政府
> committee〔kəˈmɪtɪ〕*n.* 委員會

10. (**B**) Children under five years old <u>must not</u> swim without an adult. It's dangerous for them to swim alone.

五歲以下的小孩子，絕對不可以在沒有大人的陪同下去游泳。小孩子單獨去游泳，是很危險的。

> 依句意，選 (B) ***must not*** + *V.*「絕對不可以」，表「強烈禁止」。而 (A) 不必，(C) be supposed to「應該」，(C) 不必，(D) 必須，均不合句意。
>
> adult〔əˈdʌlt〕*n.* 成人
> dangerous〔ˈdendʒərəs〕*adj.* 危險的
> alone〔əˈlon〕*adv.* 單獨地

TEST 50

Directions: *Of the four choices given after each sentence, choose the one most suitable for filling in the blank.*

1. If he _____ you, he would be angry.
   - (A) is
   - (B) be
   - (C) were
   - (D) being   ( )

2. You must have your car _____ regularly.
   - (A) check
   - (B) checks
   - (C) checked
   - (D) checking   ( )

3. Luke wasn't able to go with me.
   - (A) He wasn't supposed to go.
   - (B) He wasn't ready to go.
   - (C) He didn't want to go.
   - (D) He couldn't go.   ( )

4. My friends _____ when I came into the room.
   - (A) sung
   - (B) were singing
   - (C) are singing
   - (D) have been singing   ( )

5. _____ you know her well, you can ask her for help.
   - (A) In case of
   - (B) In spite of
   - (C) Because of
   - (D) Now that   ( )

6. Vincent hasn't made his application for a loan yet, but he _____.

   (A) is planning
   (B) plans doing
   (C) plan to do
   (D) plans to   ( )

7. I've been invited _____ dinner by the Joneses, but I'm not going.

   (A) by
   (B) for
   (C) with
   (D) in   ( )

8. The deaf _____ with each other by using sign language.

   (A) communication
   (B) communicative
   (C) communicate
   (D) communicates   ( )

9. The professor didn't come so the students _____ that the class was dismissed.

   (A) were told
   (B) told
   (C) tell
   (D) were telling   ( )

10. Unlike adults, young children can easily _____ the sounds in a foreign language.

   (A) imitating
   (B) to imitate
   (C) imitate
   (D) imitated   ( )

TEST 50 詳解

1. (**C**) If he <u>were</u> you, he would be angry.

如果他是你的話，他會很生氣。

由 would be 可知，本句為「與現在事實相反」的假設語氣，

其公式為：

$$\text{If} + \text{S.} + \begin{Bmatrix} \text{were} \\ \text{過去式動詞} \end{Bmatrix} \cdots, \text{S.} + \begin{Bmatrix} \text{should} \\ \text{would} \\ \text{could} \\ \text{might} \end{Bmatrix} + \text{V.}$$

angry〔'æŋgrɪ〕*adj.* 生氣的

2. (**C**) You must have your car <u>checked</u> regularly.

你必須讓車子定期接受檢查。

have（使）為使役動詞，其用法為：

$$\begin{cases} \textbf{\textit{have}} + 人 + 原形動詞（表主動）\\ \textbf{\textit{have}} + 物 + 過去分詞（表被動）\end{cases}$$

依句意，車子「被檢查」，故選 (C) *checked*。

check〔tʃɛk〕*v.* 檢查

regularly〔'rɛgjələlɪ〕*adv.* 定期地

3. (**D**) Luke wasn't able to go with me.

路克不能和我一起去。

依句意，選 (D) He couldn't go. (他不能去。)

be able to V. 能夠~ (= *can* + *V.*)

be supposed to V. 應該~

ready〔'rɛdɪ〕*adj.* 準備好的

4. (**B**) My friends <u>were singing</u> when I came into the room.
當我進入房間的時候，我的朋友正在唱歌。

依句意，表「在過去某個時間正在進行的動作」，應用
過去進行式，即「was/were＋現在分詞」，故選 (B)。

5. (**D**) <u>Now that</u> you know her well, you can ask her for
help. 既然你跟她很熟，就可以向她尋求協助。

空格應填引導子句的連接詞片語，選 (D) *Now that*
「既然」。而 (A) in case of「如果」，(B) in spite of
「儘管」，(C) because of「因為」，均為介系詞片語，
後面須接名詞，在此用法不合。

ask sb. *for* sth. 向某人請求某事

6. (**D**) Vincent hasn't made his application for a loan yet,
but he <u>plans to</u>. 文生還沒申請貸款，但是他打算申請。

$\left\{ \begin{array}{l} \textit{plan} + \textit{to V.} \text{ 計劃～；打算～} \\ = \textit{plan on} + \textit{V-ing} \end{array} \right.$

plans to 是 plans to *make his application for a loan*
的省略。

application〔ˌæpləˈkeʃən〕*n.* 申請
loan〔lon〕*n.* 貸款　　yet〔jɛt〕*adv.* 還（沒）

7. (**C**) I've been invited <u>to</u> dinner by the Joneses, but I'm
not going. 瓊斯一家人邀請我去吃晚餐，但是我不會去。

invite sb. *to dinner* 邀請某人吃晚餐
invite〔ɪnˈvaɪt〕*v.* 邀請

the Joneses 瓊斯一家人

8. (**C**) The deaf <u>communicate</u> with each other by using sign language. 聾人藉由使用手語來彼此溝通。

本句缺乏動詞，又主詞 The deaf「聾人」(= *Deaf people*) 代表全體，須視為複數，故空格填入複數動詞，選 (C) ***communicate*** 〔 kəˈmjunəˌket 〕 *v.* 溝通。而 (A) communication 〔 kəˌmjunəˈkeʃən 〕 *n.* 溝通，(B) communicative 〔 kəˈmjunəˌketɪv 〕 *adj.* 愛說話的；交際的，均不合句意。

deaf 〔 dɛf 〕 *adj.* 聾的　　***sign language*** 手語

9. (**A**) The professor didn't come so the students <u>were told</u> that the class was dismissed.
教授沒有來，所以學生被告知下課。

依句意，學生「被告知」下課，為被動語態，即「be 動詞 + 過去分詞」的形式，故選 (A) ***were told***。

professor 〔 prəˈfɛsɚ 〕 *n.* 教授
dismiss 〔 dɪsˈmɪs 〕 *v.* 解散；下 (課)

10. (**C**) Unlike adults, young children can easily <u>imitate</u> the sounds in a foreign language.
和大人不一樣，小孩可以輕易模仿外語的聲音。

助動詞 can 後面須接原形動詞，故選 (C) ***imitate*** 〔ˈɪməˌtet 〕 *v.* 模仿。

unlike 〔 ʌnˈlaɪk 〕 *prep.* 不像　　adult 〔 əˈdʌlt 〕 *n.* 成人
young 〔 jʌŋ 〕 *adj.* 年幼的　　easily 〔ˈizɪlɪ 〕 *adv.* 輕易地
sound 〔 saʊnd 〕 *n.* 聲音　　foreign 〔ˈfɔrɪn 〕 *adj.* 外國的
language 〔ˈlæŋgwɪdʒ 〕 *n.* 語言

TEST 51

Directions: *Of the four choices given after each sentence, choose the one most suitable for filling in the blank.*

1. I look forward to _____ you soon.
   - (A) visited
   - (B) having visited
   - (C) visiting
   - (D) visit   (   )

2. Both _____ will take the driving test.
   - (A) you and I
   - (B) my brothers
   - (C) we
   - (D) them   (   )

3. I prefer the black coat to the blue one.
   - (A) I like one more than the other.
   - (B) I like the black coat just as well as the blue one.
   - (C) To me, one color is as pretty as the other.
   - (D) I like the black one more.   (   )

4. Cathy doesn't buy _____.
   - (A) somewhere
   - (B) anywhere
   - (C) anything
   - (D) nothing   (   )

5. He _____ several paintings when he was in Italy.
   - (A) have done
   - (B) had done
   - (C) done
   - (D) did   (   )

6. _____ Laura's request for leave was against my better judgment.

(A) To denying
(B) Deny
(C) Denies
(D) To deny   ( )

7. Select the correct sentence.

(A) We will go hiking if it doesn't rain.
(B) If we will go hiking it doesn't rain.
(C) If we doesn't go hiking it will rain.
(D) We if it will rain doesn't go hiking.   ( )

8. Avoid _____ embarrassing questions at the formal party.

(A) ask
(B) to ask
(C) asking
(D) to asking   ( )

9. Mother had me _____ the helmet before leaving.

(A) wear
(B) wore
(C) to wear
(D) worn   ( )

10. All you have to do _____ a letter of complaint to the manager of that company.

(A) are to write
(B) are writing
(C) is write
(D) write   ( )

TEST 51 詳解

1. (**C**) I *look forward to* <u>visiting</u> you soon.

   我期待很快能拜訪你。

   look forward to + *V-ing* 期待~

   visit〔'vɪzɪt〕*v.* 拜訪

2. (**B**) Both <u>my brothers</u> will take the driving test.

   我的兩個哥哥都要參加路考。

   both「兩者都」的位置：

   ① both + the/these/those/所有格 + 名詞

   ② 人稱代名詞主格（we, you, they）+ both

   ③ both + of + 人稱代名詞的受格（us, you, them）

   take a test 參加考試

   driving test 拿取汽車駕照的考試；路考

3. (**D**) I prefer the black coat to the blue one.

   我喜歡那件黑色外套，甚於藍色那一件。

   依句意，選 (D) I like the black one more.

   （我比較喜歡黑色那一件。）

   prefer〔prɪ'fɝ〕*v.* 比較喜歡 的用法為：

   prefer A *to* B 喜歡 A 甚於 B

   coat〔kot〕*n.* 外套　　*as···as~* 像~一樣···

   pretty〔'prɪtɪ〕*adj.* 漂亮的

   one···the other （兩者中）一個···另一個

4. (**C**) Cathy doesn't buy <u>anything</u>.

凱西沒有買任何東西。

依句意為否定，故選 (C) *anything*「任何東西」。而 (A) somewhere「在某處」，(B) anywhere「任何地方」，(D) nothing「（什麼也）沒有」，句意均不合。本句可改寫成：Cathy buys nothing. (凱西什麼也沒買。)

5. (**D**) He <u>did</u> several paintings when he was in Italy.

他在義大利的時候，畫了幾幅畫。

when 引導的子句中，動詞 was 的時態為過去簡單式，故空格應填動詞 do「作（畫）」的過去簡單式，故選 (D) *did*。

painting〔'pentɪŋ〕 *n.* 畫　　*do a painting* 作畫
Italy〔'ɪtḷɪ〕 *n.* 義大利

6. (**D**) <u>To deny</u> Laura's request for leave was against my better judgment.

拒絕蘿拉請假的要求，並非是我的本意。

動詞須以動名詞或不定詞的形式，才能做主詞，
故選 (D) *To deny*。　　deny〔dɪ'naɪ〕 *v.* 拒絕給予
request〔rɪ'kwɛst〕 *n.* 請求　　leave〔liv〕 *n.* 休假
against〔ə'gɛnst〕 *prep.* 違反
judgment〔'dʒʌdʒmənt〕 *n.* 判斷
against one's judgment 非本意地；不情願地

7. (**A**) Select the correct sentence. 選出正確的句子。

 We will go hiking if it doesn't rain.

 如果沒有下雨的話，我們會去健行。

 go hiking 去健行

8. (**C**) Avoid <u>asking</u> embarrassing questions at the formal

 party. 要避免在正式的宴會上，問令人尷尬的問題。

 avoid + V-ing 避免～

 embarrassing〔ɪm'bærəsɪŋ〕*adj.* 令人尷尬的

 formal〔'fɔrml〕*adj.* 正式的

9. (**A**) Mother had me <u>wear</u> the helmet before leaving.

 媽媽要我在出門前，先戴上安全帽。

 have「要；叫」為使役動詞，其用法為：

 ⎰ have + 人 + 原形 V. (表主動)
 ⎱ have + 物 + p.p. (表被動)

 helmet〔'hɛlmɪt〕*n.* 頭盔；安全帽

 leave〔liv〕*v.* 離開

10. (**C**) All you have to do <u>is write</u> a letter of complaint to

 the manager of that company.

 你所必須做的，就是寫一封投訴信，給那家公司的經理。

 All one has to do is + 原形 *V.* 某人所必須做的是～

 letter〔'lɛtɚ〕*n.* 信

 complaint〔kəm'plent〕*n.* 抱怨；投訴

 manager〔'mænɪdʒɚ〕*n.* 經理

 company〔'kʌmpənɪ〕*n.* 公司

TEST 52

Directions: *Of the four choices given after each sentence, choose the one most suitable for filling in the blank.*

1. Never _____ a lamp too near a curtain.

   (A) set
   (B) sit
   (C) sat
   (D) seat   (   )

2. Jamie saw the accident. The accident _____ by Jamie.

   (A) is seen
   (B) seeing
   (C) had seen
   (D) was seen   (   )

3. Not much _____ about the event since that time.

   (A) to say
   (B) is saying
   (C) has been said
   (D) have to say   (   )

4. We'd better try to straighten _____ this living room.

   (A) off
   (B) to
   (C) up
   (D) down   (   )

5. The Nile River is the _____ river in the world.

   (A) long
   (B) longest
   (C) longer
   (D) more long   (   )

6. The students who are standing outside _____ come in now.
   - (A) can
   - (B) had
   - (C) may have
   - (D) would   (   )

7. We demanded that he _____ the bill by the end of the month.
   - (A) pays
   - (B) pay
   - (C) paid
   - (D) has paid   (   )

8. Helen says that she's _____ English very well now.
   - (A) can speak
   - (B) spoke
   - (C) spoken
   - (D) speaking   (   )

9. Our sales _____ for months, so we are now in great financial difficulties.
   - (A) have been dropping
   - (B) had been dropped
   - (C) had been dropping
   - (D) are dropping   (   )

10. Gary : Did they get any cigarettes there?
    Alan : Yes, they got _____.
    - (A) any
    - (B) some
    - (C) much
    - (D) nothing   (   )

TEST 52 詳解

1. (**A**) Never <u>set</u> a lamp too near a curtain.

絕對不要把燈放在太靠近窗簾的地方。

祈使句的否定，有兩種寫法：

$$\begin{cases} \text{Don't} + 原形 \text{ V.} \quad 不要～ \\ \text{Never} + 原形 \text{ V.} \quad 絕對不要～ \end{cases}$$

故 (C) sat 為 sit 的過去式，(D) seat〔sit〕*n.* 座位，

為名詞，用法皆不合；(B) sit「坐」，不合句意，故選

(A) *set*〔sɛt〕*v.* 放置。

lamp〔læmp〕*n.* 燈　　curtain〔'kɜtn̩〕*n.* 窗簾

2. (**D**) Jamie saw the accident. The accident <u>was seen</u> by Jamie.

潔咪看見了那場車禍。那場車禍<u>被</u>潔咪<u>看見</u>了。

依句意為過去式，且「被」潔咪「看見」，須用被動

語態，故選 (D) *was seen*。

accident〔'æksədənt〕*n.* 意外；車禍

3. (**C**) Not much <u>has been said</u> about the event since that time. 從那時起，人們就不太談論那個事件了。

由 since「自從」可知，主要子句須用現在完成式，

又依句意，為被動語態，故選 (C) *has been said*。

event〔ɪ'vɛnt〕*n.* 事件

since that time 從那時起

4. (**C**) We'd better try to *straighten **up*** this living room.
我們最好整理一下這間客廳。

> *straighten up* 整理
>
> *had better V.* 最好~　　*try to V.* 試圖~；努力~
> *living room* 客廳

5. (**B**) The Nile River is the <u>longest</u> river in the world.
尼羅河是全世界<u>最長的</u>河。

> 依句意為最高級，形容詞 long 的最高級是 *longest*，
> 故選 (B)。
>
> Nile〔naɪl〕*n.* 尼羅河　　*in the world* 在全世界

6. (**A**) The students who are standing outside <u>can</u> come
in now. 站在外面的學生，現在可以進來了。

> 依句意為現在式，故用現在式助動詞 *can*，選 (A)。
> 而 (C) may have + p.p.「可能已經」，表對過去的
> 推測，在此不合。
>
> outside〔'aʊt'saɪd〕*adv.* 在外面

7. (**B**) We demanded that he <u>pay</u> the bill by the end of the
month. 我們要求他，月底之前，要把帳單付清。

> demand「要求」，為慾望動詞，其後接 that 子句，子
> 句中的動詞，須用「should + 原形 V.」的形式，又助
> 動詞 should 可省略，故選 (B) *pay*〔pe〕*v.* 付（錢）。
>
> demand〔dɪ'mænd〕*v.* 要求　　bill〔bɪl〕*n.* 帳單
> *by the end of* 在~結束前

8. (**D**) Helen says that she's <u>speaking</u> English very well now.
海倫說，她現在英文說得非常好。

依句意為現在進行式，故選 (D) *speaking*。

9. (**A**) Our sales <u>have been dropping</u> for months, so we are now in great financial difficulties.
我們的銷售量已經持續好幾個月都下降了，所以我們現在陷入了嚴重的財務困難。

由副詞片語 for months「持續好幾個月」可知，是從過去一直持續到現在，須用「現在完成式」，即「have + p.p.」，如強調動作仍在持續進行中，則用「現在完成進行式」，即「have been + V-ing」，故選 (A) *have been dropping*。
drop〔drɑp〕v. 下降（詳見「文法寶典」p.349）

sales〔selz〕n. pl. 銷售量　　great〔gret〕adj. 很大的
financial〔faɪˋnænʃəl〕adj. 財務的
difficulty〔ˋdɪfəˏkʌltɪ〕n.（財務上的）困境；危難

10. (**B**) Gary : Did they get any cigarettes there?
Alan : Yes, they got <u>some</u>.
蓋瑞：他們在那裡有買任何香菸嗎？
艾倫：有，他們有買一些。

cigarettes 為可數名詞，故 (C) much 用法不合，選 (B) *some*（= *some cigarettes*）。

get〔gɛt〕v. 買　　cigarette〔ˋsɪgəˏrɛt〕n. 香煙

TEST 53

Directions: *Of the four choices given after each sentence, choose the one most suitable for filling in the blank.*

1. _____ go to the movies?
   - (A) Do you
   - (B) How about
   - (C) How often
   - (D) How   (   )

2. The police _____ to find the murderer.
   - (A) has still trying
   - (B) have still trying
   - (C) are still trying
   - (D) is still trying   (   )

3. The officer is busy _____ for the important exam.
   - (A) preparing
   - (B) to prepare
   - (C) with preparing
   - (D) prepare   (   )

4. The storm prevented our family _____ yesterday.
   - (A) leave
   - (B) to leave
   - (C) of leaving
   - (D) from leaving   (   )

5. The circus was _____.
   - (A) delighting
   - (B) delight
   - (C) delightful
   - (D) delighted   (   )

6. In a bakery, Patty bought not only toast _____.
   - (A) or bread
   - (B) but other kinds of bread
   - (C) and a hamburger
   - (D) also a hamburger   ( )

7. I _____ here since 1995.
   - (A) am living
   - (B) live
   - (C) have lived
   - (D) lived   ( )

8. The teacher told the student _____ in class.
   - (A) not daydreaming
   - (B) not to daydream
   - (C) don't daydream
   - (D) not daydream   ( )

9. When I had a dog, I always _____ him out for a walk in the evening.
   - (A) take
   - (B) took
   - (C) had taken
   - (D) was taking   ( )

10. A new amusement park _____ here next year.
    - (A) was built
    - (B) will going to build
    - (C) is going to be built
    - (D) is going to build   ( )

TEST 53 詳解

1. (**A**) <u>Do you</u> go to the movies?

你要去看電影嗎？

> 從 go 判斷，選 (A) ***Do you***。而 (B) How about 後面接
> （動）名詞，表「～如何？」，(C) How often「～多久
> 一次？」、(D) How「如何」為疑問副詞，缺少主詞，
> 均不合。
>
> ***go to the movies*** 去看電影

2. (**C**) The police <u>are still trying</u> to find the murderer.

警方仍然正在努力尋找謀殺犯。

> the police「警方」表「全體警員」，視為複數，空格
> 須填複數動詞，故 (A)(D) 不合；現在完成式的形式為
> 「have/has＋過去分詞」，故 (B) 不合，選 (C) ***are still***
> ***trying***，符合現在進行式的形式：「be 動詞＋現在分詞」。
> ***try to V.*** 努力～；試圖～
> murderer〔'mɝdərə 〕 *n.* 謀殺犯

3. (**A**) The officer is busy <u>preparing</u> for the important exam.

那名軍官正忙著準備重要的考試。

> $\begin{cases} \textbf{\textit{be busy}} + (\textbf{\textit{in}}) + \textbf{\textit{V-ing}} \ \ 忙於～ \\ = \textbf{\textit{be busy}} + \textbf{\textit{with}} + \textbf{\textit{N.}} \end{cases}$
>
> prepare〔 prɪ'pɛr 〕 *v.* 準備 <*for*>
> officer〔'ɔfəsə 〕 *n.* 軍官
> important〔 ɪm'pɔrtṇt 〕 *adj.* 重要的
> exam〔 ɪg'zæm 〕 *n.* 考試

4. (**D**) The storm prevented our family <u>from leaving</u> yesterday. 昨天的暴風雨讓我們全家不能出發。

> ***prevent*** + 受詞 + ***from*** + ***V-ing*** 阻止…做～
> prevent〔prɪ'vɛnt〕*v.* 阻止　　leave〔liv〕*v.* 出發
> storm〔stɔrm〕*n.* 暴風雨

5. (**C**) The circus was <u>delightful</u>.
馬戲團表演是令人愉快的。

> 依句意，選 (C) ***delightful***〔dɪ'laɪtfəl〕*adj.* 令人愉快的。
> 而 (A) delight〔dɪ'laɪt〕*v.* 使高興，(B) delight〔dɪ'laɪt〕
> *n.* 欣喜，(D) delighted〔dɪ'laɪtɪd〕*adj.* (人) 高興的，
> 均不合句意。
>
> circus〔'sɝkəs〕*n.* 馬戲團表演

6. (**B**) In a bakery, Patty bought not only toast <u>but other kinds of bread</u>. 在麵包店裡，派蒂不僅買了吐司，還買了其他種類的麵包。

> ***not only…but*** (***also***)～　不僅…而且～
> bakery〔'bekərɪ〕*n.* 麵包店　　toast〔tost〕*n.* 土司
> kind〔kaɪnd〕*n.* 種類　　bread〔brɛd〕*n.* 麵包
> hamburger〔'hæmbɝgɚ〕*n.* 漢堡

7. (**C**) I <u>have lived</u> here since 1995.
我從一九九五年起，就住在這裡。

> 介系詞 since「自從」，與現在完成式連用，即
> 「have/has + 過去分詞」的形式，故選 (C)。

8. (**B**) The teacher told the student <u>not to daydream</u> in class.
　　　　老師告訴學生，不要在課堂上做白日夢。

> ⎰ *tell sb.* *to V.* 告訴某人做～
> ⎱ *tell sb.* *not to V.* 告訴某人不要做～

> daydream〔'de͵drim〕*v.* 做白日夢

9. (**B**) When I had a dog, I always <u>took</u> him out for a walk in the evening.
　　　　我以前養狗的時候，我總是在傍晚帶牠出去散步。

> 依句意為過去式，又頻率副詞 always 須置於一般動詞
> 之前，助動詞或 be 動詞之後，故 (D) 不合，選 (B) *took*。

> *take～out* 帶～出去　　walk〔wɔk〕*n.* 散步

10. (**C**) A new amusement park <u>is going to be built</u> here next year.　這裡明年將會建造一座新的遊樂場。

> 依句意，為被動語態，須用「be 動詞＋過去分詞」
> 表示，又 next year「明年」為表未來的時間副詞，
> 須與未來式連用，故選 (C) *is going to be built*，
> 在此等於 will be built。

> build〔bɪld〕*v.* 建造（三態變化為：build-built-built）

> amusement〔ə'mjuzmənt〕*n.* 娛樂

> *amusement park* 遊樂場

TEST 54

Directions: *Of the four choices given after each sentence, choose the one most suitable for filling in the blank.*

1. I may _____ if I fall behind.
    (A) not catch up be able to
    (B) be not able to catch up
    (C) be able to not catch up
    (D) not be able to catch up ( )

2. I don't know _____.
    (A) whom is he
    (B) who is he
    (C) who he is
    (D) whom he is ( )

3. _____ jeans need to be cleaned.
    (A) This
    (B) These
    (C) Such
    (D) Any ( )

4. _____ it was raining, we decided to go out.
    (A) If
    (B) Despite
    (C) Though
    (D) Unless ( )

5. He is a very good friend _____ mine.
    (A) of
    (B) in
    (C) to
    (D) with ( )

6. I am afraid that my shoes need _____.

   (A) mending
   (B) to be mending
   (C) to be fixing
   (D) adjust   (   )

7. Marco Polo, _____ traveled to the Orient with his father and uncle, wrote a book about his travels.

   (A) that
   (B) whom
   (C) who
   (D) which   (   )

8. If I _____ enough money then, I would have bought that fancy car.

   (A) have
   (B) had
   (C) have had
   (D) had had   (   )

9. Joan is in her car. She is on her way to work. She _____ to work.

   (A) have driven
   (B) is driving
   (C) drives
   (D) drove   (   )

10. My friend told me that the country is rich _____ natural resources.

    (A) in
    (B) on
    (C) with
    (D) of   (   )

TEST 54 詳解

1. (**D**) I may <u>not be able to catch up</u> if I fall behind.
   我如果落後了，可能就無法跟得上。

   > 否定的 not 應與助動詞連用，故本題選 (D)。
   > ***be able to V***. 能夠　　***catch up***　跟上；趕上
   > ***fall behind***　落後

2. (**C**) I don't know <u>who he is</u>.
   我不知道他是誰。

   > 空格為疑問句，在此做 know 的受詞，為間接問句，
   > 主詞和動詞不需要倒裝，故選 (C) ***who he is***。

3. (**B**) <u>These</u> jeans need to be cleaned.
   這條牛仔褲應該清洗了。

   > jeans「牛仔褲」、pants「褲子」、shoes「鞋子」等
   > 名詞，都是兩兩成雙，應用複數，故本題選 (B) ***These***。
   > jeans〔dʒinz〕*n. pl.* 牛仔褲　　clean〔klin〕*v.* 清洗

4. (**C**) <u>Though</u> it was raining, we decided to go out.
   雖然在下雨，我們還是決定外出。

   > 前後兩子句均為完整句，且語氣有轉折，應用連接詞
   > ***Though***，故選 (C)。而 (A) If「如果」和 (D) Unless「除
   > 非」，句意不合。而 (B) Despite「儘管」為介系詞，
   > 不能接子句，用法不合。
   > decide〔dɪˈsaɪd〕*v.* 決定

5. (**A**) He is a very good friend <u>of</u> mine.

他是我非常好的一個朋友。

> 本句為雙重所有格的用法，形式要寫成：
> 「*a* (this, that) + 名詞 + *of* + 所有格名詞」，
> 故本題選 (A)。

6. (**A**) I am afraid that my shoes need <u>mending</u>.

恐怕我的鞋子需要修補。

> need（需要）的用法為：
>
> $\begin{cases} 人 + \textbf{\textit{need}} + \textbf{\textit{to}}\ \textbf{\textit{V}}. \ 某人需要～ \\ 物 + \textbf{\textit{need}} + \textbf{\textit{V-ing}} \ 某物需要被～ \end{cases}$
>
>   （= 物 + *need to be* + *p.p.*）
>
> that 引導的名詞子句中，主詞 my shoes 為物，故選 (A)
> ***mending***。而 (B) 須改為 to be mended，(C) 須改為 to be
> fixed 或 fixing，(D) 須改為 to be adjusted 或 adjusting，
> 才能選。 mend〔mɛnd〕*v.* 修補；縫補
>
> fix〔fɪks〕*v.* 修理   adjust〔əˋdʒʌst〕*v.* 調整

7. (**C**) Marco Polo, <u>who</u> traveled to the Orient with his
father and uncle, wrote a book about his travels.

馬可波羅和他的父親及叔叔到東方旅行，寫了一本
相關的遊記。

> 空格引導形容詞子句，補充說明先行詞 Marco Polo，
> 先行詞為「人」，且形容詞子句中缺乏主詞，故本題
> 選 (C) ***who***。
>
> Orient〔ˋorɪ͵ɛnt〕*n.* 東方（與 the 連用）
> travel〔ˋtrævl̩〕*n. pl.* 遊記

8. (**D**) If I <u>had had</u> enough money then, I would have bought that fancy car.

如果我當時有足夠的錢，我就會去買那部高級車。

由主要子句中的 would have bought 可知，本句為「與過去事實相反的假設語氣」，公式為：

$$\text{If} + \text{S.} + \text{had} + \text{p.p.}\cdots, \text{S.} + \left\{ \begin{array}{l} \text{would} \\ \text{could} \\ \text{should} \\ \text{might} \end{array} \right\} + \text{have} + \text{p.p.}\cdots$$

if 子句應用過去完成式，選 (D) ***had had***。

fancy〔'fænsɪ〕*adj.* 高級的

9. (**B**) Joan is in her car. She is on her way to work. She <u>is driving</u> to work.

瓊坐在她的車上。她在去上班的途中。她正開車去上班。

由前兩句可知，瓊「正在開車」，用現在進行式，選 (B) ***is driving***。

on *one's **way to***~ 在某人去~的途中

10. (**A**) My friend told me that the country ***is rich <u>in</u>*** natural resources.

我的朋友告訴我，這個國家有豐富的天然資源。

表示某個地方「有豐富的…」，英文可寫成 be rich ***in***…，選 (A)。

natural〔'nætʃərəl〕*adj.* 天然的

resource〔rɪ'sors〕*n.* 資源

TEST 55

Directions: Of the four choices given after each sentence, choose the one most suitable for filling in the blank.

1. The history of nursing _____ the history of man.
   - (A) as old as
   - (B) is as old as
   - (C) is as older as
   - (D) that is as old as   (   )

2. Do what I tell you, _____ you will be in trouble.
   - (A) so
   - (B) why
   - (C) or
   - (D) and   (   )

3. If I had some money, I _____ go abroad.
   - (A) am
   - (B) have
   - (C) will
   - (D) would   (   )

4. They call him Isaac.
   - (A) He has called Isaac.
   - (B) He will call Isaac.
   - (C) He is called Isaac.
   - (D) He is calling Isaac.   (   )

5. I hope I will _____ enter a good college.
   - (A) able to
   - (B) be able to
   - (C) being able to
   - (D) to be able to   (   )

6. They are making their cities _____.
   - (A) cleaner and beautiful
   - (B) cleanly and beautifully
   - (C) cleaner and more beautiful
   - (D) more cleanly and more beautifully   ( )

7. While we watched TV, Monica _____ on her computer.
   - (A) was working
   - (B) will work
   - (C) works
   - (D) is working   ( )

8. I don't think Miranda will show up, but I know you _____, won't you?
   - (A) will
   - (B) won't
   - (C) would
   - (D) would, too   ( )

9. Ellen bumped into a childhood friend _____ the party.
   - (A) at
   - (B) on
   - (C) in
   - (D) by   ( )

10. The most efficient way _____ is by teamwork.
   - (A) work
   - (B) worked
   - (C) to work
   - (D) working   ( )

TEST 55 詳解

1. (**B**) The history of nursing <u>is as old as</u> the history of man.
    護理的歷史和人類的歷史一樣久。

> ***as*** + 原級形容詞 + ***as*** … 如同 … 一樣 ~
>
> 依句意，空格也須填入動詞，故選 (B) ***is as old as***。
>
> history〔'hɪstrɪ〕*n.* 歷史   nursing〔'nɜsɪŋ〕*n.* 護理
> man〔mæn〕*n.* 人類

2. (**C**) Do what I tell you, <u>or</u> you will be in trouble.
    照我告訴你的話去做，否則你會有麻煩。

> ⎰ 祈使句, ***or*** + S. + V. (or 表「否則」)
> ⎱ 祈使句, ***and*** + S. + V. (and 表「就會」)
>
> 本句等於：***If*** you ***don't*** do what I tell you,
> you will be in trouble.
>
> ***in trouble*** 有麻煩

3. (**D**) If I had some money, I <u>would</u> go abroad.
    我如果有一些錢，我就會出國。

> 由 had 可知，本句為「與現在事實相反」的假設語氣，
> 其公式為：
>
> If + S. + ⎰ were   ⎱ ··· , S. + ⎧ should ⎫
>   ⎱ 過去式動詞 ⎰   ⎪ would ⎪ + V.
>   ⎨ could ⎬
>   ⎩ might ⎭
>
> abroad〔ə'brɔd〕*adv.* 到國外

4. (**C**) They call him Isaac. 他們叫他以薩。

> 依句意，選 (C) He is called Isaac. (他名叫以薩。)
>
> call〔kɔl〕v. 稱呼；打電話給～
>
> **be called** 被稱為；名為 (= be named)

5. (**B**) I hope I will be able to enter a good college.

> 我希望我能進入一所好的大學。
>
> 助動詞 will 後面接原形動詞，故選 (B) **be able to**「能夠」。
>
> enter〔'ɛntɚ〕v. 進入　　college〔'kɑlɪdʒ〕n. 大學

6. (**C**) They are making their cities cleaner and more beautiful. 他們正在使他們的城市更乾淨、更漂亮。

> make (使) 的用法為：「make + 受詞 + *adj.*」，又 and 為對等連接詞，前後須連接文法地位相等的單字、片語或子句，依句意為比較級，故選 (C) **cleaner and more beautiful**。
>
> clean〔klin〕*adj.* 乾淨的
>
> cleanly〔'klinlɪ〕*adv.* 乾淨地

7. (**A**) While we watched TV, Monica was working on her computer.

> 我們在看電視的時候，莫妮卡正在她的電腦上工作。
>
> 依句意，表「在過去某個時間正在進行的動作」，應用過去進行式，即「was/were + 現在分詞」，故選 (A)。
>
> computer〔kəm'pjutɚ〕n. 電腦

8. (**A**) I don't think Miranda will show up, but I know you
<u>will</u>, won't you?

我認爲米蘭達不會出現，但是我知道你會出現，不是嗎？

連接詞 but 前面句意爲否定，故空格須爲肯定，用
助動詞 *will* 代替 will show up。

show up 出現

9. (**A**) Ellen bumped into a childhood friend *at the party*.

愛倫在宴會上，碰巧遇到她一個兒時的朋友。

「在」宴會上，介系詞用 *at*，故選 (A)。

bump into sb. 碰巧遇到某人
childhood〔'tʃaɪld,hʊd〕n. 童年時期

10. (**C**) The most efficient way <u>to work</u> is by teamwork.

做事情最有效的方式是團隊合作。

不定詞片語 *to work* 當形容詞，修飾前面的名詞 way。

efficient〔ɪ'fɪʃənt〕adj. 有效率的
way〔we〕n. 方式
teamwork〔'tim,wɜk〕n. 團隊合作

TEST 56

Directions: Of the four choices given after each sentence, choose the one most suitable for filling in the blank.

1. If Emily needs your help, I _____ you at once.
    - (A) going to tell
    - (B) am telling
    - (C) will tell
    - (D) had told   (   )

2. Arnold decided _____ Rachel to the party.
    - (A) inviting
    - (B) invited
    - (C) to invite
    - (D) invite   (   )

3. Did the maid _____ a lot of work last week?
    - (A) has
    - (B) had
    - (C) have
    - (D) having   (   )

4. The army surgeon will see you as soon as he _____.
    - (A) can
    - (B) could
    - (C) possible
    - (D) will be able   (   )

5. _____ many small rooms similar to this one.
    - (A) It is
    - (B) They are
    - (C) There is
    - (D) There are   (   )

6. Our students _____ many new words since they began their language training.

   (A) learn

   (B) learned

   (C) has learned

   (D) have learned   ( )

7. A: Are there any other boys in Jimmy's family?
   B: Yes, he _____.

   (A) has two brothers

   (B) has one sister

   (C) has a grandmother

   (D) is the only child   ( )

8. I don't think he can make it, but you _____.

   (A) could, too

   (B) would

   (C) can't

   (D) can   ( )

9. The thermometer sometimes _____ below zero.

   (A) has read

   (B) is reading

   (C) is read

   (D) reads   ( )

10. The cheapest way _____ is by airplane.

   (A) travel

   (B) traveled

   (C) traveling

   (D) to travel   ( )

TEST 56 詳解

1. (**C**) If Emily needs your help, I <u>will tell</u> you at once.
    如果愛蜜莉需要你的幫助，我會立刻告訴你。

    > 由 If 子句用現在式可知，主要子句應用未來式，
    > 選 (C) *will tell*。
    >
    > *at once* 立刻

2. (**C**) Arnold decided <u>to invite</u> Rachel to the party.
    阿諾決定要邀請瑞秋去參加舞會。

    > 表示「決定要～」，應用 decide to + V.，
    > 故本題選 (C) *to invite*。　invite〔ɪn'vaɪt〕v. 邀請

3. (**C**) Did the maid <u>have</u> a lot of work last week?
    女傭上星期有很多工作嗎？

    > 由時間副詞 last week 可知，本句為過去式，而疑問
    > 句中，將過去式助動詞 Did 置於句首，空格用原形
    > 動詞，選 (C) *have*。
    >
    > maid〔med〕n. 女傭

4. (**A**) The army surgeon will see you as soon as he <u>can</u>.
    陸軍軍醫會盡快來看你。

    > $\begin{cases} \textit{as soon as one can} \ 儘快～ \\ = \textit{as soon as possible} \end{cases}$ 　依句意為現在式，選 (A)。
    >
    > army〔'ɑrmɪ〕n. 陸軍
    > surgeon〔'sɝdʒən〕n. 外科醫生；軍醫
    > *army surgeon* 陸軍軍醫

5. (**D**) <u>There are</u> many small rooms similar to this one.

　　有很多小房間都和這個房間很類似。

　　　表示「存在有～」的概念，應用「There + be 動詞」，
　　　本句空格後是複數名詞，be 動詞也應該用複數，故
　　　選 (D) ***There are***。

　　　similar (ˈsɪmələ) *adj.* 類似的

6. (**D**) Our students <u>have learned</u> many new words since
　　they began their language training.

　　我們的學生，自從開始作語言訓練後，已經學會很多
　　生字了。

　　　由過去某時一直持續到現在的動作，應用「現在
　　　完成式」，選 (D) ***have learned***。

7. (**A**) A: Are there any other boys in Jimmy's family?
　　B: Yes, he <u>has two brothers</u>.

　　甲: 吉米家裡還有其他的男孩嗎？
　　乙: 有，他有兩個兄弟。

　　　由答句 Yes 可知，他家裡還有其他男孩，選 (A) ***has***
　　　two brothers。而有姊妹、有祖母、是獨生子，均不合。

8. (**D**) I don't think he can make it, but you <u>can</u>.

　　我不認為他做得到，但是你可以。

　　　由連接詞 but 可知，前後兩句意思相對，前句為否定，
　　　故後句應為肯定，且前後時態相同，故選 (D) ***can***。

　　　make it 成功；辦到

9. (**D**) The thermometer sometimes <u>reads</u> below zero.
氣溫有時會降到零度以下。

表示「（儀器等）顯示；（告示、書信中）寫著」，
動詞用 read，而且用主動，在此主詞為單數，且由
頻率副詞 sometimes 可知，此處用現在簡單式即可，
故選 (D) *reads*。本句字面意思是「溫度計有時會顯示
零度以下」，引申為「氣溫有時會降到零度以下。」
thermometer 〔θə'mɑmətə 〕 *n.* 溫度計
below 〔 bə'lo 〕 *prep.* 在～之下
zero 〔'zɪro 〕 *n.* 零；零度

10. (**D**) The cheapest way <u>to travel</u> is by airplane.
旅行最便宜的方法是搭飛機。

表示「～的方法」，可用 the way $\begin{cases} + \textbf{\textit{to V.}} \\ + \text{of} + \text{V-ing} \end{cases}$

故選 (D) *to travel*。 travel 〔'trævl̩ 〕 *v.* 旅行
way 〔 we 〕 *n.* 方法
airplane 〔'ɛr͵plen 〕 *n.* 飛機

TEST 57

Directions: *Of the four choices given after each sentence, choose the one most suitable for filling in the blank.*

1. Who prepared _____?
   - (A) have all these delicious cookies
   - (B) these all delicious cookies
   - (C) all these delicious cookies
   - (D) eat all these delicious cookies ( )

2. I always have my brother _____ the car.
   - (A) wash
   - (B) washing
   - (C) to have washed
   - (D) to be washed ( )

3. When I mentioned her name, I noticed _____.
   - (A) he smiling
   - (B) him smiles
   - (C) he smile
   - (D) him smile ( )

4. The world news _____ every morning at 7:00.
   - (A) is reported
   - (B) are reported
   - (C) have reported
   - (D) to report ( )

5. The bag was heavy, so I helped her _____ the garbage.
   - (A) taking
   - (B) take out
   - (C) to taking out
   - (D) from taking ( )

6. Don't make me _____! I'm trying to concentrate on my work.
   - (A) laugh
   - (B) to laugh
   - (C) laughing
   - (D) laughed   ( )

7. Luther : Will you and your friend both join the party?
   Martin : Yes, _____ will come.
   - (A) you
   - (B) she
   - (C) we
   - (D) I   ( )

8. Five students made this model; one was a boy and _____ were girls.
   - (A) others
   - (B) the others
   - (C) the other
   - (D) some   ( )

9. I want to make sure if Sabina _____ to the meeting tomorrow.
   - (A) comes
   - (B) will come
   - (C) came
   - (D) has come   ( )

10. Sandy : Does your brother brush his teeth every day?
    Rick : Yes, he always _____ his teeth.
    - (A) brush
    - (B) brushes
    - (C) brushed
    - (D) brushing   ( )

TEST 57 詳解

1. (**C**) Who prepared <u>all these delicious cookies</u>?

誰準備了所有這些好吃的餅乾？

> prepare〔prɪˋpɛr〕v. 準備 在此題為及物動詞的用法，後
> 面直接接受詞，又 all 要放在指示代名詞 these 的前面，
> 故選 (C) *all these delicious cookies*。
> delicious〔dɪˋlɪʃəs〕adj. 好吃的
> cookie〔ˋkʊkɪ〕n. 餅乾

2. (**A**) I always have my brother <u>wash</u> the car.

我總是要我弟弟洗車。

> have「使；要」的用法為：
> $$\begin{cases} have + 人 + 原形動詞 \\ have + 物 + 過去分詞 \end{cases}$$
> 受詞為 my brother，故接原形動詞 *wash*，選 (A)。

3. (**D**) When I mentioned her name, I noticed <u>him smile</u>.

當我提到她的名字時，我注意到他在微笑。

> notice「注意到」為感官動詞，其用法為：
> $$notice + 受詞 + \begin{cases} 原形 V. （表主動） \\ 現在分詞 （表主動進行） \\ p.p. （表被動） \end{cases}$$
> 依句意，「他微笑」為主動，故選 (D) *him smile*。
> smile〔smaɪl〕v. 微笑
> mention〔ˋmɛnʃən〕v. 提到；說起

4. (**A**) The world news <u>is reported</u> every morning at 7:00.
世界新聞每天早上七點鐘報導。

> The world news (世界新聞) 爲單數主詞，又依句意爲被
> 動，即「be 動詞＋過去分詞」的形式，故選 (A) *is reported*。
> report〔rɪ'port〕*v.* 報導

5. (**B**) The bag was heavy, so I helped her <u>take out</u> the
garbage. 那個袋子很重，所以我幫她倒垃圾。

> $\begin{cases} \textbf{\textit{help}} + sb. + \textbf{\textit{(to)}} \, \textbf{\textit{V.}} \ \text{幫忙某人做某事} \\ = \textbf{\textit{help}} + sb. + \textbf{\textit{with}} + sth. \end{cases}$
>
> ***take out*** 帶…出去
>
> heavy〔'hɛvɪ〕*adj.* 重的　　garbage〔'gɑrbɪdʒ〕*n.* 垃圾

6. (**A**) Don't make me <u>laugh</u>! I'm trying to concentrate on
my work. 不要讓我笑！我正努力想專心工作。

> make 爲使役動詞，其用法爲：「make＋受詞＋原形 **V.**」，
> 故選 (A) ***laugh***〔læf〕*v.* 笑。
>
> concentrate〔'kɑnsn̩ˌtret〕*v.* 專心 <*on*>

7. (**C**) Luther : Will you and your friend both join the party?
Martin : Yes, <u>we</u> will come.
路得：你和你的朋友兩個人都會來參加派對嗎？
馬汀：會的，我們都會來。

> 問句中 you and your friend 對馬汀而言，就是「我和
> 我的朋友兩個人」，故代名詞用 ***we*** 表示。
>
> join〔dʒɔɪn〕*v.* 參加

8. (**B**) Five students made this model; one was a boy and the <u>others</u> were girls.

有五名學生製作這個模型；一個是男生，其他則是女生。

> 有限定指這五名學生時，用 ***the others*** 表示「剩下的其餘部分」。本句中，the others 等於 the other students。而 (A) others、(D) some 則用於「some…others~」的句型，表「有些…有些~」，(C) the other 「（兩者中）另一個」，均不合句意。
>
> model〔'mɑdl̩〕*n.* 模型

9. (**B**) I want to make sure if Sabina <u>will come</u> to the meeting tomorrow.

我想確定，莎賓娜明天是否會來參加會議。

> if（是否）所引導的名詞子句是直述句，故有表示未來的動作或狀態，須用未來式。依句意，tomorrow 為未來時間，須用未來式，故選 (B) ***will come***。
>
> ***make sure*** 確定   meeting〔'mitɪŋ〕*n.* 會議

10. (**B**) Sandy : Does your brother brush his teeth every day?
Rick　: Yes, he always <u>brushes</u> his teeth.

珊蒂：你弟弟每天都刷牙嗎？
瑞克：有，他總是會刷牙。

> 依句意，為現在簡單式，又主詞 he 為第三人稱單數，故動詞用 ***brushes***。   brush〔brʌʃ〕*v.* 刷
>
> teeth〔tiθ〕*n. pl.* 牙齒（單數是 tooth〔tuθ〕）

TEST 58

Directions: *Of the four choices given after each sentence, choose the one most suitable for filling in the blank.*

1. Why _____ Max when you see him?
   - (A) weren't you calling
   - (B) don't you call
   - (C) you don't call
   - (D) haven't you called   (   )

2. You shouldn't have much trouble getting around here.
   - (A) Finding your way will be difficult.
   - (B) You will get lost very easily.
   - (C) You should be able to find your way.
   - (D) Your movements here will be restricted. (   )

3. I told Helen _____ oversleep again.
   - (A) mustn't
   - (B) had to
   - (C) not
   - (D) not to   (   )

4. The new co-worker _____.
   - (A) in the office at all this morning wasn't
   - (B) wasn't in the office at all this morning
   - (C) at all wasn't this morning in the office
   - (D) this morning at all wasn't in the office (   )

5. My father plays basketball _____ than me.
   - (A) good
   - (B) well
   - (C) better
   - (D) best   (   )

6. _____ Mississippi River flows _____
   southward.
   (A) X , the
   (B) The, the
   (C) The, X
   (D) X , X   (   )

7. The old man entered the room _____ by his
   grandson.
   (A) supporting
   (B) supported
   (C) supports
   (D) support   (   )

8. The regulation requires that cars _____ before
   a safety test.
   (A) not be driven
   (B) are not driving
   (C) be not driven
   (D) should not drive   (   )

9. Some people considered _____ be cruel to send
   animals in rockets into outer space.
   (A) to
   (B) that
   (C) it to
   (D) that to   (   )

10. The rich woman _____ to the department store
    every day.
    (A) goes
    (B) will go
    (C) is going
    (D) has gone   (   )

TEST 58 詳解

1. (**B**) Why <u>don't you call</u> Max when you see him?
你看到馬克斯的時候，為何不叫他呢？

> $\begin{cases} \textbf{\textit{Why don't you}} + 原形動詞？\quad 你為何不～？ \\ = \textit{Why not} + 原形動詞？ \end{cases}$

call〔kɔl〕*v.* 叫喊；呼叫

2. (**C**) You shouldn't have much trouble getting around here.
你在這附近走動，應該不會太困難。

> 依句意，選 (C) You should be able to find your way.
> (你應該可以找到路。)

> ***have trouble*** + (*in*) + *V-ing* 做…有困難
> ***get around*** 到處走動 (= *walk around*)
> ***be able to V.*** 能夠 (= *can*)
> way〔we〕*n.* 路
> difficult〔'dɪfə͵kʌlt〕*adj.* 困難的　　***get lost*** 迷路
> easily〔'izɪlɪ〕*adv.* 輕易地
> movement〔'muvmənt〕*n.* 行動
> restrict〔rɪ'strɪkt〕*v.* 限制

3. (**D**) I told Helen <u>not to</u> oversleep again.
我告訴海倫，不要再睡過頭了。

> $\begin{cases} \textit{tell sb. to V.} \text{ 告訴某人做～} \\ \textit{tell sb. not to V.} \text{ 告訴某人不要做～} \end{cases}$
> 不定詞的否定，否定的字須放在不定詞前面。
> oversleep〔'ovɚ'slip〕*v.* 睡過頭

4. (**B**) The new co-worker <u>wasn't in the office at all this</u> <u>morning</u>. 那位新同事今天早上根本沒在辦公室。

> ***not…at all*** 一點也不…
>
> co-worker〔'ko,wɜkə〕*n.* 同事
> office〔'ɔfɪs〕*n.* 辦公室

5. (**C**) My father plays basketball <u>better</u> than me.
我爸爸籃球打得比我好。

> 修飾動詞 plays，須用副詞，又由連接詞 than 可知，
> 此為比較句型，故選 (C) ***better*** (是 well 的比較級) 。

6. (**C**) <u>The</u> Mississippi River flows southward.
密西西比河往南流。

> 河流的專有名詞前，須加定冠詞 ***the***，而 southward
> 〔'sauθwɜd〕*adv.* 向南為副詞，直接放在動詞 flows
> 後面，故選 (C)。
>
> Mississippi〔,mɪsə'sɪpɪ〕*n.* 密西西比河 (= *Mississippi*
> *River*)   flow〔flo〕*v.* 流

7. (**B**) The old man entered the room <u>supported</u> by his
grandson. 老人由孫子扶著進了房間。

> 本句已有動詞 entered，又兩個動詞之間若沒有連接詞，
> 第二個動詞須改為分詞，從 by 與句意判斷，為被動，
> 故選 (B) ***supported***。   support〔sə'port〕*v.* 扶持
> enter〔'ɛntə〕*v.* 進入
> grandson〔'grænd,sʌn〕*n.* 孫子

8. (**A**) The regulation requires that cars <u>not be driven</u> before a safety test.

規定要求，車輛在接受安全測試之前，不能行駛。

require〔rɪ'kwaɪr〕v. 要求 爲慾望動詞，其用法爲：

S. + *require* + *that* + *S.* + (*should*) + 原形動詞

（詳見文法寶典 p.372）

又被動語態的否定字 not，須置於 be 動詞前面，故選 (A)。

regulation〔͵rɛgjə'leʃən〕n. 規定

safety〔'seftɪ〕n. 安全   test〔tɛst〕n. 測試

9. (**C**) Some people considered <u>it to</u> be cruel to send animals in rockets into outer space.

有些人認爲，用火箭把動物送到外太空，是很殘忍的事情。

consider〔kən'sɪdə〕v. 認爲 的用法爲：

consider + 受詞 + (*to be*) + 形容詞

若受詞過長，可用虛受詞 it 代替，此題的 it 代替後面的

不定詞片語 to send animals in rockets into outer

space，做 consider 的眞正受詞。

cruel〔'kruəl〕adj. 殘忍的   send〔sɛnd〕v. 送

rocket〔'rakɪt〕n. 火箭   *outer space* 外太空

10. (**A**) The rich woman <u>goes</u> to the department store every day. 那位有錢的女士每天去百貨公司。

從時間副詞 every day 判斷，「去百貨公司」爲固定的

習慣動作，故動詞時態用現在簡單式，選 (A) *goes*。

rich〔rɪtʃ〕adj. 有錢的   *department store* 百貨公司

TEST 59

Directions: *Of the four choices given after each sentence, choose the one most suitable for filling in the blank.*

1. My brother used to _____ when he was a schoolboy.
   - (A) be timid
   - (B) being timid
   - (C) timid
   - (D) have been timid   (   )

2. We _____ go to the club last night.
   - (A) couldn't
   - (B) won't
   - (C) shouldn't
   - (D) can't   (   )

3. I'm used to drinking tea for breakfast.
   - (A) I don't like tea.
   - (B) I am accustomed to drinking tea in the morning.
   - (C) I never drink tea.
   - (D) I do not enjoy tea for breakfast.   (   )

4. I cannot find my ticket; I _____ it.
   - (A) haven't lost
   - (B) must have lost
   - (C) should
   - (D) should have lost   (   )

5. You can't swim, _____?
   - (A) can't you
   - (B) can you
   - (C) don't you
   - (D) do you   (   )

6. Our workers are packing the _____ fruit into boxes.

   (A) for drying
   (B) which dries
   (C) dries
   (D) dried   (   )

7. The policeman stopped the man to search _____.

   (A) him of a hidden weapon
   (B) him a hidden weapon
   (C) a hidden weapon on him
   (D) him for a hidden weapon   (   )

8. Nancy gets paid twice a month. She receives her pay _____.

   (A) once a month
   (B) two times a month
   (C) once every ten days
   (D) every weekend   (   )

9. Bob wrote letter after letter, and it was well past midnight when he finished _____.

   (A) to write
   (B) written
   (C) have written
   (D) writing   (   )

10. The retiring teacher made a speech _____ she thanked the class for the gift.

   (A) which
   (B) what
   (C) in which
   (D) that   (   )

TEST 59 詳解

1. (**A**) My brother *used to **be** timid* when he was a
schoolboy. 我弟弟以前唸書的時候很膽小。

> *used to V.* 以前 (表以前的狀態或習慣，但現在已經沒有了)
> timid ('tɪmɪd) *adj.* 膽小的
> schoolboy ('skul͵bɔɪ) *n.* 男學生

2. (**A**) We <u>couldn't</u> go to the club last night.
我們昨天晚上沒辦法去俱樂部。

> 依句意為過去式，故選 (A) *couldn't*。而 (B) won't
> 「將不會」，用於未來式，(C) shouldn't「不應該」，
> (D) can't「無法」，則用於現在式，在此不合。
> club (klʌb) *n.* 俱樂部；社團

3. (**B**) I'm used to drinking tea for breakfast.
我吃早餐時習慣喝茶。

> $\begin{cases} \textbf{\textit{be used to V-ing}} \ 習慣於 \ \textbf{【}used\ to\ V.\ 表「以前」\textbf{】} \\ = be\ accustomed\ to\ V\text{-}ing \end{cases}$
> 依句意，選 (B) I'm accustomed to drinking tea in
> the morning. (我早上習慣喝茶。)

4. (**B**) I cannot find my ticket; I <u>must have lost</u> it.
我找不到我的票：我一定是把它弄丟了。

> $\begin{cases} \textbf{\textit{must have}} + \textbf{\textit{p.p.}} \ 當時一定 \ (\ 現在推測過去\ ) \\ \textbf{\textit{should have}} + \textbf{\textit{p.p.}} \ 早該 \ (\ 表過去該做而未做\ ) \end{cases}$
> 依句意，選 (B) *must have lost*。 lose (luz) *v.* 遺失

5. (**B**) You can't swim, <u>can you</u>?

你不會游泳，不是嗎？

前句為否定，附加問句須用肯定，又助動詞為 can，代名
詞為 you，故選 (B) **can you**，是 can you *swim* 的省略。

6. (**D**) Our workers are packing the <u>dried</u> fruit into boxes.

我們的工人，正在把乾燥的水果裝入箱子裡。

空格應填形容詞，修飾其後的名詞 fruit（水果），
故選 (D) **dried**〔draɪd〕*adj.* 乾燥的。

worker〔'wɝkə〕*n.* 工人　　pack〔pæk〕*v.* 包裝

7. (**D**) The policeman stopped the man to ***search*** <u>him ***for*** a
hidden weapon</u>.

警察將那人攔下來，搜查他身上，尋找藏匿的武器。

search〔sɝtʃ〕*v.* 搜查
***search* sb. *for* sth.** 搜查某人，以尋找某物
hidden〔'hɪdn̩〕*adj.* 隱藏的　weapon〔'wɛpən〕*n.* 武器
policeman〔pə'lismən〕*n.* 警察　　stop〔stɑp〕*v.* 攔下

8. (**B**) Nancy gets paid twice a month. She receives her pay
<u>two times a month</u>.

南西每個月領兩次薪水。她一個月領兩次薪水。

⎰ twice a month　一個月兩次
⎱ = ***two times a month***

pay〔pe〕*v.* 付薪水　*n.* 薪水　twice〔twaɪs〕*adv.* 兩次
receive〔rɪ'siv〕*v.* 收到；得到
once〔wʌns〕*adv.* 一次

9. (**D**) Bob wrote letter after letter, and it was well past midnight when he finished <u>writing</u>.

鮑伯一封信接一封信地寫著，當他寫完時，早已過了半夜十二點。

> ***finish + V-ing*** 完成～
> enjoy，finish，avoid，mind 這四個字，
> 後接動名詞，常考。
>
> ***letter after letter*** 一封信接一封信地
> well〔wɛl〕*adv.* 相當；大大地；遠遠地
> past〔pæst〕*prep.* 超過
> midnight〔'mɪd,naɪt〕*n.* 半夜；半夜十二點

10. (**C**) The retiring teacher made a speech <u>in which</u> she thanked the class for the gift.

那位即將退休的老師發表演說，她在演說中，感謝全班同學送禮物給她。

> 依句意，「在演說中」，選 (C) ***in which***。關代 which
> 代替先行詞 speech。
>
> retiring〔rɪ'taɪrɪŋ〕*adj.* 即將退休的
> ***make a speech*** 發表演說　　thank〔θæŋk〕*v.* 感謝
> ***the class*** 全班同學　　gift〔gɪft〕*n.* 禮物

TEST 60

Directions: *Of the four choices given after each sentence, choose the one most suitable for filling in the blank.*

1. Would you like _____ for a walk?
   - (A) go
   - (B) to going
   - (C) going
   - (D) to go   ( )

2. Food spoils _____ if it is not in a fridge.
   - (A) ease
   - (B) easy
   - (C) easily
   - (D) easing   ( )

3. My brother is very good _____ music.
   - (A) at
   - (B) on
   - (C) for
   - (D) in   ( )

4. If I had had time, I _____ you.
   - (A) would have visited
   - (B) will visit
   - (C) would visit
   - (D) will have visited   ( )

5. There was hardly _____ money left in my pocket.
   - (A) some
   - (B) any
   - (C) few
   - (D) no   ( )

6. _____ in one place for such a long time was pretty uncomfortable.
   - (A) Sitting
   - (B) Sit
   - (C) Sat
   - (D) For sitting   (   )

7. He is acting _____ his father day by day.
   - (A) like most
   - (B) more like
   - (C) like to
   - (D) as likely   (   )

8. I have a girlfriend, _____ name is Patty.
   - (A) her
   - (B) who's
   - (C) whose
   - (D) which   (   )

9. Joyce _____ by the dentist the other day.
   - (A) was examining
   - (B) examined
   - (C) was examined
   - (D) did examine   (   )

10. Select the correct sentence.
   - (A) The gas tank will 16 gallons hold.
   - (B) The 16 gallons gas tank will hold.
   - (C) The gas tank will hold 16 gallons.
   - (D) The gas tank 16 gallons will hold.   (   )

TEST 60 詳解

1. (**D**) Would you like <u>to go</u> for a walk?
   你想要去散步嗎？

   would like to V. 想要～

   go for a walk 去散步

2. (**C**) Food spoils <u>easily</u> if it is not in a fridge.
   食物如果沒有放在冰箱裡，很容易腐壞。

   修飾動詞應用副詞，故選 (C) ***easily***。

   spoil〔spɔɪl〕*v.* 腐壞　　fridge〔frɪdʒ〕*n.* 冰箱

3. (**A**) My brother is very good <u>at</u> music.
   我的哥哥非常擅長音樂。

   be good at 擅長

4. (**A**) If I had had time, I <u>would have visited</u> you.
   如果我當時有時間，就會去拜訪你。

   If 子句中的 had had 可知，本句為「與過去事實相反
   的假設語氣」，公式為：

   $$\text{If} + \text{S.} + \text{had} + \text{p.p.}\cdots, \text{S.} + \begin{cases} \text{would} \\ \text{could} \\ \text{should} \\ \text{might} \end{cases} + \text{have} + \text{p.p.}\cdots$$

   故選 (A) ***would have visited***。　visit〔ˈvɪzɪt〕*v.* 拜訪

5. (**B**)   There was hardly <u>any</u> money left in my pocket.

我的口袋裡幾乎沒剩下什麼錢了。

> 句中有 hardly「幾乎不」，即視為否定句，要用 ***any***，
> 選 (B)。而 (A) some「一些」用於肯定句，(C) few「很少」
> 用於修飾可數名詞，(D) no 即為否定，不再與否定字連用。
>
> hardly〔'hɑrdlɪ〕*adv.* 幾乎不   left〔lɛft〕*adj.* 剩下的
> pocket〔'pɑkɪt〕*n.* 口袋

6. (**A**)   <u>Sitting</u> in one place for such a long time was pretty
    uncomfortable.

坐在同一個地方這麼久，非常不舒服。

> 動詞片語做主詞，應用動名詞或不定詞，故本題
> 選 (A) ***Sitting***。
>
> pretty〔'prɪtɪ〕*adv.* 非常地
> uncomfortable〔ʌn'kʌmfɚtəbḷ〕*adj.* 不舒服的

7. (**B**)   He is acting <u>more like</u> his father day by day.

他的行為舉止日漸和他的父親相像。

> 依句意，他的行為舉止日漸和他的父親「相像」，故選
> (B) ***more like***，like 作「像」解，為介系詞。而 (D)
> likely 作「可能的」解，若前面用 as，後面應再接 as，
> 在此句意、文法皆不合。
>
> act〔ækt〕*v.* 舉止；表現   ***day by day*** 一天天

8. (**C**) I have a girlfriend, <u>whose</u> name is Patty.

我有個女朋友，她的名字是派蒂。

空格引導形容詞子句，補充説明先行詞 girlfriend，
表示「她的」名字，爲所有格，故選 (C) ***whose***。

girlfriend〔'gɝl͵frɛnd〕*n.* 女朋友

9. (**C**) Joyce <u>was examined</u> by the dentist the other day.

喬依絲前幾天接受牙醫的檢查。

由空格後用 by the dentist 可知，此處爲被動語態，
故選 (C) ***was examined***。 examine〔ɪg'zæmɪn〕*v.* 檢查

dentist〔'dɛntɪst〕*n.* 牙醫 ***the other day*** 前幾天

10. (**C**) Select the correct sentence. 選出正確的句子。

The gas tank will hold 16 gallons.

這個油箱可以容納十六加侖的油。

gas〔gæs〕*n.* 汽油 (是 gasoline〔'gæsl͵ɪn〕的縮寫)
tank〔tæŋk〕*n.* (油) 箱 ***gas tank*** 箱
hold〔hold〕*v.* 容納；裝入
gallon〔'gælən〕*n.* 加侖 (容量單位，約 3.8 公升)

特別推薦

全國最完整的文法書 ★★☆

文法寶典

▶ 劉 毅 編著

　　這是一套想學好英文的人必備的工具書，作者積多年豐富的教學經驗，針對大家所不了解和最容易犯錯的地方，編寫成一套完整的文法書。

　　本書編排方式與眾不同，首先給讀者整體的概念，再詳述文法中的細節部分，內容十分完整。文法說明以圖表爲中心，一目了然，並且務求深入淺出。無論您在考試中或其他書中所遇到的任何不了解的問題，或是您感到最煩惱的文法問題，查閱**文法寶典**均可迎刃而解。例如：哪些副詞可修飾名詞或代名詞？(P.228)；什麼是介副詞？(P.543)；那些名詞可以當副詞用？(P.100)；倒裝句(P.629)、省略句(P.644)等特殊構句，爲什麼倒裝？爲什麼省略？原來的句子是什麼樣子？在**文法寶典**裏都有詳盡的說明。

　　例如，有人學了**觀念錯誤的**「假設法現在式」的公式，

> If + 現在式動詞……，主詞 + shall (will, may, can) + 原形動詞

只會造：If it rains, I will stay at home.

而不敢造：If you *are* right, I *am* wrong.

　　　　　If I *said* that, I *was* mistaken.

　　　　（If 子句不一定用在假設法，也可表示條件子句的直說法。）

可見如果學文法不求徹底了解，反而成爲學習英文的絆腳石，對於這些易出錯的地方，我們都特別加以說明（詳見 P.356）。

　　文法寶典每冊均附有練習，只要讀完本書、做完練習，您必定信心十足，大幅提高對英文的興趣與實力。

◉ 全套五冊，售價**900**元。市面不售，請直接向本公司購買。

||||||||||||||||● **學習出版公司門市部** ●||||||||||||||||

台北地區：台北市許昌街 10 號 2 樓 TEL：(02)2331-4060‧2331-9209
台中地區：台中市綠川東街 32 號 8 樓 23 室
　　　　　 TEL：(04)2223-2838

||||||||||||||||||||||||||||||||||||||||||||||||||||

ECL 文法題庫①

主　　　編／林銀姿
發　行　所／學習出版有限公司　　　　☎ (02) 2704-5525
郵 撥 帳 號／0512727-2 學習出版社帳戶
登　記　證／局版台業 2179 號
印　刷　所／裕強彩色印刷有限公司
台 北 門 市／台北市許昌街 10 號 2 F　　☎ (02) 2331-4060‧2331-9209
台 中 門 市／台中市綠川東街 32 號 8 F 23 室　　☎ (04) 2223-2838
台灣總經銷／紅螞蟻圖書有限公司　　☎ (02) 2795-3656
美國總經銷／Evergreen Book Store　☎ (818) 2813622
本公司網址　www.learnbook.com.tw
電 子 郵 件　learnbook@learnbook.com.tw

┌─────────────────────────┐
│ 售價：新台幣三百八十元正 │
└─────────────────────────┘
2003 年 9 月 1 日初版

ISBN 957-519-724-0
版權所有‧翻印必究